TOO LONG A STRANGER

W0009395

Books by Janette Oke

Janette Oke's Reflections on the Christmas Story

Janette Oke: Heart for the Prairie
Biography of Janette Oke by Laurel Oke Logan

The Oke Family Cookbook
by Barbara Oke and Deborah Oke

TOO LONG A STRANGER

STRANGER

JANETTE OKE

BETHANY HOUSE PUBLISHERS
MINNEAPOLIS, MINNESOTA 55438

Cover by Dan Thornberg,
Bethany House Publishers staff artist.

Copyright © 1994
Janette Oke
All Rights Reserved

Published by Bethany House Publishers
A Ministry of Bethany Fellowship, Inc.
11300 Hampshire Avenue South
Minneapolis, Minnesota 55438

Printed in the United States of America

Library of Congress Cataloging-in-Publication Data

Oke, Janette, 1935–
   Too long a stranger / Janette Oke.
     p. cm.

   I. Title
PR9199.3.O38T66 1994
813'.54—dc20   94–7586
ISBN 1-55661-456-X   CIP
ISBN 1-55661-457-8 (Large Print)

To all mothers and daughters—

May God bless your relationships,
Heal any wounds,
Enhance understanding,
And multiply love in your hearts.

JANETTE OKE was born in Champion, Alberta, during the depression years, to a Canadian prairie farmer and his wife. She is a graduate of Mountain View Bible College in Didsbury, Alberta, where she met her husband, Edward. They were married in May of 1957, and went on to pastor churches in Indiana as well as Calgary and Edmonton, Canada.

The Okes have three sons and one daughter and are enjoying the addition of grandchildren to the family. Edward and Janette have both been active in their local church, serving in various capacities as Sunday school teachers and board members. They make their home near Calgary, Alberta.

Contents

Chapter One

Sarah

"I've got to think. I've got to—to plan."

Sarah lifted a trembling hand to press the palm against her brow. Her delicate face looked pinched and pale. Her lip quivered in spite of persistent efforts to keep it under control by holding it firmly between evenly spaced teeth. She brought the hand at her forehead down and clasped it with her other in hopes of stilling the tremors.

Her world—her whole secure world—had come tumbling in upon her. She needed to think, to make some sense of it all, but her mind failed to work. *What will I do? Where will I go?* whirled around in her thoughts. She had to make plans—but her brain refused to cooperate.

A soft cry came from the room next to her own. *Rebecca. Rebecca needs me.* That much she could still understand.

She left her bedroom and went quickly to the little room that was Rebecca's nursery. They had been so proud of the room. So excited about fixing it up to welcome their newborn. They had teased each other about choosing the color. Michael had insisted that the new baby would be a boy, and Sarah had been just as strong in her resolve that it was a girl. Both of them knew it did not matter. Any child would be more than welcome in this little room, in their lives and hearts.

But as Sarah entered the room and crossed swiftly to the cradle, she did not think of the decor. She thought only of the small child, little more than a year old, and now without a father.

It had been so unexpected, Michael's death. He had been so strong. So independent. Sarah still couldn't believe it was really so—that she and her baby Rebecca were now alone in the world.

"Mama's here," she whispered to her little one, a catch in her voice as she lifted the infant from the cradle and held her tightly against her shoulder.

But your papa will never be here again, her heart cried. To Sarah's memory came the image of the tall, strong young man who had been Rebecca's father, bending over this same small bed to lift his tiny daughter up against his own shoulder. Even with her eyes squeezed shut, she could see him. The imprint of his face was as detailed and real as if he were standing before her. His firm, square chin. His slightly crooked nose. He had broken it as a twelve-year-old determined to ride one of the bulls on his father's ranch. Over the years the incident, and the nose, had become the butt of many little jokes on the part of his friends. Michael had not seemed to mind, laughing along with them.

But Sarah had scarcely noticed the nose when she first met the tall young man. She had been much too fascinated by his eyes. Brown eyes, framed with long, dark sweeping lashes.

"His eyes look like melted chocolate," she had gushed to her closest girl friend, and Jane had giggled at her remark and later embarrassed her by telling some others. Even now Sarah blushed at the remembrance.

She lifted her chin slightly in stubborn defiance. "He did have beautiful eyes," she murmured softly as though defending herself. Then her own eyes filled with tears and she pressed little Rebecca closer to her. Those brown eyes so filled with love would never look on her or on their baby girl again.

"I must get hold of myself," Sarah chided quietly. "I must. I have to plan. For the sake of Rebecca."

The baby squirmed in her arms, and Sarah realized she had been holding her too tightly. She blinked away her tears as best she could, swallowed the difficult lump in her throat, and forced a smile to her lips before she turned the child to where she could look into her face.

"Are you hungry?" she managed, her voice sounding remarkably controlled. "Mama has your dinner waiting for you in the kitchen. You've had a nice long nap."

In answer, Rebecca squirmed again and grinned at her mama. Then she reached for a handful of her mother's shiny dark hair and gave a tug. To Sarah's dismay the pins pulled loose and soft curls were soon spilling over her left ear.

"Now see what you've done," she scolded gently, but Rebecca squealed and reached for the mass, tangling her tiny fingers in the softness.

"It was my fault," Sarah conceded as she carried the child toward the small kitchen at the rear of the house. "I pinned it carelessly." She sighed and her slim shoulders seemed to sag with a sudden weight.

"Don't eat it," she told her young daughter, who

was trying to stuff a fistful of the tresses into her mouth.

"You think everything is to eat—don't you?" she continued, smiling wanly as she tried to ease the hair from the tightened fist. It was a difficult task, for Rebecca had the strands all entangled in tiny fingers.

Sarah finally deposited her daughter in her high chair and, bending over her, tried to finish the task of freeing her hair from the little one's grasp.

"There," she said at last, able to straighten up again and reach to pin the hair haphazardly in place. Then she went to the cupboard for Rebecca's meal and moved to the wood-burning stove to reheat the mashed vegetables and gravy.

Rebecca squealed. She was never patient, which was especially true where her dinner was concerned.

"Mama's coming," Sarah assured her. "You don't want your dinner cold, do you?"

But Rebecca was in no mood to wait. She thumped on the tray of the chair and squealed loudly again. Sarah knew if she didn't hurry, the child would soon be crying—and then screaming. What was it Michael had said? That she was an angel—until it came to food. Then she suddenly turned into a little terror. In spite of her aching heart, Sarah smiled. The child's papa had known her well.

Rebecca began the second stage of her protest, and Sarah hurried toward the high chair. The food would have to be served as it was. She felt she could not endure a childish tantrum now. In her present state her nerves were raw, her heart near breaking, and she feared she might find herself screaming and crying right along with her offspring.

"You shall have it," she informed her small daughter. "If it isn't quite warm enough—then you've your-self to thank."

But Rebecca did not complain as Sarah spooned the food into her small mouth.

At first Sarah was absorbed in her task, but grad-ually troubling thoughts came back to fill her mind and heart again.

What will I do? I must make some plans.

Her whole person staggered under the weight of de-cisions to be made, but she seemed no nearer to any answers.

———

"What do you plan to do?"

It was Mrs. Galvan who asked the question. Sarah had regarded Mrs. Galvan as a pleasant neighbor—nothing more, since she was at least thirty-five years Sarah's senior. According to the neighborhood report, the woman had borne six children. She had lost twins, one after the other, soon after their birth, and her only daughter to whooping cough at the age of two. One of her sons had been killed in a lightning storm and her two remaining sons were now young men. The younger of the two had recently married and was on his own; the other still lived at home and helped his father run the local hardware store. Sarah had thought of the Gal-vans as fellow worshipers at the little church they at-tended. She met them on the streets of the little town and was always greeted warmly, but they had never been included in Sarah's small circle of close friends.

Now the older woman sat across from her at her kitchen table, a cup of tea growing cold in front of her as she cuddled small Rebecca in her arms.

"I—I don't really—know." Sarah tried hard to control her voice. She had to think. But it was so—so soon. Her head still refused to work. It was as though she was in a daze.

"If there's any way I can help—" There was such kindness in the voice that Sarah found it hard to fight the tears that surged behind her eyes. She nodded mutely.

"There may be someone who would like to buy the dray business," Mrs. Galvan went on. "That would—"

Sarah shook her head slowly. She already knew that wasn't the answer. "I—I talked to the banker," she said slowly. "He said—" She gulped and tried to go on, her voice little more than a whisper. "He said—it isn't likely. That—that anyone who wants to haul freight wouldn't need to buy but—but could just go ahead and start their own. He said—" But Sarah could not continue. It seemed that Michael's carefully built and maintained business of hauling freight from the train station in West Morin into their own small town of Kenville was really of no monetary value to her.

"Then what—?"

"I don't know. I just don't know."

Sarah shook her head, her hair threatening to spill about her ears again. She chided herself. She really had to start taking better care of her appearance. She would come to be known as the town frump. Quite a change from her reputation as a most proper young wife. She reached up to push the pins in more securely.

"I would be most happy to help in any way I can," declared Mrs. Galvan, and Sarah knew from the tone of her voice and the look in the sympathetic eyes that the woman meant every word.

"Thank you," she whispered, her head lowering. "I—I appreciate that more than . . ." But Sarah could

not go on. Her chin trembled and she pressed her lips
together and willed self-control.

"Why don't you try to get some rest," the older
woman said, rising to her feet. "I know it's hard with
a baby to care for but—" Then she checked herself.
"Why don't I just take little Rebecca on home with me
for the night?" she went on. "That way you can get
some undisturbed sleep."

"Oh, but—"

"Now, I've cared for babies before," the woman
quickly cut in.

"But she—she doesn't seem to manage sleeping
through the night. She did before, but—I think she
must sense . . ."

Again Sarah could not finish her thought.

"Well, perhaps *you* could sleep the night through—
given a chance," assured the woman. "And if you are
ever to get things sorted out, you need to be able to
think. And to think, one must have rest."

Sarah knew this was so, but she did hate to give
Rebecca up—even for a night. How could she bear to
lose her one connection with reality? She was still
shaking her head. She was sure she would sleep even
less with her baby gone from the house.

But Mrs. Galvan, with Rebecca in her arms, was
moving toward the nursery bedroom. "I'll just pick up
a few little things and—"

"Where will she sleep?" Sarah asked hastily.

"I still have the crib from my own babies," Mrs.
Galvan answered over her shoulder.

"But—" began Sarah again.

"Now don't you worry none. She'll be pampered
aplenty. My husband and boy both love babies. Truth
is, she'd likely be spoiled beyond bearin' if she stayed
with us for long."

The woman laughed softly as she spoke the words. Sarah's thoughts still spun around. She was beyond rational thinking. Almost beyond caring. Maybe it would be okay—for just one night. Maybe she could sleep. She wasn't sure. She didn't know. She didn't seem to know much of anything at the moment. Numbly she followed the woman into Rebecca's bedroom and absentmindedly packed a small bag with the things necessary for the child's overnight stay. Almost before she could take in what was happening, the woman left the house with Rebecca in her arms. "I'll bring her back tomorrow afternoon," she called over her shoulder. "You get some sleep."

Sarah nodded, her eyes filling with long-resisted tears. Rebecca was grinning back at her, one chubby hand waving a cheerful goodbye just as she had waved to her papa as he left the home on his last morning run with the freight wagon.

Sarah felt the sobs working their way into her throat, nearly choking her. She pressed her fingers over her mouth and turned from the door, closing it firmly behind her. She leaned against it, trying hard to get control of her overwhelming emotions.

"Why? Why?" she cried into the emptiness of the little house. "Why, *Michael*? Why?"

She leaned more heavily against the door and let the sobs shake her body. She had not let herself grieve so freely before. She'd had to be strong for Rebecca. Now Rebecca was in the care of another, and Sarah found that she could no longer be strong. She allowed herself to slowly slide down the door's surface until she crumbled on the floor. Her sobs shook her whole being. "Why?" she cried again and this time there was anger in her voice. "Why? Why take Michael? You know we need him. You know. How can I go on? Why should I go on? What is there to live for? Answer me. *Answer me!*"

The last words were flung toward the ceiling. Sarah lifted a face filled with agony and streaked with tears.

"Answer me," she cried again. "What is there to live for with Michael gone?"

Through tear-blurred eyes Sarah saw the open doorway that led to the nursery. Rebecca's cradle, the one Michael had brought home on his freight wagon, stood near the window, the blanket she had stitched tossed carelessly over the side. The little toy top Michael had purchased on one of his many trips to the neighboring town lay lopsidedly on the floor beside the rag doll Granny Whitcomb had sent. Sarah could not see the simple chest that held the tiny garments—but she was conscious of its presence. She knew every drawer and exactly what each one held. She knew the picture on the wall. The pair of tiny shoes that sat on the window ledge. The rocker in the corner with the multi-color cushion on the hard-polished oak. Sarah's breath caught in her throat. She pushed back her tumbled hair and turned her face toward the ceiling. He had answered. She knew He had. It was Rebecca. Rebecca was her reason for living. Rebecca was the reason she must somehow put her life back together and go on. Rebecca—a very real and very living part of Michael.

Sarah lowered her face into her hands and sobbed, but her crying was now controlled. She had a right to grieve. She had lost much. She had to grieve. Her loss had to be expressed. She would suffer. There would be many days when the hurt would be there—real and painful and so big she would wonder if she would be able to bear it. But she had to go on. For Rebecca.

Chapter Two

Sorting It Through

Somehow Sarah managed to get herself to her bed, fall upon it, and allowed herself to cry until she was completely drained of all tears—all emotion. Exhausted, she at last fell asleep, her last thought being a little prayer, "Oh, God. Help me. I—I need you like I never have before."

She was shocked when she awakened to find the sun already high in the sky. Her bedside clock indicated that it was twenty minutes past ten. She could not believe it. She scrambled up with a pounding heart. Why hadn't Rebecca cried? Had she cried and not been heard? Sarah was about to dash for the door when she remembered that Rebecca was safely cared for at the Galvan home. With a sigh she laid her head back on the pillow and rubbed a hand over her eyes. She wondered if they were red and swollen from her night before.

"I must make some plans," she said aloud as she lifted herself from her bed.

To her surprise she felt prepared to think. Was it the long sleep—or was it the fact that she had finally accepted Michael's death? She did not know. She only knew that she had Rebecca to care for and she did not intend to let her down.

She left the comfort of her bed, washed her puffy face in cold, clear water, forced herself to eat some breakfast, then carefully pinned her hair as she had done each morning in what now seemed the distant past. Then drawing her only black dress from the closet, she slipped it over her head, blinking back the tears that wished to come.

She pinned her hat securely in place, took up her gloves and handbag, and proceeded out to face her difficult day of decisions.

———

"Have you made any plans?"

There was genuine kindness in the eyes and voice of the man as he leaned slightly toward Sarah over the counter between them. He spoke softly, seeming to will her some of his own strength for her ordeal.

Sarah managed a wobbly smile and shook her head slowly. "I am going to see the banker again this morning. Mrs. Galvan has little Rebecca. I—I need to use this time to—to work things through."

The man nodded solemnly. "If there is anything I can—" He seemed to choke up. His gaze dropped and he did not go on. Sarah noticed that the hands that clasped on to the counter top were trembling. She was deeply touched by his obvious concern.

Mr. Murray, whom the whole town, except for Sarah, called Alex, was also a member of the local church congregation. He was a cheerful young fellow, always polite and eager to serve. Michael had wondered why the man was still a bachelor. "Surely some woman should realize his worth," Sarah recalled Michael saying. "It may be true that he's not striking in appearance," her husband had admitted, "but he is not unpleasant to look at."

Sarah had never troubled herself with the affairs of others, so she had given little thought to the matter. "Perhaps he does not wish to marry," she had responded casually and pushed the matter aside.

Michael had laughed at that and pulled Sarah into his arms. "Then he doesn't know what he's missing," he teased and plucked the pins from her hair, sending it tumbling down over her shoulders.

At the memory of the conversation, Sarah felt her face grow warm. *Would every little thing that happened in life trigger some memory of her deceased husband?* she wondered. She dropped her gaze and stirred restlessly as she toyed with the white hanky in her hands and shifted her slight weight to her other foot. Mr. Murray cleared his throat. Sarah lifted her eyes again.

"I wish I could help," he said hesitantly, and Sarah recognized the sincerity in his voice.

She tried another smile and managed quite admirably. "Thank you. People have—everyone has been— most kind. I really don't know how I would manage without—friends."

She turned her eyes to the floor again and swallowed. The tears were threatening to come. *I must not give in to them. I must not!* She had thought she had used up all her tears the night before.

Feeling slightly giddy with the burden of many decisions still before her, Sarah calmly ordered sugar and flour, eggs and baking powder so she might replenish the supplies in her cupboards. Rebecca must eat, and life must go on.

"I know that—it must be hard—to sort things out,

but if there is anything—anything at all that I can—"
the man repeated.

"Thank you," said Sarah again. "I do appreciate
your kindness."

She dropped the coins for the purchases on the
counter and was about to leave when he spoke again.

"Are you sure—I mean—if you—"

Sarah turned back to him and saw the sympathy in
the hazel eyes.

He flushed slightly, and Sarah knew he was embarrassed, though she could not imagine why. At last he
took a deep breath and blurted out hurriedly, "I'm not
good with words, Mrs. Perry. But I would—would like
to offer you—credit here at the store until—until you
get things under control."

Sarah was deeply touched and managed a sincere
smile. "Thank you," she replied, her voice only a whisper. "Thank you very much. I—I do have funds on
hand—at present."

"Well, if you ever—please, please don't hesitate to
ask."

He sounded so sympathetic, so sincere. Sarah
smiled again and nodded. It was a relief for her to
know that she and Rebecca would not go hungry.

———

"As—ah—I said before, Mrs. Perry, I really—ah—
don't know just how much—ah—could be realized
from the sale of—ah—your husband's business."

The banker cleared his throat and shuffled some
papers on his desk. It seemed to Sarah that he kept
rearranging them from one stack to another. She distractedly wondered if he would need to sort through
the whole pile after she left.

"Well—at least there should be something from—from the sale of the wagon and the horses," she dared to venture.

"Well—ah—I'm afraid that—that the—ah—wagon and horses—ah—still belong in good part to the—ah—bank."

"The bank?"

He refused to look at her as he shuffled the pages again.

"What do you mean?" asked Sarah, leaning forward, demanding by her very stance that the man stop his fumbling around and get to the heart of the matter.

"Well—ah—" He pushed his spectacles higher on the bridge of his nose.

"Yes?" prompted Sarah. She finally seemed to have captured his attention.

"The bank—ah—holds a note—a loan," he managed to get out before he dropped his gaze again.

"How—how large a note?" asked Sarah directly.

"Well—ah—Mr. Perry was doing well in paying it off." The man stopped and went back to shifting piles of paper nervously again. Sarah was sorely tempted to reach out a hand to still the restless documents.

"How much?" she asked again.

"Well—ah—"

"How much did Michael still owe?" she said, and marveled at the steadiness of her own voice.

"Well—ah—if we could sell them—everything—at a reasonable price—then—ah—you would realize a sum of—ah—say—twenty-five or thirty dollars."

Sarah gasped. Twenty-five—even thirty dollars—would not care for her and Rebecca for any time at all.

"But—" she began but didn't know where to go with her exclamation. Her denial. Her protest.

"I—I admit—ah—that it doesn't sound like much

but—Michael was making the payments with—ah—no difficulty. He would have soon—"

Sarah did not let him finish. "You are saying that it is a solid business?"

He looked at her then. But he still did not speak.

"Are you?" she demanded.

"Well—ah—yes. Solid but not—not—ah—high paying."

"But sound?" She insisted that he give her a straightforward answer.

"Solid and sound," he admitted with a nod of his head.

"So I have a good business—that is worth—*nothing*?" she pushed further.

He shifted his feet and the papers.

"Is that it?" asked Sarah, trying hard to keep her voice under control.

"Well—ah—"

"Is it?" She had to guard herself. She did not want to become hysterical. She lowered her voice and spoke again. "Is it?"

"Well—ah—a man could—"

"A man?" demanded Sarah. She could feel her head spinning again. The whole world seemed to be going off into the distance. Nothing seemed real. Nothing seemed tangible. She clasped her handbag for something to make contact with, trying to bring things back into proper relationship. Then she reached out from somewhere within her and clutched onto a single thought that made sense.

"Then I'll hire a man," she said evenly. Her head seemed to clear. The world stopped spinning for just a minute.

The banker was shaking his head. "You'd have to

pay wages," he told her plainly, without his customary pauses of speech.

Sarah's head went spinning again. "Wages?" she said dumbly.

"Wages—ah—to the driver," he went on, grabbing some pages. Sarah thought she would go mad with the rustling of the paper, the nervous gestures of the man.

"The—ah—bank payments—ah—plus the man's wages—ah—would leave you—ah—little—for your livelihood," the man said frankly. His words seemed brutal—wrenching apart the only shred of hope she had held.

She swallowed and tried to get her head working—understanding. "You're saying," she said slowly, "that the business is profitable—but not so profitable that it could—could handle a—a salaried man—as well as pay off the debt?" she repeated.

He nodded.

She lowered her gaze and twisted her gloved hands together.

"I—ah—see the freight wagon is—ah—still making the run," remarked the banker.

"Yes," breathed Sarah, her head coming up. "Through the kindness of the parson who has arranged for volunteers to take turns with the driving. But I have presumed on their kindness long enough. I must—must make other plans—soon."

"I—ah—see," said the banker and cleared his throat again.

"There is—is a matter of a—ah—payment due next—ah—week," he offered.

For one brief instance she was tempted to pick up the piles of shuffled papers and fling them in the face of the man who stolidly sat opposite her. Did he realize how vulnerable she was? Did he know the pain she was in? Was he really giving her straight answers? She had no way of knowing. She only knew that she was boxed in a tight corner and there seemed to be no way out.

"I—I may be able to find a buyer—ah—with luck," the man said calmly.

Sarah looked at him evenly. He squirmed slightly and reached out for the nearest sheet of paper. "Of course—ah—as I said—it wouldn't be much—but—ah—it should care for the—ah—bank loan."

He's anxious to sell, thought Sarah. *I can see it in his eyes. He already has a buyer, eager to get his hands on Michael's hard-won business—his team and wagon. I can sense it.*

She stood shakily. What recourse did she, a young, slight, unskilled woman have? It seemed that the banker had won. She would need to put Michael's business assets up for sale at a despicably low price, take the few dollars and try to find some other way to provide a living for herself and her baby girl. She could not take advantage of her friends forever. Nor could she accept the offer of credit at the local grocer's—kind as it had been. No, she had to figure some way to provide for Michael's daughter. Her daughter. Little Rebecca needed her mother's strength. Her provision.

She stood, straightened her shoulders, and lifted her chin slightly, hoping that it was not trembling.

"I—I will be back tomorrow with—with my decision," she said evenly.

Did she see a slight glint in the eyes of the man before he lowered them and reached to shift and straighten the pile of papers for one last time?

Mrs. Galvan brought Rebecca home around four o'clock.

"My, she is a bright little thing," she said as Sarah reached out for the comfort of her baby girl. "Kept us entertained the whole time. We haven't had so much fun since I don't know when."

Sarah managed a smile.

"Even Boyd was taken with her. But then, Boyd likes young'uns. He can hardly wait for his brother to get him a niece or nephew. Hammers on about it all the time. Ralph says, 'Why don't ya marry and get your own?' but Boyd, he says he still hasn't found him the right girl."

Sarah could not help but smile in spite of the heaviness of her heart.

"Did you get some sleep?" asked the older woman with concern as she moved to place the little bag of Rebecca's belongings on a nearby chair.

"I did," admitted Sarah. "I could not believe how late I slept. It was nearing noon. I've never—"

"You needed it," spoke the woman softly. "You were beginning to look like a ghost."

"Let me put on the teakettle," said Sarah in answer. She did not wish to discuss what she had begun to look like—nor how she felt about it.

The woman eased herself into a kitchen chair, and Sarah placed Rebecca in the high chair and offered her a cookie from the tin on the cupboard counter.

"I went to see the banker again today," Sarah began slowly.

The woman lifted her eyes and they mirrored the young, pale face before her. "I'm guessing he didn't have good news for you, did he?" she commented.

"He says that there isn't much money. . . ." Sarah

hesitated. She did hope she wouldn't have to explain the whole story.

"You'll need something—" began Mrs. Galvan.

Sarah nodded as she sliced from the loaf of cinnamon bread sent in by one of her thoughtful neighbors.

"Have you any ideas?" spoke the woman as she reached to retrieve the cookie that Rebecca had dropped and was scrambling around for among the folds of her full pinafore.

Sarah shook her head. "I'm not much at sewing," she admitted. "And I don't think this town would be interested in baking. All the women do their own. I've never—never been anything but—but a—Michael's wife. I—" She couldn't go on. All afternoon she had been sorting through her life—her accomplishments, her abilities. It seemed that she had no skills with which to care for herself and her baby girl.

"Is there any way to—any place to go back to?" Mrs. Galvan asked.

Sarah shook her head. After her mother had passed away, her father had moved back to live with her aunt and uncle. It was enough to crowd him into the small home. She couldn't ask for refuge for herself and Rebecca as well.

Sarah lifted the teapot from the shelf. She dreaded the woman's next question. She hated to admit out loud that she really had no way out of her predicament.

But rather than a harsh question, a soft chuckle reached her ears. She looked up quickly to see Mrs. Galvan bent over Rebecca. "That's right. You show Mama what Boyd taught you."

Sarah looked at her daughter. She was sitting in her chair, her hand tightly clutching the crumbling cookie. Sarah found herself wondering what was so smart about that and then her eyes lifted to Rebecca's face. The child was sticking out her little tongue. Sarah was about to rebuke her, then watched as the tiny tongue reached upward toward the little pug nose. Then Rebecca reached up one pudgy hand and pressed the little nose downward to meet the tongue.

"There—you did it!" cried Mrs. Galvan and clapped her hands together at the accomplishment. "You touched your nose with your tongue." Mrs. Galvan laughed joyously. "Or your tongue with your nose—I'm not quite sure which."

Rebecca beamed, turning her gaze from one woman to the other. She giggled and chortled and did the trick again.

Sarah had no desire to have her daughter learning that sticking out her tongue was acceptable—even admired—no matter for what reason. But Mrs. Galvan was thoroughly enjoying the baby's new game, and Rebecca seemed so very pleased with herself. Sarah could resist no longer. She put the teapot down and smiled at her daughter.

"Did Boyd teach you that?" she asked half teasingly. She wished to add, "Naughty Boyd," but the words couldn't pass her lips. It was likely that her own beloved Michael would have taught Rebecca the trick—had he thought of it.

Sarah watched as Rebecca performed the little stunt again.

"I do hope she won't do that in church!" she exclaimed in alarm, and Mrs. Galvan laughed heartily.

Sarah poured the tea. For some reason she couldn't explain, a little of the heavy weight had lifted from her slumping shoulders.

"She is such a dear," enthused Mrs. Galvan. "I had

quite forgotten how wonderful it is to have a baby in the house."

Sarah glanced in her neighbor's direction.

"We were talking about it last night," went on Mrs. Galvan as she accepted the cup of tea. "All of us—think that—well—we were wondering if it would—be of any help to you if we sorta helped with the care of Rebecca. I mean, when you find whatever way you need to care for the two of you. Like—well—I was wondering if someone might need a clerk in their store or something. It wouldn't be much but it might get you by until— Anyway, Rebecca would be more than welcome at our house. We wouldn't expect pay. We'd be glad to do it as a neighbor. As a part of the church family. And for the enjoyment of it. We'd—"

Sarah stopped pouring her cup of tea and looked at the kind woman at her table. She hated to lose even a moment with the growing Rebecca, but—but this might be the way. The "out." Maybe with Mrs. Galvan caring for Rebecca for part of the day the two of them could make it. Maybe she would be able to get enough work to keep body and soul together. She felt her head spinning again. There was so much to think about. So many tough decisions. But maybe—just maybe there'd be a way.

She blinked back tears and reached out to wipe cookie crumbs from the face of her baby girl. "Thank you," she managed to say to Mrs. Galvan. "Thank you. I'll—I'll give it careful thought."

Chapter Three

The Solution

Sarah worked at her laundry the next day. In spite of what she was going through, she and Rebecca needed clean clothes. It took her all morning bending over the scrubboard before she had the lines filled with fluttering garments. It was early afternoon when she delivered a sleepy Rebecca to Mrs. Galvan, then hurried home to prepare for another trip to the banker. She had spent much of the previous night working through her problem and finally, near dawn, she had come to a conclusion. She felt she knew what had to be done.

But she dreaded what lay ahead. She blinked back tears and determinedly straightened her shoulders as she cast one last glance in the mirror. Her blue eyes looked strangely dark, rimmed with fatigue and sorrow. Her cheeks looked gaunt and pale. In spite of her resolve, she still looked fragile and vulnerable, but her hair was put carefully in place and her chin was set decisively.

"I expect some opposition," she announced to her reflection. "However, I have quite made up my mind."

She drew on her gloves, picked up her parasol to protect herself from the shimmering sun, and stepped out into the hazy afternoon.

"It will surely bring a thunderstorm," she murmured, lifting her eyes to the sky. "Such intense heat. I do hope it doesn't hail."

Sarah cast a quick glance toward her vegetable garden. She had fussed over it and pampered it all spring and now was about to reap the benefits on her dinner table. "We will soon have all the fresh vegetables we can eat and plenty for the root cellar," she had confidently announced to Michael just two short weeks earlier. Now as she let her gaze travel over the rows of growing vegetables, a little stab of guilt passed through her. She had given no thought to her garden in the last ten days. Ever since—ever since the morning of Michael's tragic and untimely death.

"I will need that garden—now more than ever," she reminded herself. "At least Mr. Murray should not have to put vegetables on my account."

And Sarah determined to check her garden as soon as she returned from her trip up the dusty street.

At the entrance to the bank she paused to shake the powdery dirt from the hem of her skirts, took a deep breath, and stepped calmly inside.

Two gentlemen who were just leaving the premises lifted their hats and nodded a good morning. Sarah could see the sympathy in their eyes. Even though she scarcely knew either of them, she knew that they had heard the news of her widowhood.

She nodded acknowledgment and moved quickly past them. She did not want to give opportunity for them to express their condolences.

"Is Mr. Shuster in?" she asked the man who stood in the teller's cage.

"Yes, ma'am," he answered. "I'll tell him you're here."

"Never mind," responded Sarah quickly. "I'll announce myself."

The man nodded mutely, and Sarah moved toward the small office at the back of the bank.

"Mr. Shuster?" said Sarah in the open door and found herself tempted to smile, recalling the name Michael had called the man in private. "Shuster," Michael had said, "should be called Shyster." And thereafter, in the privacy of their own home, Michael had referred to the man as "Mr. Shyster at the bank."

The man behind the desk lifted his head and stumbled quickly to his feet. A false smile pulled stern, thin lips back in an expression that looked more like a leer than a welcome. He waved his hand and motioned her to a chair. Sarah looked at his desk to assess the number of loose papers that he would be toying with while they had their little chat. For her part, she planned to say quickly what she had come to say and then make her departure. She had no wish for confrontation or argument. She had made her plans, chosen her path, and now determined to proceed as quickly as possible. The answer had suddenly presented itself as she had struggled and prayed for guidance in the long, empty hours of the night.

"Mr. Shuster," Sarah began even before she reached the chair that he had indicated, "I have come to inform you of my decision."

He nodded, his eyes seemingly taking on that faint glow again.

"Please sit down," he invited, and the smile looked almost genuine.

"I—I really am not in need of a seat," said Sarah. "I must go pick up my daughter who is with the Galvans. It will not take me long to say what I have come to say."

Mr. Shuster looked perplexed, no doubt thinking that if Sarah were not to sit, he could not sit. He could not reach his papers that provided his hands with something to do. His hands fluttered this way, then that, reached toward a pocket, then reappeared. He really looked most uncomfortable.

He pointed toward the chair again and licked his lips.

"You will be more comfortable—ah—sitting to sign the forms," he advised her.

"Forms?"

"Authorizing me to make the sale."

"Oh, but I'll not be selling," replied Sarah evenly.

"I don't mean—ah—the house. Mr. Perry was quite determined to have the house paid for with clear title. You'll not need to concern yourself with that. Unless, of course, you—ah—desire to leave our area. But the—ah—business assets, they—ah—we'll need to have forms signed for them—even—ah—if the bank already has legal claim—ah—until the notes are repaid. I'll have Sawyers bring the papers. I've taken the liberty to—ah—have them prepared so that I wouldn't need to—ah—detain you unnecessarily."

He pasted on his smile again. Sarah felt annoyance.

"But I will not be signing *any* papers," she said evenly, still refusing the proffered chair.

"But you do not understand—ah—" he said in a voice that placed her in the same category as an uninformed child. "We do need forms to proceed with the sale."

"But I am not selling," she repeated firmly.

He looked at her with a puzzled expression on his face, and she held the gaze steadily. "Anything," she added emphatically. "I am not selling anything. Not the house—which I own. Not the wagon or the horses. Not my husband's business—nothing."

"But, Mrs. Perry," he said, and he seemed to strain for patience, his face at first pale, now slightly flushing with the effort. "I thought that you—ah—that we understood that the business would not make—ah—sufficient return to merit a paid driver—"

"I do not plan to hire a driver," said Sarah quietly.

"Then—I thought you said you had accepted the help of your friends for quite long enough."

Sarah nodded. "That is so," she agreed.

He looked further puzzled.

"But the team and wagon—ah—will make no money sitting in the barn!" he exclaimed, irritation in his voice.

She nodded. "Quite so," she agreed.

"They certainly can't—ah—make the trips for freight on their own." Now sarcasm edged his words and tone. Sarah bit her tongue and nodded again.

"So—if you are not going to hire—ah—not going to presume on the kindness of your friends, who will drive the freight wagon?" he demanded.

"I will," said Sarah evenly.

His head jerked up quickly and his eyes traveled up and down her small frame. Sarah found herself straightening to her full five feet three inches. She hoped that her hat added to her stature.

"You?" He could not hide his amazement. Then he lowered his head and Sarah saw amusement threatening to spill over into laughter, twisting his lips first this way and that as he fought against it.

"I have driven horses before," declared Sarah. "I can handle a team."

He managed to get himself under control. He even

tried to look sympathetic and thoughtful. "Mrs. Perry, please—ah—please have a seat," he implored her.

"I don't need to sit, thank you," she replied, her voice rising. "I have informed you of my decision; my business is now complete. You may—may tear up those—those forms—whatever they are. I will see that your payments are made each month—and on time."

"But, Mrs. Perry—I don't think that you fully understand the nature of draying. The freight—it is—ah—not an easy business—for—ah—a man. And hardly the kind of work suitable for a genteel woman."

"I thank you for your concern," said Sarah coolly, "but it is unwarranted."

"But, Mrs. Perry. Draymen not only haul—they load. They—ah—have all of the heavy freight to get on the—ah—wagon and off the wagon. And—ah—"

Sarah had not thought about the loading and unloading. For one moment her face blanched; then her chin came up again.

"I will care for the loading and unloading, Mr. Shuster," she declared. "You just prepare the papers for me as Mr. Perry's widow to take over the business with the same terms you had given to him. I'll drop by to sign them tomorrow."

Sarah spun on her heel and left the office. She stepped briskly, her head up, her chin set, but inside she suffered. She had not thought of the loading and unloading. She had seen some of the heavy crates and bundles that Michael unloaded when he drove his wagon to the local businesses. Even he had strained under the weight of them. How would she ever manage to get the freight on and off the wagon?

"I'll manage," she whispered to buoy up her courage. "I'll manage—somehow." But inwardly she had some nagging doubts. Doubts that brought tears to her eyes in spite of her strong resolve. Would she really be able to take on the awesome task? Would she really be able to provide for Rebecca?

————

"You've been to see Mr. Shuster?" asked Mrs. Galvan as Sarah came to pick up Rebecca.

"I have," she answered, trying to put some bounce into her voice but failing. "I have everything arranged."

"Come in and sit," said Mrs. Galvan. "Rebecca is still having a nap. Sit and rest for a bit and have a glass of lemonade. You look about done in."

Sarah did not protest. She felt done in as well. A sigh escaped her lips as she lowered herself to a chair. "I didn't sleep well last night," she admitted. "I had too much on my mind. Now that it's settled, I'll sleep better tonight."

Mrs. Galvan looked as if she wanted to ask what was "settled" but changed her mind. When silence continued between them, Sarah spoke again. She felt the need to share her decision with someone. She had become so used to talking over every thought with Michael.

"I'm not selling," she said, hoping that her friend would understand her meaning.

Mrs. Galvan looked surprised but nodded.

"I don't blame you for wanting to keep the horses," she said. "A fine team. Boyd says they're the best team around. He would have been tempted to offer for them hisself—had he a real use for them."

"It isn't that I'm attached to the team," admitted Sarah. "Though I would hate to lose them. Michael—" She stopped that train of thought and continued. "It's just that it seemed the only way to keep things going. Mrs. Galvan—if you still think you could keep Rebecca, I'd—I'd sure be beholden to you."

"I'm right glad to keep her," she said as she stirred about her kitchen preparing the lemonade. "She's such a little sweetheart," she added with a smile.

"Unless she's hungry," put in Sarah. "When she's hungry—she's the most impatient little thing you've ever seen. Just opens right up and whoops at times. Michael always said . . ." Sarah's voice trailed off.

Mrs. Galvan filled the awkward silence.

"You've found work?" she asked.

"I've had work all along—so to speak," Sarah replied, her eyes on her hands.

"You're going to try baking?"

"No-o. No, I still don't think there would be a sale for baked goods. I—I am going to—to continue the freight run."

"The freight run? But I thought the banker said it wouldn't pay to hire—"

"I'm not going to hire," said Sarah. "I'm going to drive the team myself."

The older woman stopped mid-stride and stared at Sarah. Not with a look of frustration. Not with a look of amusement—but with a look of honest concern. She finally moved forward and placed the glasses of lemonade on the table. "Oh, Sarah," she said softly, "do you really think—that it's wise?"

"I don't see any other choice," Sarah replied quietly. "There is nothing much that I can do. Michael's business is there. The horses and wagon are there. If we continue, we can pay off the loan. It's enough for Rebecca and me to live on. We have the house—the garden. We'll make out fine."

"But the work. Do you think you can—I mean—it's

hard work, Sarah. Hard work for a burly man. You saw the muscles it built for Michael. I mean—you're a woman. And you are of slight frame even for a woman."

Sarah nodded and fought against the tears that threatened to spill. She had thought of all those things. Since the banker had thrown them in her face, she had mentally tossed them this way and that. There didn't seem to be any other answer than just to go at it. Hard as it seemed, she had to try.

"Maybe Boyd—" began the woman.

"No," said Sarah firmly. "No, I will not be laying my responsibility on another. Either I make a go of it on my own—or I sell."

Mrs. Galvan nodded. She understood Sarah's need for independence.

"When do you plan to start?" she asked simply as she pushed the lemonade toward Sarah.

"I thought I'd ride along with the other drivers for a morning or two until I learn about the pick-ups. Then I'd take over on my own."

Mrs. Galvan nodded and patted Sarah's arm encouragingly.

"They leave rather early," she said very matter-of-factly. "Rebecca won't be awake yet. Best I come to your house and stay with her there until she wakes up. Then I'll bring her on over here, and you can pick her up when you get back in the afternoon."

Sarah nodded. She hadn't thought about the unearthly hour that she would need to be on her way.

"I'd appreciate that," she said simply. "Michael always left early so he could be home and unloaded in plenty of time to have time for Rebecca and me. I'd— I'd like to have that time with Rebecca, too."

" 'Course," said the woman. " 'Course." Then she

added emphatically as though to lift Sarah's troubled spirit, "It'll work just fine. Just fine."

Sarah felt a tremble go through her body. She did so hope that the older woman was right. She wanted with all her being for the plan to work. Because if it didn't—what was she ever going to do to provide for Rebecca?

———

"I've heard you are taking over the freight run," Mr. Murray said to Sarah the next time she entered his store. She had already made one trip with Mr. Curtis. It hadn't seemed so bad. Sarah had even tried to help with the loading, though most of the crates and bags had been too heavy for her.

"I'll soon build up my muscles," she had stoutly declared, and Mr. Curtis had smiled sympathetically.

Now she looked at Mr. Murray and nodded her reply. She even tried a brave smile. "It was Michael's business," she declared. "He left it to me—so it seems only right that I make use of it."

He nodded, but his face looked pained. Sarah knew that he was studying the size of her frame but in a much different way than had the banker.

"I've been thinking," the man went on. "This here store doesn't really make enough to merit another clerk—but it sure would be nice to get out for some fresh air now and then. Do you suppose that—that you and I could—could do a swap. I mean—I'll teach you to run the store—and I'll—haul the freight. You know—a swap."

For one brief instance Sarah was awfully tempted to jump at the opportunity. It would be so much easier to mind the store. And she would be so much nearer to Rebecca. Why, she could even see her in the daytime now and then. But then Sarah looked back at the kind gentleman before her and realized he had made the offer, not to get fresh air, but because he felt sorry about her circumstance. *He doesn't think I can do it,* she said to herself. Indeed, she wasn't sure yet that she could. Though she appreciated the concern of the storekeeper, she was not ready to accept charity—even if it was well meant.

"I—I do appreciate that, Mr. Murray," she managed to say. "I really do—but—well—I have a need for a little fresh air myself. If—if I find that—that this— doesn't work well—well, then I just might remind you of your offer." Her smile was a little wobbly.

"You won't forget?" he prompted. "You'll feel free to speak?"

"I'll feel free to speak," she promised and nodded her good-day.

Why should he care—that much? she puzzled as she went to pick up her young daughter from the Galvans'.

"Well, he has always been a caring person," she concluded under her breath. "I have just never thought of it before. I should have realized. At church—he's always helping this person or that person. That's why everyone says he makes such a good usher. He's—what do they say? He's—in tune—that's what the pastor says. In tune—always with an eye for a need. I just never paid much attention before. My own eyes were always so—so filled with Michael and Rebecca, I never paid much mind to anyone else."

And Sarah pushed the thoughts of the kind offer from her mind and hurried to pick up her little girl.

Chapter Four

First Day

Sarah tiptoed to the cradle and pressed a kiss on the softness of Rebecca's silken hair, whispering in the stillness that Mama would soon be home again. Then she went to open the door for Mrs. Galvan, whom she had heard on the boardwalk.

The woman entered the house quietly so as not to disturb the sleeping child, placed a small package on the table, and proceeded to the stove to put another stick in the firebox and push the kettle forward for coffee.

"Have you eaten?" she asked Sarah in a motherly way.

"Yes," she replied softly.

"Enough?" continued the older woman, "or did you just grab a slice of bread?"

Sarah's cheeks flushed. That was exactly what she had done.

"You need a full stomach to begin that task," the woman insisted gently, then went on. "Here—I've brought you some lunch."

Sarah accepted the older woman's thoughtfulness

with a murmured thanks. "I hadn't thought of a lunch," she admitted. "From now on I'll fix myself one."

Mrs. Galvan nodded.

"And I'll eat a proper breakfast, too," Sarah continued, feeling much like a little girl making promises to her mother again.

Mrs. Galvan did not respond, but her kind eyes looked at Sarah. For one moment Sarah thought the older woman might step forward and gather her into her arms against her shoulder. For the same length of time, Sarah hoped she would. Then she straightened her shoulders with a little shake, stepped back, and lifted her chin. She was not a child who needed comforting. She was a grown woman with a baby of her own to care for. She reached for the package of lunch from the table and fixed a wan smile firmly in place.

"I'll be off. I want to get back early."

Mrs. Galvan nodded and moved back toward the kitchen stove.

Rebecca slept on, oblivious to the change that had taken place in her home—in her world.

———

Sarah had watched carefully as Mr. Curtis harnessed the team, led them out of the barn, and hooked the two horses to the wagon. Even so, a few days later when it came time for her to do the hitching, she found the task much more difficult than she could have imagined.

Sarah had always admired horses—but at a distance. She had never handled the big animals before. A sense of fear filled her at being up close. For one thing, the heavy team of draft horses were taller than

she was, and though they were gentle and patient, she
had a struggle lifting the heavy collars and getting
them fastened properly around the thick necks. She
had to resort to standing on an upturned oat bucket to
get the job done. Then came the task of lifting the harness up and over the broad backs. In the process everything seemed to tangle in a confusing mess. It took
a good deal of work to get things straightened and in
proper place; and by the time she had completed the
job, her carefully fastened hair was drooping over one
ear, her skirt torn at the hem, and her shirtwaist
smeared with dirt from the harness.

She glanced down at herself and felt ready to weep.
But there was no time for weeping. She brushed at her
clothing the best she could, pinned her hair more securely, then led the big team over to the wagon. She
felt so small in comparison to Gyp and Ginger and
feared that they might suddenly bolt for some reason
and run over her, leaving her bruised and tattered, perhaps even dead. She couldn't die. Not now. Rebecca
needed her.

At length Sarah managed to get the team lined up
properly along the tongue of the wagon and bent to lift
the heavy pole. It was all she could do to snap the yoke
to the harness breast strap while hoisting the tongue
into the air. She was panting and sweaty by the time
she was done. The final task was to get the tugs hooked
to the singletrees.

At long last the team was hitched to the wagon, but
it had taken her much longer than it should have. It
meant a late start in getting off. She wouldn't have as
much time with Rebecca as she had hoped. She bit her
lip as she climbed up over the high wagon wheel, took
up the reins, and spoke to the horses.

Both Gyp and Ginger leaned into the harness at her

command. The wagon seemed to sit and tremble. The
horses appeared as confused as Sarah felt. She saw
them lean forward again, straining at the tugs, strong
muscles rippling as they threw their weight against the
resisting force.

The wagon began to slide forward. Sarah noted
that the front wheels were not rolling as wheels should.
She looked about her, perplexed. She would never
make any time if the wagon refused to cooperate. And
then with a flush of her cheeks and a prayer of thankfulness that nobody was watching her, she reached
down and released the hand brake.

The wheels began to roll, and Sarah was finally on
her way. Already she felt that she had put in a day's
hard work, and she had just begun.

Sarah's thoughts turned to her sleeping child. How
she prayed that when the little one awoke, she would
not feel afraid to find Mrs. Galvan with her rather than
her own mother. *She has even stopped asking for Papa,*
her thoughts continued, and a tear slid down her cheek
and splashed on the hands that held the reins. Then
she gave her full attention back to the team.

It had looked so easy when Sarah had watched Big
John, as everyone called Mr. Curtis, drive the team of
muscled bays. The horses were responsive to the reins,
well-trained and obedient. But Sarah found the task
far more difficult than she would have imagined.

The constant jarring and rumbling of the wagon
soon had every muscle in her body aching, and the constant pull of the horses against the reins made her
arms hurt all the way to her shoulders.

"Relax," Big John had instructed her. "Don't fight

agin the reins. Just hold 'em light like and guide the team. They won't bolt. But you gotta be firm. Horses are smart. They sense things. They like to know you have everythin' under control."

Everything under control! Sarah almost laughed as she repeated the thought. Then she felt like crying. Nothing was under control. The horses were the least of it. Her whole world had gone spinning off in some foreign direction, totally beyond her wishes or sense of rightness. Would things ever be controlled again?

Sarah stopped herself with the thought that God was in control. He had not lost His grip on her world. Though her way looked dark and clouded at the moment, He knew exactly what lay ahead. All she had to do was to trust Him. Trust Him in all things. Sarah decided that the long, slow rides to and from the Jackson train depot would be wonderful opportunities to talk to her heavenly Father. Forgetting that she was in charge of a team of horses, she bowed her head and closed her eyes.

A sharp jolt made her eyes fly open. She could not believe how far she had drifted from the proper track. She was indeed fortunate it was only a large stone that had passed under the wagon wheel. A few more feet and she could have found herself in great difficulty. From there on, Sarah decided to do her talking to God with her eyes wide open.

———————

Sarah was glad she had traveled with Big John on a few trips so she knew the daily procedure. By the time she eased her team up to the hitching rail at the depot, the sun was high in the sky.

"A little late this mornin'," a man called out, but he

spoke cheerily. Sarah nodded her head ruefully and wrapped the reins around the upright rein pole.

The man looked more carefully toward the wagon seat. He saw Sarah as she stiffly lifted herself from the hard board seat and attempted to shake the road dust from her skirts.

His eyes opened, his jaw dropped, exposing his chewing tobacco. Then he reached upward as he jerked off his hat, and his head lowered slightly. "Ma'am," he said to her as he had been taught to greet a woman.

Sarah responded with a nod of her head and moved to climb down over the high wheel with as much decorum as she could muster.

The man was still staring. Slowly he replaced his hat, and as Sarah brushed past him to tie her team, he seemed to finally find his tongue.

"Something wrong with the mister this mornin'?" he asked.

Sarah did not even turn to look at him. "Meaning?" she flung over her shoulder. She knew he had heard what had happened to Michael. He had seen Big John and the other volunteer drivers since that time. He had even seen Sarah as she accompanied Big John. Perhaps he gathered that she was Big John Curtis's wife. Well, he was wrong. Sarah had not stopped to explain to the stationmaster the future plans for her business. It was her right to run things as she saw fit.

He acted totally flustered. "Well—I—I was—I mean I heerd thet Mike was—well—I know other men been drivin' since—I jest—jest thought—thet—well, I didn't suppose—I mean—"

Sarah finished tying her horses and stepped back to look at the man. "I am Michael's widow," she said as evenly as she could. "I will be hauling the freight from now on. You must be Mr. Parker."

The man nodded his head, though his eyes still showed disbelief. Sarah saw him swallow, and then his face turned reddish purple. She wondered if she had caused him to lose his chewing tobacco. He leaned over slightly and spit on the ground. He looked further embarrassed.

"Best we git her loaded," he said without looking at her. "Got a full load this mornin'."

Sarah hiked up her drooping hem and moved to follow.

"Just back thet there wagon up to the platform here," he went on hurriedly, as though in a great rush to get the job done.

Sarah stopped mid-stride, her skirts still in her hands. She looked first at the man and then to the platform he had indicated with a casual wave of his big, gnarled hand.

Her confusion must have been obvious, for he repeated again in the same hurried manner, "Jest back 'er up agin the platform."

This time Sarah did speak, and her voice showed her total alarm. "Back up? How?"

Her eyes traveled back to the team that was now hitched to the rail. She knew how to go ahead. She could even turn corners reasonably well, but how on earth did one ever reverse horses *and* a wagon?

The man stopped and gave Sarah a head-to-toe study. He seemed to draw some conclusions. She was a woman. She was a small woman. She really had no business trying to take over a job meant for a man. Here was trouble—and he was the one who was going to suffer for it.

He gave a sigh that looked like it came from his toes up, shook his head as though to accept his unwanted, undeserved burden, and took on the tone of one speaking to a small child or to a dog that needed training.

"Just take the reins, tug back and say—say . . ." He hesitated. Each driver had his own way of speaking to his team. "Say whatever ya like," he finished lamely, "but ya gotta git 'em from here over to there." He jerked his head at the platform where the formidable stack of freight stood waiting.

Sarah already was aching all over, and the sight of the huge pile of boxes and bags was enough to bring tears to her eyes. But she blinked them away, took a deep breath, and moved toward the waiting team and wagon.

Carefully and slowly she untied the horses, her head busy with the thought of what she must do and trying to quickly devise a plan for the doing.

She had seen Michael back the horses with no difficulty. She had seen Big John back the horses with the same ease. How had they done it? Why hadn't she watched more closely? What did one do?

She climbed stiffly over the wheel rim and settled herself on the board seat. What did she say? She lifted the reins and opened her mouth, still without formulated words when, miraculously, the horses began to reverse.

Sarah blinked. Apparently the horses were smarter than she was. When up against the hitching rail, they seemed to know that the only way to go was backward. At once Sarah felt both tremendously relieved and just a mite smug.

But the feeling did not last long.

"Now jest back 'em up to the platform here," the man behind her called.

The platform was not in the right place, Sarah quickly concluded. There was no way she could simply keep backing straight back and arrive at the proper destination. How did one do that? She would have to maneuver the wagon this way, then that way, then over there. She couldn't do that. She knew she couldn't.

Well—she could try. Bottom lip secured between her teeth, she determinedly began to work with the reins and the horses. "This way, Gyp. No—no. Over there. Here, Ginger. Easy, girl. No, this way. Gyp—turn. Hi-ya. Gyp. Gyp. You're cutting too sharp. Easy."

It was soon apparent Sarah would never be able to get the team properly positioned at the platform, and at that moment she did have sense enough to ask for help.

Turning to the stationmaster, she said as simply and straightforward as a woman on the verge of frustrated tears was able, "Could you back them please, Mr. Parker?"

The man nodded grimly, clambered up over the wheel, and took the reins Sarah extended.

Sarah realized very quickly that backing was not such an easy thing. Even the man had to do some shifting and repositioning and inching forward, then swinging back before he had the team properly in place. Sarah watched closely to see how it was done. She studied the team, the wagon wheels as they moved this way, then that, and the movement of the team and wagon. She would not find herself in this embarrassing situation again, she purposed, and made a mental note to practice backing when she got back to the stables with her team. She would work at it until no man could fault her. She would keep on until she could get it perfectly right—every time.

Once the team had been brought to a halt at the platform, Sarah stood up and again climbed down over the wheel, watching her skirts so they would not trip her up.

What a huge pile of freight faced her. What a discouragement with her already sore muscles. But it
must be loaded. That was part of the task. Sarah forced
herself toward the smallest crate of the lot. She would
load it all—somehow.

The man flushed, then stepped forward and hoisted
the largest crate with a grunt and a straining of muscles. "Best to load the biggest stuff first, ma'am," he
said around his new tobacco nip.

Now it was Sarah's turn to flush. She placed the
small box back on the wooden boards of the platform
and reached for a larger one.

"I'll git thet, ma'am," said a voice behind her, and
a broad shoulder brushed past her. Soon two burly men
were loading her freight. The red in Sarah's cheeks
deepened. This was to have been her job. If the men
had to load the boxes and barrels each time she came
for pickup, they would soon be complaining and she
might lose the route.

"Really—I—I will do the loading," she managed to
say. "I'm—I'm sure that you have your own work to be
tending to."

The nearest man just grunted and lifted another
heavy drum, and the man from the depot did not even
look her way.

Sarah stepped back and brushed her sweat-sticky
hands against her skirt. Already they felt burned and
blistered from the rough leather of the reins. How
would she ever continue to drive? Had the banker been
right? Was she incapable of keeping Michael's run going? Maybe she would lose it after all—her livelihood,
her only means of caring for baby Rebecca.

No. She would not. She refused to let it go. She
would manage on her own. She would find a way. She
would work it through. And she would not be beholden

to strange men. If she could not load the freight herself, then obviously she would need to find help. But she had to be in charge—herself.

She flicked her dusty skirt and squared her shoulders. She would talk to the stationmaster. She would make the proper arrangement. Perhaps he knew of a boy—strong and willing to load her freight each day. She would pay him. She cringed at the thought. It would bite harshly into the little bit she and Rebecca would have to live on. But if it had to be done—then it had to be done. She would still make her payments to the banker each month. She would. And with stubbornness lifting her chin and determination causing her blue eyes to intensify, Sarah grabbed up her skirt, ignoring the sagging hemline, and made her way to the little shed marked "Office."

She—and Rebecca—were not to be defeated.

It was later than Sarah would have liked when she finally pulled up in front of the Kenville hardware and began the difficult task of sorting through crates and drums and bundles to select the ones to be delivered there.

The door slammed in front of her, and she looked up to see Mr. Galvan looking at her strangely.

He didn't speak—just stood there studying her face, her dirty, dangling skirt, her stained shirtwaist, and her bedraggled hair. Then he nodded slowly, turned and called to Boyd, and moved forward to sort through the stacks of freight.

Boyd was not quite so open as he studied Sarah. She felt his eyes turn her way, slide over her quickly as though he wished to deny what he was seeing, and then busied himself helping his father.

Sarah knew better than to move forward to help. This was her town. These men were her neighbors. They would not feel that she was in their debt because of their manly concern.

When the last of their items had been lifted off and Sarah climbed wearily back up over the large wheel, about to lift the reins to move on down the street, Boyd stepped forward. He reached out a hand to pat Gyp on his muscular rump, making the dust fly in little swirls around his fingers.

"How's it goin'?" he asked simply.

Sarah shrugged. She looked down at her skirts, turned one stinging hand upward so she could study the blistered palm, and tried to lift bone-weary shoulders.

"I found a boy to help with the loading," she answered him.

He nodded and thumped the horse with a firm, flat-handed pat again. "You should be wearin' gloves," he informed her gently, not allowing his eyes to travel to her hands.

Sarah nodded back.

He fumbled with the harness, at first maybe just for something to do. But then his hands seemed to sense something wrong and he turned his attention to the straps.

"Got a tug twisted here," he said as his eyes and his hands traveled on and down the pieces of leather. He leaned to unsnap the offending piece and gave it half a turn, snapping it back in place. Sarah assumed he then would move away and she would be free to go. She was anxious to finish her deliveries and get home to little Rebecca. But Boyd did not step away from the team. Instead, he moved closer, his big, work-hardened hands traveled over the muscled side of the horse with a keen sensitivity. Sarah's eyes followed.

"Got a bit of a harness sore here," he said without a change of tone.

"Harness sore?" Sarah could vaguely remember Michael talking of harness sores. He checked his team carefully each night when he brushed them down and put them in their stall.

"Guess that tug jest rubbed a bit. You got anything to put on it?"

"Well—I'm—I'm sure that Michael has—had. He—he talked about—I think he kept something in the barn. I'm sure—"

"I'll slip over after work tonight and check on it," Boyd said simply, and without even glancing up at Sarah he stepped back from the team.

She lifted the reins and spoke to the horses, who immediately moved forward.

"Thet little Rebecca—she's somethin'," the man called after her.

A smile lifted Sarah's tired features. "She is," she called back to him. "She really is. I can hardly wait to get home."

And she flicked the reins to hurry up the team. Suddenly she had renewed strength to finish the tasks of the day.

Chapter Five

Adjustments

By the time Sarah had unhitched the team, rubbed them down, pumped enough water into the trough to give them a long drink, measured out their oats, and filled their manger with hay from the loft, her back was aching so badly that she wondered if she could make it to the house upright.

"I still need to go get Rebecca," she whispered to herself. "But first I need to clean up some. The way I look, she'd not even know me."

But when Sarah entered her kitchen by the back door, Rebecca toddled toward her with a glad cry. Sarah forgot her dirty dress. She even forgot her aching back. She hurried to sweep the infant into her arms. Tears filled her eyes and ran in streaks down her cheeks as she crooned words of love to her little girl.

"Mama missed you," she said over and over. "I missed you so much."

A movement caught Sarah's attention. Mrs. Galvan stood at the kitchen stove stirring something delightfully inviting in a cooking pot.

"Thought you might be tired out on yer first day," she offered.

Sarah sighed deeply. "I didn't imagine it would be so hard," she admitted.

"I did," the woman said with a nod. "I did. But then—you'll gradually git used to it. It'll git easier—with time."

"I certainly hope so." Sarah rose from her kneeling position and lifted Rebecca up in her arms. "Oh," she groaned with the movement, "I ache from top to bottom. I hurt in muscles I didn't even know I had."

"You'll be good and stiff tomorrow," went on the older woman. "I've fixed you a hot bath with Epsom Salts in yer room. You run along and soak an' I'll tend Rebecca."

"But your own supper—" began Sarah.

"Got it fixed and on the back of the stove. Men can help themselves if I'm missin'. They've done it before. Never have starved either."

Sarah glanced down at her rumpled, dirty shirtwaist. "I'll never get this clean again," she murmured sadly as she moved stiffly toward her bedroom and the welcoming bath.

While she soaked she listened to Rebecca's happy chatter from the kitchen. Mrs. Galvan's low voice spoke often to the little girl, but Sarah did not even try to understand the words. She was so tired. So weary. It seemed that she had dragged the entire weight of a troubled world around in that freight wagon all day long. She tried to shrug it away and relax. Surely, as Mrs. Galvan had said, it would get easier.

———

Knowing that another long day faced her, Sarah

was about to retire. The light rap on her front door stopped her in her steps toward her bedroom.

"Who can that be?" she muttered to herself, and the thought of the banker checking up on her entered her mind. Her shoulders straightened unconsciously and she crossed swiftly to the door.

But it was Boyd who stood there. At the sight of him she remembered his promise. She also remembered her neglect.

"Oh—the harness sore—I forgot all about it."

"I checked on it," he said easily. "I rubbed some salve into it and padded that piece of harness. I don't think it will be a problem."

Sarah stepped back, nodding acknowledgment and murmuring her thanks. "Come in," she invited, feeling embarrassed about her lack of courtesy.

"I won't be stoppin'," he said and stepped back rather than forward. "Jest wanted to let you know it's been cared for."

"Thank you. Thanks so much," Sarah managed to say. "I—I had forgotten—"

"You have a lot on your mind. I'll check on the horses now and then. They look sound right now."

Sarah frowned. "Check? What—?" She had no idea what to watch for. Hadn't even realized that it was part of the task.

"Jest run a hand over them now and then. See if they flinch. That means sore spots."

"Sore spots? Like—from the harness?"

"And muscles an' things."

Sarah's head started to spin. The freight-hauling itself had turned out to be much more complicated than she had imagined. Now this.

"An' check their feet to—"

"Check their feet?" Sarah was aghast.

Boyd nodded.

"What—? How do you do that?" Sarah thought of the large, hair-covered hooves of the pair of animals. How would one ever go about checking them? And what did one check?

"Never mind," he said hurriedly. "I'll drop by and check them."

He appeared to feel it was settled and nodded as he turned to go. Sarah spoke quickly. She had to get things clearly settled before they got out of hand.

"No," she said, reaching her hand out as though to hold him in place. "No—they are my team. I must learn to care for them myself."

He looked up at her from his place on the step below the open doorway where she stood, a shadow in his eyes.

"I mean—I—I really need to know how to care for my own horses," she repeated more gently. "I—I can't—can't live—dependent on them—if—if I don't even know how to care for them. Don't you see?" she finished lamely.

He nodded.

Sarah swallowed and felt the color flushing her cheeks. As much as she hated to be in anyone's debt, she knew that she needed this man's help.

"But—I—I would be—be forever grateful if you could—could teach me what I need to know. That is— if you have the time," she hurried on.

He nodded again. His troubled eyes seemed to brighten.

"I'll teach ya," he said simply, and Sarah knew it was a promise that would not be broken.

One day seemed to slide into another, losing its own identity in the sameness of the routine. Sarah did gradually get used to wrestling the harness over the broad backs, and she did learn to wear tough leather gloves that helped with the bruises and blisters of her slowly toughening hands. She paid the strong-backed boy who daily loaded her freight, and managed, with the help of the kind hometown folk, to get it unloaded at the other end.

She even learned to dress more appropriately for the task at hand, choosing skirts that were darker and not as full and shirtwaists that wouldn't show the dirt as readily and had no ribbons or frills to catch on the bundles and boxes that she endeavored to maneuver into organized place. Her abundant hair, that Michael had always adored, was pulled back out of her way in a much simplified fashion. She often wanted to weep as she surveyed herself in the mirror. She felt as if she had forsaken her femininity—but that was the price to pay for survival. This was the only way she knew of to provide for Rebecca.

"How are you?"

Sarah had been asked the question many times over the past few weeks, but perhaps never with such sincere concern. Mr. Murray, who stood beside her in the churchyard, held her eyes steadily, so she was reluctant to give a quick reply.

"I'm—I'm doing—fine," she finally answered. She felt that the answer was a truthful one, though it didn't reveal her discouragement concerning the long, difficult days on the road or her regret at needing to miss so much of young Rebecca's daily growing up.

He looked at her steadily. His gaze seemed to rest for a moment on her small, toughening hands. She quickly pulled on her Sunday gloves with a nervous gesture.

"I will still be happy to teach you the clerking," he said in a soft voice so it would not carry to the other members of the congregation who stood around them chatting.

"You are kind," she whispered back. "I—I do appreciate it."

"You will feel free to let me know if there is ever—anything that I can do?"

His direct question called for an honest answer. She wished to say, "No. No, I will never feel free to ask for anyone's help. I want to make it on my own." But his gaze made her change her mind. Perhaps—perhaps she would need someone—sometime. And if she did, she knew of nowhere else to turn. She lowered her head to avoid the penetrating eyes and said softly, "I promise."

When she lifted her eyes again to look at him, he was still studying her. He nodded slightly, his eyes still showing concern even though a bit of a smile played about his lips; then he lifted his hat and bid her a good-day.

"A funny little man," Sarah breathed to herself as he walked away. "So—so intense."

But it gave her a good feeling to know that she had someone on whom she could count. Someone to turn to.

She called to Rebecca, who was playing nearby with another child, waved to Mrs. Galvan, and started for home.

———

Each month—on time—Sarah met the bank payment, and she couldn't help but feel a bit smug as she counted out the money onto the desk of the solemn banker.

And every Sunday was her day. Her own special day with Rebecca. After the morning church service they ate their simple dinner together, chattering and laughing. Sarah tried hard to fill the huge gap in their home and the place in their hearts that had once been filled by Michael.

Rebecca was growing quickly. She was now steady on her feet and rarely tumbled as she ran about the house or yard. And daily she seemed to add new words to her limited vocabulary. Mrs. Galvan always seemed to have some amusing little anecdote to tell Sarah when she returned home, shoulders weary, body dragging from another difficult day on the dray wagon.

Boyd had kept his promise. Sarah knew more about Gyp and Ginger than she had thought possible to know about horses. She no longer felt so intimidated as she worked with them. They were more than just animals. More than just big animals. They were part of her team. Necessary for her livelihood. Needed for her very survival. It was vital to keep them well and strong.

She checked them carefully each night and each morning. She went over the harness, the wagon, each working part of the partnership. She prayed as she studied carefully each part of her equipment and team that Boyd had not forgotten any detail. She did not know what she would have done without him—but she was independent now. She had learned what must be done. She was on her own. And making it. They had little income to spare—but they were making it.

———

A long, pleasant fall was roughly pushed aside by a sudden winter storm. From her bed Sarah knew the howling wind and the slashing of snow against the windowpane meant that the day would not be an easy one. She hated the thought of pulling herself from her bed. She dreaded hitching the team in the tearing wind. She hated the thought of the cold, bitter miles of travel to pick up the freight and then deliver it all.

But she forced herself out of the warmth of the heavy comforter and pushed her feet into the depth of the wool rug by her bed. She shivered as she struck a match and held it to the wick of the kerosene lamp, the cold globe in her left hand.

Hurriedly she dressed in her warmest skirt and pulled a sweater over her shirtwaist.

"I'll need every shred of warmth I can find today, I'm thinking," she said under her breath as she ran a comb through her hair and wound it securely at the nape of her neck.

Quietly she left her room and tiptoed past the bed where Rebecca slept. "Poor Mrs. Galvan," she said to herself. "I do hate getting her up and out into this."

As often in the past, Sarah again thanked God for the good neighbor. "I sure don't know what I would ever have done without her," she murmured and hurried to light the fire.

But it was Boyd who stood at the back step when she answered the door a few moments later.

"Ma has a bit of rheumatism this mornin'," he informed her gently. "Didn't think it wise to go out in the weather. I'll wait for Rebecca to wake up and take her on over home."

Sarah felt a frown wrinkling her brow. He seemed to notice it.

"Ma'll be fine," he quickly informed her. "Jest

didn't think it wise to come out."

"But—but you need to—to get to work," Sarah managed.

"Rebecca doesn't sleep late. Pa will mind the store until I get there. No one'll be stirrin' in this weather anyway."

Sarah cast a glance out the window and nodded in mute agreement.

"Fact is," Boyd went on, his tone casual, "I sorta figured that I might—that you might let me take the run this mornin'. I mean with Ma sorta down, maybe you should jest stay on home with Rebecca yerself."

Sarah looked at him. Was Mrs. Galvan really sick?

" 'Course Ma'll be fine," he added quickly at her concerned look. "Jest didn't think it wise to come out. So it would work fine for you to stay on home with the little one and I'll jest take—"

"But your father will need you at the store," Sarah reminded him.

"Well—like I said, not much chance anyone'll be stirrin' about today—in this weather."

"Then you really don't mind staying until Rebecca wakens?"

"Not a'tall. If thet's what you're wantin'."

"It is," said Sarah simply and moved to get her coat. He seemed to know that he had lost.

"Maybe you should show me Becky's clothes," he said to her retreating back. Sarah turned and looked at him in surprise. She had never heard her little girl called Becky before.

"They are all laid out," she answered him. She always prepared the child's clothes for the next day before they retired at night.

He watched as she shrugged into her heavy long coat.

"Got anything better for your feet?" he asked solicitously, his gaze moving to her shoes.

Sarah shook her head.

"They're likely to freeze in those—those flimsy little things. At least pull some heavy socks over them."

"I—I don't have any," Sarah responded.

"Hasn't Michael—?" He stopped.

It had been some months since anyone had spoken of Michael in Sarah's presence. It brought her up short. When she managed to breathe again she spoke, trying to keep her voice controlled, even. "There are likely some in his drawer."

"Best use them," he responded, and she noted that his voice had a quiver.

She turned to go for the heavy socks.

"Be a good idea to pull on a heavy pair of pants, too," he added quietly so as not to awaken Rebecca.

Sarah half turned to look at him to see if he was serious. A woman—in a man's pants. Hardly. But he was serious. She could tell it by the look on his face. "Never!" she muttered softly to herself.

"I'll take a heavy robe," she said to the man, and he seemed to know that it would have to do.

"Take two robes," he replied. "One to throw over the seat and hang down to protect the back of your legs and one to throw over you."

It sounded sensible to Sarah. She determined to take two heavy robes from those stacked in the back closet.

———

The wind was even more fierce than Sarah had thought. She struggled to make her way against it, fighting to secure her long coat about her and hold tightly to the heavy robes in her arms. She dreaded the thought of harnessing the team and hitching them to the wagon, but as she arrived at the barn, she was surprised to find them already hitched and tied to the hitching post.

"Boyd shouldn't do that," she mumbled to herself. "He shouldn't pamper me. I can quite look after myself."

But she quickly chided herself. "He is a good neighbor. His mother has brought him up to be mannerly. Proper. No—more than proper. *Christian,*" she admitted. "I don't know how I ever would manage without her. She likely was the one who sent Boyd out to care for me."

Tears overflowed onto Sarah's cheeks. She did not know if they had been caused by emotions or the biting wind.

———

"Mornin', ma'am."

The voice behind her caused Sarah to whirl around. She had not expected someone to be standing near her team, especially on such a cold, stormy morning. She drew in her breath sharply.

"Didn't mean to startle you, ma'am," the low voice continued but there was really no apology in the tone.

"What do you—?" began Sarah, clutching the robes tightly in her arms.

"Nasty mornin'," the voice drawled slowly, and the man in the deep shadows stepped forward.

Sarah found herself wishing to retreat but she held her ground.

"I don't believe I know you," she managed to say and was surprised at the control of her own voice.

"I been around," the man answered carelessly.

"Heerd you been takin' the freight run."

Sarah nodded, even though she knew the morning darkness likely hid the motion.

"Hardly a job fer a little lady," the voice went on. "I was jest thinkin' thet I'd be glad to take yer line off yer hands. Even willin' to buy up yer team and wagon—at a fair price."

"I've no intention to sell," responded Sarah quickly and moved forward to deposit the heavy lap robes on the wagon seat.

"I could even start this mornin'," the voice went on. "No need fer you to go out in this storm."

"I'm prepared," said Sarah simply, nodding her head toward the heavy blankets.

The tone of the voice seemed to change. "Heerd ya was a mite hardheaded. I been patient long enough. If one can't hear good reason," the voice went on, and Sarah noted a threat in the words. She felt a finger of fear trace all the way down her spine.

She spun on her heel and faced the man still shrouded in darkness. "What are you meaning, mister?" she demanded, her own voice deepened with emotion.

"Nothin' a'tall, ma'am. Jest seems a little lady like yerself might take a bit of good advice and give in to reason. Never know what could happen."

"Meaning?"

"Well—" he drawled. "Banker says it jest keeps you scrapin' to meet those payments. Seems more sense to sell—and git somethin'—than lose the route and git nothin'." His voice sounded like a smirk in the darkness. Sarah shivered.

So that was it. The banker was somehow involved with this vile man and his threats.

"I've no plans to lose the route," she said firmly.

"Perhaps the banker also told you that I have never been late with a payment."

"So far," he responded easily. "So far."

Was he seriously threatening her or was he just talking idly to try to frighten her? She chose to believe the later and moved past him to untie her team.

"If you'll excuse me," she said, her head high, "I have a run to make."

The man chuckled softly. His laugh brought the fear to her soul more than his words had. She tried to still the rapid pounding of her heart as she climbed up into her wagon and eased the team away from the hitching rail. In the blackness of the winter morning with its sweeping storm of white, Sarah could see the outline of the man, dark against the darkness of her barn. Who was he? Why was he speaking to her as he had? Who was behind all this? Why had he mentioned the banker? She was making the payments. What more could the banker gain from the freight business than what he was already realizing? Sarah felt very unnerved. Should she tell someone about the threats? Or should she keep them to herself? And if she shared her fears, to whom should she talk? It was all so disturbing.

Chapter Six

Difficulties

Sarah was glad her team knew the road even better than she did. For much of the trip to the train depot, she simply slackened the reins and let the horses find their way through the storm. The wind whipped around her, threatening to tear the heavy rug from off her. She was forced to warm her hands under the robe, one at a time, in order to keep them from freezing; and she feared that her face might freeze even though her back was to the wind.

"How will we ever get home to Kenville in this storm?" she asked herself. "It's bad enough traveling with it at our back." The horses' broad backs and plodding gait were some comfort.

When they finally reached the depot, the station-master looked up sharply when Sarah forced her way into the small office. The snow swirled about her long skirts as she leaned back heavily to push the door shut against the force of the wind.

"You out in this storm?" he asked incredulously.

Sarah looked blank.

"Don't you have freight to be delivered?" she asked

through stiff lips. She was so cold she no longer shivered.

If I have driven all the way through this storm and there is no freight to haul—she began her mental protest.

" 'Course there's freight. But it coulda waited. Weather out there's not fit fer man nor beast. Coulda made the haul tomorra."

"I'm here now," said Sarah weakly. "Is Hank around?"

"He was hangin' around for part of the mornin'. Think he mighta gone on home now."

Sarah's shoulders slumped. She had freight to load and no lad for the loading.

"I'll give ya a hand this mornin'. Not as much to load up as some days."

Wordlessly he pulled on his heavy mackinaw and then grabbed his fur-lined mitts.

"Never seen such a storm to start the winter," he yelled as the two of them left the warmth of the little building and struggled against the force of the wind.

It was impossible to converse further. The storm took their words—and almost their breath—away on its angry blast. They were both exhausted and breathing heavily by the time the freight was loaded.

At least I've warmed up a bit, Sarah thought as she went to gather the reins.

"Sure you shouldn't be stayin' here till this lessens up?" the man yelled almost in her ear.

"I can't," Sarah shouted back at him. "I have to get the freight out."

"It'll wait," he said loudly. "Nobody will be out lookin' fer it today anyway. Leave the deliveries till tomorrow and stay here till the storm dies down."

"I've got a baby girl waiting for me," Sarah yelled again.

"She'll be taken care of," the man replied.

Yes. Rebecca would be quite safe with Mrs. Galvan. Still, Sarah's mother-heart felt compelled to get back home. She gave the man one last look, hoping that he would understand her stubbornness, then gathered the reins and climbed aboard.

The trip home was even worse than she would have dared to think. She could not see the team in front of her through the driving snow. Perhaps the man had been right. The storm seemed to have worsened. She should have stayed where she was safe until the height of the fury had passed. Now she was halfway between nothing and nowhere. There were not even any shacks in which to take shelter as far as she knew.

At length she wrapped the reins around the rein pole, letting the team forge ahead on their own, curled up in a ball in the bottom of the wagon, her feet tucked firmly beneath her, and bundled herself as securely as she could in the heavy robes.

It seemed that the trip would never end. At times Sarah felt as if she had lost all control of her senses. She knew she had lost track of time. Sometimes she even wondered if they were still moving, but then another jolt of the wagon would assure her that the team was steadily plodding on.

"I wonder where we're going?" she whispered to herself through frozen lips. "Where will we end up when this is over? If it ever ends. Oh, God, please— please—if I don't make it—take care of Rebecca. Take care of my little girl."

Sarah dozed off, then awoke with a start and stirred slightly. Her whole body felt numb. "I must stay awake. I must try to move," she told herself. But she was beyond moving.

Suddenly she realized that the team was no longer trudging through the storm. The wagon was no longer rumbling its way over the rutted road. They had come to a standstill.

"Thank God you're home," a familiar voice spoke through the still-whirling snow. It was Boyd.

"I am? I am home?"

Sarah could not believe it. She turned her head to look about her. The team of bays had stopped in front of their own barn door.

For reasons Sarah could not have explained, she buried her head on the heavy rug and wept.

———

Boyd took the wagon for the rest of the week. Sarah was not prepared to argue. Mrs. Galvan sided with her son and insisted that Sarah stay put until she fully recuperated from the ordeal. There was concern about frostbite, but after some miserable, painful days, Sarah seemed to have fared quite well.

"I'll never know how you ever made it through," said the kind neighbor woman. "I prayed all day."

"I guess that's how I made it," replied Sarah. "I was doing a good deal of praying myself."

Sarah had almost forgotten about the threatening man who had appeared as though out of the storm. Now and then his words came back to haunt her. She still puzzled over their meaning. But with Boyd driving the wagon until she was again able to resume the run, Sarah pushed the matter from her mind.

The next week the weather had settled down to being just cold and bleak, and Sarah picked up the reins again to take back the freight route. But by then she was willing to lay aside her pride. She rummaged through the drawer still filled with Michael's clothes and came up with heavy woollen trousers. She pulled the sturdy pair of pants over her woollen stockings and refused to look at herself in the hall mirror. She did not wish to see the unsightly, unladylike figure she had become. Instead, she turned her back on her own reflection, pulled one of Michael's bulky sweaters over her own, and looked down at her heavily stockinged feet.

"It will only be until the weather turns warm again," she promised herself. "Then I can go back to being a lady."

She stepped into the small nursery room and pressed a kiss on Rebecca's soft head. She was glad the child was still sleeping. Surely she would have found it difficult to recognize her own mother in such a getup.

"Have you heard the news?" Mrs. Galvan asked when Sarah went to reclaim Rebecca at the end of an early spring day.

Sarah lifted her eyes to the older woman's face to judge if the news forthcoming would be good or bad.

"What news?" she asked, though from the look on the woman's face she knew it was not to be good news.

"You're to have some competition."

"Competition?"

The woman nodded her head. Sarah could hear the irritation in Mrs. Galvan's voice when she spoke.

"Some fella is runnin' around town tryin' to git folks to hire him to haul their freight."

Sarah could not believe her ears.

"Stopped by the store. Guess Boyd let 'im know where he stood on the matter."

"But—who—?" began Sarah.

"Some fella by the name of Williams or Wilson or somethin'. He's fairly new in town—though Boyd says he's seen him hangin' around some."

Sarah's mind flew back to the stranger who had presented himself in the storm. Over the months that had followed she had had only fleeting thoughts about his challenge.

"Been makin' all sorts of wild promises. Promises earlier delivery—lower rates—free unloadin'."

"Folks don't pay for the unloading now," cut in Sarah.

"No—but most of them do their own," rejoined Mrs. Galvan.

Sarah had to admit it was true. When Michael had done the hauling, he had also done the unloading. Since Sarah had taken over the route, folks had just started out giving her a hand. Now she thought nothing of it as they unloaded their own freight.

"I should be doing the unloading myself," she murmured quietly.

"Nonsense," said Mrs. Galvan. "No one in this here town minds lendin' a hand."

Sarah felt her shoulders slump. She had made it through her first winter. She had never missed a payment at the bank. She had thought they were over the worst hurdle. Even though she was always exhausted when she arrived home at the end of a long day, yet she was gradually getting used to the wearisome grind.

And Rebecca seemed to be doing fine. She babbled and chatted and showed her mother all the new tricks she learned at the Galvan household. Rebecca did not seem to be suffering at all in spite of her disjointed home life. For that, Sarah was the most thankful.

"Do you think—? Do you think it is a real— threat?" Sarah managed to ask, her voice a bit husky. She didn't know what she would do if she lost her customers.

"Boyd—Boyd thinks it's a matter for concern," Mrs. Galvan said honestly.

Sarah allowed herself the support of a nearby kitchen chair.

"What can I do?" she asked wearily.

"Well—you will never lose some of your customers. In fact, I would suspect a good number of the folks will stand behind you. But—well—it could be harder to meet those bank payments each month."

Sarah nodded. She had taken great pride in being able to meet the payments—even over the tough winter months. But there had been very little to spare for their other needs. On two occasions she had been afraid she might have to accept the credit at Alex Murray's store.

"I—I can't afford to lose *any*," she managed. "I—I just barely make it now."

"I don't know how important it is to get the freight in earlier," Mrs. Galvan went on.

"I can always leave earlier in the morning," answered Sarah.

"You don't get enough sleep now," interposed Mrs. Galvan.

"Rebecca has been a bit fussy the last two nights. She's had a bit of a tummy upset. She'll soon be sleeping fine again."

"It's more than one or two nights of lost sleep. You've been pushing too hard, Sarah. We are all worried about you. Look at you. You're near skin and bones."

Sarah looked down at her loosely hanging garments. "It's just these big clothes of Michael's," she
argued. "If I were in my own things, I wouldn't look
like this."

"You wear your own things on Sunday, Sarah. The
folks at church are really worried. You look thinner
every week."

Sarah had to admit that she had lost weight. But
she didn't think she looked so bad that the entire congregation should be fretting over her.

She attempted to change the subject. "What do you
think I can do about this new—this competition?"

"Can you afford to take a cut in your hauling
rates?" the older woman asked.

Sarah thought about it. "I am operating on a narrow margin now," she admitted. "I don't know how I'd
ever manage to make it on any less."

"Then I guess we've got some real prayin' to do,"
Mrs. Galvan said seriously.

The two women looked at each other for a long moment. That seemed to be the only answer.

Sarah called to Rebecca, who was playing with a
kitten and a spool of thread.

"Come, love. Time to go home now."

For the first time ever Rebecca did not instantly
run to her mother, anxious to go home.

"Rebecca," called Sarah to the busy little figure.
"It's time to go home."

Rebecca lifted her head long enough to look
squarely at her mother. "Wanna play," she said plainly.
"Wanna stay with Auntie Min. You go."

She waved a tiny hand toward the door, her eyes
still on her mother's face. "You go," she said again.

Sarah could not have described the pain that
pierced her heart. This was worse then losing the

freight route. Her own daughter—the child she loved
with all her heart was calmly dismissing her in favor
of Auntie Min. She was no longer the most important
person in Rebecca's world. It hurt so badly that it took
her breath away.

"Come on, Rebecca," Mrs. Galvan called, seeming
to sense Sarah's deep pain. "Yer mama is ready to go
home now. You can play with Tiger in the morning."

She did not wait for the child to respond favorably
but crossed the room and lifted her up in her arms.

"Remember what you have to take home? Remember the cookies that we baked especially for your supper?"

Rebecca immediately became excited. "We baked
cookie for you," she said to Sarah. "Me can carry. Me."

The fact that the small child had been placated and
agreed to accompany her mother home did very little
to ease the hurt in Sarah's heart.

———

It had not been a false rumor. The next day as
Sarah pulled into the station to pick up her load, she
spotted another wagon there ahead of her, the team
already tied and a man loading barrels. Sarah was
nearly positive it was the man who had spoken to her
through the darkness. She was sure if he were to speak
now, she would recognize his voice.

Her manner was cool as she approached the depot
office.

"Miz Perry," Mr. Parker said, as though surprised
to see her there or embarrassed to be discovered giving
business to another in her place. "Didn't know iffen
you'd be in today."

"I am in every day, Mr. Parker," Sarah reminded him evenly.

"Well—er—of course. 'Cept we heerd ya might be turning over yer route."

"I've no idea who started that rumor," Sarah replied, her back straight, her chin up. "It certainly didn't come from me."

"Well, I wouldn't be faultin' ya for it none, ma'am. Mighty tough job fer a woman."

"I think I've been doing the job," Sarah said in a rather loud voice. She hoped with all her heart that her words carried to the man hoisting the barrels. "I've heard no complaints from my customers. No complaints at all. Have you, Mr. Parker?"

"No—no, none at all," the man was quick to assure her.

"Then I am assuming that you have some freight for me to haul today," Sarah went on.

" 'Course. 'Course," replied the man. "Thet there pile right there," and he pointed to the stack to her left. Sarah noticed that it was smaller than normal. That meant that the competition had already managed to weasel away some of her business.

"Where is Hank?" she asked the depot manager.

"I—I believe he's gone on home, ma'am," said the man at the barrels.

Sarah did recognize his voice. It most certainly was the man who had accosted her during the severe winter storm. She was sure that he was responsible for sending the boy home when there was indeed freight to be loaded. Her eyes went back to the pile. Perhaps it was better that the lad was not there. At least she would not have to pay him this time.

"Fine," she said, giving the unwelcome stranger a straight look and setting about to load her own pile.

Even though the crates and bundles were not as numerous as usual, and even though the man had managed to take all the barrels she normally hauled, Sarah's back was ready to break by the time she wrestled the last crate on board. By then the other team had already pulled out and was making dust on the track that ran from the north side of the town.

He'll beat me back to town, and that's for sure, Sarah said angrily to herself. *He's got lighter, faster horses.* For the first time since she had taken on her job, Sarah felt dissatisfaction with her team. They were steady and reliable—but they were anything but fast. They plodded along in spite of her urging them to hurry.

"I might have to get some faster horses," she said to herself. "Faster horses and a lighter wagon."

But she thought of all of the rough miles of traveling and knew instinctively that she was much better off with the outfit she had. Hadn't she heard Michael say many times in the past that for hauling freight one needed a good strong, steady team and a wagon that could take the road and the weather? Had Michael been wrong? Was she about to lose her dray business to a man who seemed bent on running a race?

Sarah's eyes stung with unshed tears as she urged the horses forward. After all her hard struggles, it looked as if she might lose, after all.

Chapter Seven

Making It

"I hope you do not see it as interference, but I— I've talked to some of the men in town—about the freight line."

Sarah looked evenly at Alex Murray. He held her gaze.

"I've been concerned about you—Mrs. Perry. I thought—well, I thought it was one way that I might be—of help."

Sarah nodded slowly. Just what had Alex Murray said to the town men?

"Most of them are—are quite solid in their commitment to you—just as long as your service stays— stays acceptable. But—I'm ashamed to say—there were one or two who—who rather resent unloading their own freight. And they—they say—"

"If that is the case," put in Sarah quickly, "I'll hire a boy to help with the unloading."

"Can you afford that?" the man asked in straightforward manner.

"No—no, I really can't," Sarah said just as honestly. "But I cannot afford to lose the business either."

Alex Murray nodded his head. "Perhaps—perhaps it won't be for long. You are looking fatigued, Mrs. Perry. I do hope—"

Again Sarah cut in. "Life is a contest, Mr. Murray. My grandfather used to say that. The strong survive and the weak— I cannot beat the man in speed. I cannot meet his prices. I'm already just—just managing the loan payments. I cannot unload those heavy crates and barrels myself—not that I have any barrels to unload now—he has already taken that from me. But I can continue to give solid, dependable service. That is all that I can do and—if—if he outwits me—outlasts me—then I have done my best. I don't know what more I can do."

Silence hung between them for several minutes. Sarah stood before the man with slumped shoulders, the lines of worry creasing her forehead.

Sarah looked up suddenly, catching his own expression of worry and concern. She gave him an unexpected smile, straightened her shoulders, and gave her sweeping skirts a little shake as though in doing so she could shake some of her heavy responsibilities from her slender shoulders.

"I must hurry," she said. "I am on my way to pick up my daughter. We have precious little time together as it is. I don't want to miss one moment of it."

The man nodded. "My, she's growing," he commented. "She was in with Mrs. Galvan yesterday. Chatters along with the best of them."

Sarah beamed. "Yes. Yes—my little girl is growing up. Too fast, it seems. Each week—each day, it seems she learns something new. Sometimes she surprises even me."

"The Galvans certainly enjoy having her."

Sarah's eyes shadowed slightly. "I don't know what

I ever would have done without Mrs. Galvan," she said honestly. But in the back of her heart was the pain that she was slowly losing her importance in the eyes of her little girl. She had to change that. Had to spend more time with Rebecca. Had to do more things—find time for fun—be together. It wasn't right that a little girl should have her cookie baking, her story time, her exploration with someone other than her mother. It just wasn't right. The only answer seemed to be to leave earlier in the morning so she could be back earlier in the afternoon.

But that too posed a dilemma. How could she ask Mrs. Galvan to get up even earlier to come to her house to stay with the sleeping child? That wasn't fair. Sarah had yet to solve her problem. But she knew that the first and foremost matter was to get that loan at the bank paid off so she wouldn't be in the banker's clutches.

"I—I must hurry," she said to the man before her. Her thoughts had been miles away. She flushed slightly.

"You—you will remember," the man prompted gently. "If ever you—need a little help—?"

Sarah nodded. She prayed that day might never come. Still—if it did, she prayed also that her pride would let her accept the offer. It would be much better to take help from a brother in their little church family and provide for her little girl than to refuse help and have no means to care for Rebecca.

"I'll remember," she said solemnly and managed a grateful smile, and she turned and hurried from the store. She could hardly wait to see Rebecca. It was the moment she lived for each day.

———

"Rebecca has asked for a kitten," Mrs. Galvan informed Sarah. "Do you mind?"

Sarah did not know how to respond. A kitten would also need care.

"Well, I—" she began. She hated to refuse her little girl.

"We'll just bring it back here with her during the day—but she can take it home with her in the evening," explained Mrs. Galvan. "I thought it might give her something to—to sort of tie her two homes together. There are three of the little rascals there. The one she holds is a little female—the two tearing my rug apart are males. She can have whichever one you think best."

Sarah looked up then, her restless hands suddenly motionless. The shifting back and forth from home to home must be hard on her little daughter. Rebecca always seemed so happy. So eager to be with the Galvans. Sarah had not stopped to think that the child might have some deep emotional needs of her own.

"Of course," she answered Mrs. Galvan. "A kitten would be good for her. She loves animals so."

Michael had loved animals. Sarah had often teased that she was sure he would have filled the barn—and the house—had she permitted it. In fact, Michael was about to choose himself a dog. Sarah wasn't too fond of dogs—at least not in her house. But Michael had assured her that the dog would sleep in the barn with the horses and go with him each day to haul freight.

"If—if you are going to allow Rebecca a kitten, then—I thought you might like to be the one to—to tell her about it," went on Mrs. Galvan.

"But it's your—"

"I've just given it to you," said the woman without even looking Sarah's way.

How wise—and caring she is, thought Sarah. *She knows—she knows how I ache because—because Rebecca is slowly . . .* But Sarah did not allow herself to finish the thought. She would accept Mrs. Galvan's offer. She would take advantage of the opportunity to give Rebecca something special. She had so little chances for such expression of her love.

Sarah let her eyes rest on her little girl who sat on the floor cuddling the kitten in her arms. The child turned eyes toward her mother as though she knew she was the subject of interest. "Kitty love me," she said with confidence.

"Do you want a kitty?" asked Sarah, and she left her chair at the kitchen table and crossed the room to the little girl.

The two other kittens rolled beneath a nearby chair, clawing at imaginary somethings in the air around them.

Rebecca looked up, her large brown eyes wide as they met her mother's. Then she pressed the kitten she held against her soft baby cheek.

Sarah fought to keep the tears from falling. How like Michael's eyes were those of her little girl.

"Next week is your birthday. You'll be two years old," Sarah told her daughter. "How would you like a kitten for your birthday?"

Rebecca looked puzzled for one moment, but then her eyes lit up.

"For me?"

"Yes. For your very own."

Rebecca giggled and held the kitten out where she could get a better look at it. Then she giggled again and pulled it back to press it against her little chest.

"Aunt Min says—" began Sarah, then caught herself and started again. "You may pick whichever kitten you like the best, and we will take it home to our house. It will be yours."

Rebecca looked around her. She studied the two playing kittens, held the one in her arms out and surveyed it carefully and then looked at the other two again.

When she turned back to her mother she seemed confident of her decision. "This one," she said, holding up the kitten in her hands. "This one."

Sarah reached out her hand to stroke the softness of the kitten. She was a cute little thing.

"What shall we call her?' she asked gently.

Rebecca appeared to be thinking. "Unca Boy," she said, her eyes sparkling.

"Boyd?"

Rebecca nodded emphatically.

"But Boyd is a man's name—this little kitten is a girl."

"Unca Boy," insisted Rebecca.

Sarah shrugged and laughed gently. "Uncle Boyd it is, then. I wonder how he'll feel having a cat named after him."

Mrs. Galvan joined the laughter from the stove where she was removing loaves of bread from a hot oven.

"It is so good to hear you laugh, Sarah," Mrs. Galvan said approvingly. "Here—I baked an extra loaf for you and Rebecca to have with your supper."

———

All through the hot summer and into the fall, Sarah fought to keep her freight line going. The competition became almost unbearable. Sarah would have given up in defeat many times had it not been for little Rebecca.

But because of her love for the little girl, her commitment to provide for her, she struggled on.

"I'll never make it," she said as she counted out her monthly loan payment from her meager earnings. "I'll never make it. I have barely enough. What will we ever live on?" She looked at the few bills and coins spread out on her bed.

Sarah knew she had to swallow her pride and accept the credit offered her by Alex Murray.

The next month Sarah did not even have enough to make the loan payment. Slowly, ever so slowly, she lost additional customers to the competition.

"I'm sorry," the man at the livery stable had said, his eyes refusing to meet hers. "But I have a family to feed too. I have to take the lowest price. I have to."

Sarah had turned and left. He was right of course. She could not blame him. But there was no way she could lower her prices and survive. She didn't know how the man who billed himself as "Fast Freight Lines" could undercut her so far and continue to operate.

Sarah faced another long, difficult winter. She was praying harder than she had ever done in all her life. She couldn't go on, month after month, living on help from Alex Murray. There would come a day when those bills, too, would need to be met. Sarah sat down and did some serious calculating. She wrote down the amount still owed the bank. The debt was slowly receding, thank God for that. Then she added the amount now owed to Alex Murray. She made another column of her reasonable assets—like the team, the wagon, her barn and hay shed. Her eyes wandered about the room and she mentally calculated some of her household items. If she continued as she was, she felt she might hold out for an additional three months. Three months—no more. She would not allow herself to get into debt further than she would be able to pay off.

She stretched, lifted a thin, calloused hand to rub her aching neck. Three months. Just three more months and she and little Rebecca would be virtually penniless. What would she do then? It didn't matter about her. Sarah was past caring about herself. But what of Rebecca? What of Michael's little girl?

———————

The first good news came through Alex Murray. "Hear your competition had him a little trouble this morning."

Sarah's face registered her surprise.

"Trouble? How?"

"Seems his one horse went lame. Not surprising. He's been asking an awful lot of them over the past months. Slight horses like that were built for speed—not endurance."

Sarah thought of her own team. She had grown fond of Gyp and Ginger since she started working with them. She would hate to lose one of them. They had become more than just horses. They were like friends.

"I hadn't heard," said Sarah softly. She truly felt bad about the horse.

"He missed his freight haul yesterday. Some of his customers weren't too happy, I hear."

Alex was smiling. Sarah knew that he expected her to smile also, but for some reason the smile would not come. Should she gloat over the troubles of another? Did her Christian beliefs and behavior mean less to her than her livelihood?

"He's borrowed a horse from somewhere to make today's trip, so I guess he plans to keep on."

Sarah nodded, struggling with disappointment but relieved the lame horse would get a reprieve.

But a week later, when the winter snows made the rutted roads even more difficult to travel, Fast Freight Lines had another mishap. This time it was the wagon. It was simply built too light to withstand the constant jarring and straining of the rugged roads. It seemed that there was no wagon to borrow, and Sarah found herself hauling the man's load while he tried to get his wagon repaired and rolling again. This time Sarah felt little sympathy. There was no animal suffering.

When Fast Freight Lines returned to the road again, Sarah retained some of his customers. It was a welcome relief that when the monthly bank note was due, Sarah did not have to borrow further from Mr. Murray, though she was still unable to pay back any she owed the man.

At least I'm not going further into debt, she said to herself, and Sarah bowed her head for a quick prayer of thanks.

For three additional weeks the struggle went on. The weather did not improve, the road became even harder to travel, and week by week Sarah gradually gained back more customers from the past. At the end of the three weeks, there was no sign of Fast Freight Lines. Without giving his remaining customers notice, he simply ceased to appear. With red faces the men who had still been supporting the competition asked Sarah if she would haul for them again.

She had won. She had weathered the storm—and come out on top.

Sarah had never felt so relieved in her entire life. Nor so grateful. God—God and her friends—had seen her through. She would be able to provide for little Rebecca, after all.

————

"I've been thinking," Sarah said slowly. "I really would like more time with Rebecca. I need more time with her—but—but—I hardly know how to—to—" She stopped, then went on. "I mean—with the freight increasing more and more—it takes me longer with the loading and unloading. And she needs to go to bed early and I—well, that's when I need to do my household chores. It seems—well, it just seems that I scarcely see Rebecca anymore."

Mrs. Galvan nodded slowly in agreement. "I've wondered too—not that I don't love every minute with Rebecca," she added quickly.

She eased herself into a kitchen chair across from Sarah, drying her hands on her checkered apron. "What can we do?"

"I was thinking about leaving earlier in the morning. Now that spring is on the way, it is light earlier—and then I could get home sooner in the afternoon."

Mrs. Galvan nodded, though they were already getting up long before the sun made its appearance.

"I—I can do that," she said. "If you are sure that you—" Worry creased her features and she picked up her sentence again. "But you—"

"Oh, I couldn't—wouldn't ask you to get up any earlier than you do," quickly cut in Sarah.

Mrs. Galvan's face showed her surprise. "We can't leave her alone," she said simply.

"No. No—I'd never do that. But I wondered—if she—if she were to sleep here at your house—then you wouldn't need to rise so early—and then I'd—I'd get to spend more time with her in her waking hours."

"But—" began Mrs. Galvan. "I mean—we'd love to have Rebecca. But you—will you ever get any sleep?

You can't keep driving yerself so hard, child. You are
most worn out now."

"I'll be—I'm fine. Really, all the fresh air and—and
exercise. You know they say that's good for one."

"Fresh air and exercise, humph," snorted Mrs. Galvan. "Slave labor, you mean. Really, Sarah, I don't
think you realize what you're asking of your body.
Women weren't made for such—"

"I'm fine," Sarah interrupted again. "It's just—
just—it seems I have so little time with my baby. I—"

She was near tears. Mrs. Galvan looked as if she
wished to draw the tired mother into her arms and
hold her close. Sarah was so independent in her struggle to look after her baby Rebecca. And the baby was
quickly growing up.

"I know. I know. It's hard," Mrs. Galvan soothed.
"And if that will help—if in any way—sure, Rebecca
can sleep here. We'd love to have her."

Sarah nodded. "I—do appreciate it. I'll bring her
over at bedtime."

The tired mother stood to go, calling Rebecca to
find her kitty so they could go home.

Mrs. Galvan rose from her chair too. "Sarah," she
said as the younger woman reached for Rebecca's
hand, "why don't you just bring along your wash for
me to put through with mine? I need to git out the
scrubboard and washtubs anyway. A few more things
won't even be noticed."

"Oh, I couldn't," said Sarah softly. "I—I just
couldn't. You are already doing so much."

"I'd be glad to—"

"No. No—I couldn't. I—I'll manage—just fine."

Chapter Eight

Going On

Along with her intentions to spend more time with Rebecca, Sarah was finding that the lack of competition was a mixed blessing—the freight deliveries took a major portion of her day no matter how early she arose each morning and headed for the train depot.

Because of the complaint she had received about unloading their own freight, Sarah arranged for the young lad she had hired during the time of intense competition to continue to help her unload. Sarah's back and arms had strengthened over the months, but she still needed assistance with the heavier crates and barrels. Sometimes she and Newton had to lift the heaviest items together.

"They sure don't pack with women in mind," Sarah quipped, and the boy grinned his agreement.

At Galvan's hardware and Alex Murray's grocery, Sarah always had additional help with the unloading, even though she tried to convince the men who operated the two places of business that Newton had been hired for the task and they would manage fine.

Alex Murray replied that he had a fresh pot of tea

sitting on his table and that she should just take a minute to refresh herself. He always had more than tea prepared. Store biscuits or cookies or slices of bread often waited for her near the pot.

Boyd Galvan did not produce tea—a rather difficult feat for a hardware store. But he never failed to have a comfortable chair handy, and while he and Newton unloaded the freight, he entertained Sarah with the latest little anecdotes concerning Becky. He seemed to relate to Rebecca in an unusual way, though Sarah never felt resentment or concern. He was still the only one to refer to the child as Becky, and the little girl in turn called him Unca Boy—the same as her kitten.

For some reason that Sarah could not have explained, the combination of late afternoon tea and little stories about Rebecca were what kept her going.

As soon as the last box had been unloaded, she gathered the reins and quickly turned her wagon toward home. She did not have to urge the team. They seemed in as much of a hurry to return to their feed troughs and rest as Sarah was to clean herself up and rush over to gather her little girl back to her bosom. This was what she lived for. This was why she went on. Sarah dedicated those few, fast-fleeing hours to Rebecca. Then before she knew it, before she was even prepared to give her up, she had to bundle her up again and walk the short distance to the Galvans, where Rebecca spent the night. Sarah then returned home to the homemaker duties of laundry tubs and mending needle. She often worked long into the night even though she was up before dawn to harness the team for another freight run.

Sarah knew that the kind folks at the little community church worried and prayed for her and tried to find ways they could ease her load. There wasn't much they could do. She was aware of their own family responsibilities—and Sarah was stiff-backed in her independence.

It wasn't long until the congregation sort of settled back and breathed a collective sigh. Sarah had lost weight and she always looked tired and drawn—but she seemed to be managing. She was made of good stuff. Perhaps they had been unduly concerned after all. And life went on.

———

"Is it time to go to Auntie Min's yet?" asked Rebecca innocently.

Sarah lifted her eyes to study the little girl before her. She still ran to meet her mother when Sarah returned after a long, tiring day, but she increasingly seemed impatient to get back to the Galvans' home at day's end. A strange little fear tugged at the heart of Sarah. Was she losing her little girl's affection? Was Rebecca becoming too attached to the Galvan family?

Quickly Sarah chastened herself.

Poor little tyke, she mused inwardly. *With her life as strange as it has been, she needs all the love that any of us can give her.* She managed a smile and fought to control her voice. "Soon," she said, brushing at Rebecca's mass of curls. "Soon. Are you anxious?"

Rebecca shook her head but her words revealed the truth about her anticipation. "Unca Boy is goin' to make me a kite. He promised."

Sarah nodded. Uncle Boyd had become very important to Rebecca. Sarah was concerned that he might be spoiling her, but Mrs. Galvan assured her that Boyd did give her his undivided attention, but he also expected obedience and proper conduct. That helped to put Sarah's fears to rest. Rebecca was missing a father—though she had been too young to remember the death of Michael. Sarah grieved over that. It would have been some comfort to her to discuss the man they both had lost. Sarah's reminiscing had meant nothing to the child who looked at her with puzzled eyes. Sarah had at last dropped references to Michael. It just seemed to trouble the little girl. Now Sarah had to keep her thoughts and her feelings to herself. There was no one else with whom to share them.

"It will soon be dark," said Sarah now, her eyes lifting to the window. "We'll be seeing Auntie Min soon."

Another winter was moving toward them. Sarah dreaded the thought. Winters were so much more difficult. She hated the longer hours of darkness. It meant that she had to leave home long before the sun was there to light her way, almost requiring her team to feel their way over the country roads. And it was already dark by the time she returned home, no matter how she coaxed the horses to hurry. And the weather. Even the pelting rain did not present the same hazards as the steel-tipped driving snow.

But Sarah had no control over the seasons. She accepted them and worked with them—or against them—to the best of her abilities.

"Unca Boy said we can fly it in the mornin'," went on Rebecca. "He said he'd make it tonight an' we'd fly it tomorra. Him an' me. Together." She paused and looked at her mother to see if she was carefully following the words. Sarah was. Rebecca went on. "He said that. But he said I could see it tonight 'fore I go to bed."

Sarah nodded.

"Well—it's almost time to go to bed," went on Rebecca and pointed to the kitchen window and the shadows beyond. "See?"

Sarah nodded. She could not help but let her mind wander. She did wish that it was time for her own bed. How she longed for the comfort of the four-poster. How she ached for a good, long sleep.

She stirred herself. Her mind began to compose a long list of tasks waiting to be done before she would have the luxury of the clean sheets and fluffed pillow. And then the jarring of the alarm soon would have her on her feet again, struggling to meet the demands of a new day.

She forced her attention back to Rebecca, who was still talking. ". . . an' Unca Boy said that we should never talk like that—or even think like that. He said God doesn't like it when we be disre—disre—disre-what, Mama?"

"Disrespectful?" guessed Sarah.

"Yeah—disre—disre-that," agreed Rebecca, quite content to continue her story. "An' he said that Jimmy Sparrow should never talk like thet about anybody—ever."

Sarah made no comment. She knew now that she had missed much of Rebecca's tale.

"Isn't that right, Mama?" prompted Rebecca.

Sarah had not realized she would be expected to comment, but Rebecca was looking at her, studying her face and waiting for her response.

"I'm sure—I'm sure Uncle Boyd is right," she finally managed. *At least that is an honest answer,* she consoled herself. She had complete confidence in Uncle Boyd and his convictions concerning the right attitude and manner of children.

"Are you gonna marry Unca Boy?" Rebecca asked directly.

Sarah jerked to full attention and stared in unbelief. "Am I—? Where did you ever get an idea—?"

"He likes you," observed Rebecca with total honesty and openness.

Sarah found herself blushing in front of her infant child. The whole idea was absurd.

"I—I—don't know—where you ever got such a notion," she blurted out to the three-and-a-half-year-old who stared up at her. "Why, I have never—never even considered such a—such a thing." She stopped and brushed distractedly at the tumbling locks that had become dislodged as she and Rebecca had played with the now-grown kitten. "And I'm sure that—that Boyd has never—never given it thought either."

"Some people said—" began Rebecca and seemed to be thinking hard to remember the story. "Some ladies said that you shouldn't wait—'cause—'cause it's bound to happen someday—that Unca Boy should ask ya now and that—" She stopped and frowned more deeply as she sorted carefully through the unfamiliar phrases she was repeating. "—ya should marry Unca Boy an'—an' not drive the horses," said Rebecca, the frown creasing the smoothness of her small forehead.

Sarah, still in shock, bit her lip to fight back the retorts that wished to spill forth against the gossips. It would not do for her to vent her real feelings in front of her small daughter. She would be as bad as Jimmy Sparrow—whoever he was—in expressing disrespect—in whatever way he had done so—and bringing the displeasure of God. She swallowed and chose her words slowly, carefully.

"We must—must never pay attention to what other people say—about—about circumstances that they—they know nothing of. Those ladies—whoever they were—do not realize that I—I have no desire to marry. That I like—well, sort of like—driving the horses. It—it provides for our living. And—and Uncle Boyd has—

has no intention of marrying me."

"Well," said Rebecca, still probing her memory for the overheard conversation, "they weren't sure."

"Of course not. They—"

"They thought maybe you might marry Mr. Murray instead."

Sarah gasped. It really had gone much too far. Who were these gossipers who were trying to match her up with one of the town's young bachelors? Along with surprise and embarrassment, she now felt anger. What right did people have to be speculating about her life? What right did they have to—to talk behind her back?

And then a new thought washed through Sarah's mind, making her flush again. She did hope with all her heart that this—this despicable gossiping did not find its way to either of the men mentioned. Would they be thinking that she had anything to do with the wagging tongues? Might they think that she was misconstruing their kindness to her since the death of Michael? Oh, she hoped not. She prayed not. How embarrassing and humiliating if they should think that she, Sarah, misunderstood the kind deeds—the thoughtful acts of Christian goodwill.

Sarah's cheeks flushed deeply. Would she ever feel at ease with the men again? Would she be able to relax at Alex Murray's little kitchen table and sip the refreshing hot tea and eat slices of buttered bread and bottled jam? Would she be able to easily chat with Boyd and laugh at the stories of "his Becky" that he shared with her at each day's end?

No—likely not. At least not in comfort.

At that moment Sarah put her guard firmly in place. She must never, never do anything to feed the gossip mill. She must be doubly careful not to create an embarrassment for her two dear friends. She must be cool—and reserved—and entirely proper. There must be no reason for the gossip to continue.

And the people—whoever they were, from town or church, young or adult—knew nothing of the deep wound they had inflicted on the young, struggling widow. Now she was bereft of even her small comforts. Now she had to withdraw even further into her protective cocoon.

———

Sarah's mind was deeply troubled. Rebecca was nearing another birthday and growing up quickly. Uncle Boyd was no longer Unca Boy but Uncle Boyd, though Mrs. Galvan remained Aunt Min. Rebecca had quite properly addressed "Mr. Galvan" even when she could barely say the words. He had always been kind and good to Rebecca, but he had never fussed over the child, or any child, and Rebecca had not seemed to form a special attachment to him. But that was not what troubled Sarah. The problem was concerning Rebecca herself.

Though Sarah loved the Galvans and appreciated their kindness in caring for Rebecca more than she could ever have expressed, she was honestly concerned with Rebecca's upbringing. Though Rebecca was learning proper concern and conduct toward others, she was not learning proper etiquette and ladylike behavior. She was tomboyish, energetic, and uncontrolled. Sarah worried about it but didn't know what to do. There simply were not enough hours in her limited time with Rebecca for her to address all the things a mother should be teaching her daughter.

"What is most important after all?" she would chide herself. "That she have the proper attitudes—or that she express them in ladylike fashion?"

Of course, Sarah always convinced herself without difficulty that Rebecca was getting the most important of the two. But she still chaffed inwardly as she watched her daughter's unbridled energy spilling itself out in unladylike fashion. What could she do? What *should* she do? She hated to always be chastising Rebecca or nagging at her when they spent their brief times together. Yet—

Sarah knew that if Rebecca attended the small local classroom, she would be as unskilled in proper conduct as the local youngsters—who seemed decent and likeable enough, but who in all honesty were not trained in any social graces.

"I may not be here forever," Sarah reasoned to herself. "If—if there is ever—ever enough money—or ever the opportunity—I may sell the business and move to a city. How would Rebecca be able to cope in a society where proper manners are important?"

Sarah had to admit that in her present state, she herself might not fare so well in society. Whenever she stood before her mirror she looked at her simple, hurried hair style, her thin, pinched-looking face, her plain, patched garb, often mannish in appearance, and shuddered.

"No," she reasoned with herself on more than one occasion, "it is not the fault of the Galvans who have lived as simple, frontier folk all their lives. It is the fault of me—Rebecca's mother. I am no longer showing her how to be a proper lady. But how do I change that? What must I do?"

Sarah had no real answers. There didn't seem to be a way open to her. She had to be what she had to be in order to care for the material needs of her child—and yet in the doing, she was also denying young Rebecca the training in social graces that should also be her right. But how to balance the two tasks? It deeply troubled her.

———

Sarah was not sure if her driving skills had improved or if she simply trusted her team to a larger extent, but she found that she no longer had to keep a constant eye on the horses nor hold the reins with the same intensity. That freed her to think, to observe, and even on occasion to peruse an outdated newspaper that she picked up on the depot platform.

Since meaningful conversation was difficult in her job, she longed for some indication of what was going on in the world. So she drove, her eyes often lifting to the team and the road, but her thoughts were taken up with the bits of news she garnered from the paper she held in her hands along with the leather reins.

On one such day as Sarah scanned the paper and responded with various emotions or mental stimulation to the articles she read, her eyes drifted down the page and settled on an advertisement in the left-hand corner. "Tall Elms" was emblazoned across the top of the ad. Sarah's eyes moved on down to catch the next words. "Finishing School for Young Ladies." Sarah was immediately interested. In the midst of stately elms, here was a school that promised to educate, train in all the social graces and the arts of interest, prepare for life, and grant the poise and self-assurance needed to get a young woman launched into her world—wherever that might be. And the school started them right off as six-year-olds.

"Imagine that," breathed Sarah. "They even teach

music." Sarah had sorrowed many times at not having her piano with her in the West. As a young child, she had been given the privilege of learning to play the instrument, and had become quite skillful. She missed her music terribly, but she felt even worse that Rebecca would be denied the right.

"Imagine that," she said again.

The ad went on to explain that the school had the best of faculty, led by Miss Nola Ann Peabody. Following the name was a short list of degrees and accomplishments.

"What about the religious training?" Sarah asked herself. "I certainly don't want to send my child to a school where she will not get training in her faith. And I want to be sure that the training is in keeping with my own beliefs."

Sarah found the paragraphs that dealt with the school's position on religion. She was relieved to find that what would be "consistently and conscientiously taught" was quite in keeping with her own religious views. She breathed a deep sigh of relief and thought again of how much Rebecca could benefit from attending the school.

"Oh, if only—" began Sarah, then quickly checked herself. There was no way she would ever be able to afford such a school. No way.

She sighed deeply and allowed the newspaper to fall to the floor at her feet. She gathered the reins more firmly in her hands and sighed again. Her agitation must have traveled down the leather thongs to the horses, for Gyp tossed his head and Ginger stirred and hurried her plodding steps.

"Hi-ya," called Sarah, urging the team to faster action. Her heavy heart and troubled thoughts made her impatient with life in general and with this load of freight in particular.

There was no way that the tiresome, demanding job would ever produce enough income to give her little girl the education that she deserved. Sarah felt trapped and defeated.

"Why not?" she later reasoned as she stared again at the ad she had ripped from the pages of the worn newspaper. "At least I can write and ask." She hesitated a moment when she looked at the address and realized it was nearly a thousand miles away. "Oh, Rebecca," she mourned aloud, "how could I possibly let you go so far away—" But she thought again of the importance of a good education for her daughter, and this sounded like such an ideal school.

So Sarah got out her long-neglected writing kit and seated herself at the kitchen table. Carefully she dipped the pen in the inkwell, flexed her stiff, unyielding fingers, and began her letter. She was appalled at her penmanship. Her fingers did not respond in the neat, even script that had won her acclaim as a student in her hometown school. She stopped and worked with the fingers, trying hard to limber them up, stretching, massaging, flexing, and coaxing. By the fourth attempt she knew she had to be satisfied with her effort. Though she was still displeased with it, it did look much better than her first try.

The letter was a simple one, sent only to inquire about their school and about the fees charged for the education.

Sarah licked the flap and pressed it against the body of the envelope.

"I will post it tomorrow," she promised herself. She knew she would have many days to prepare herself for the answer. The mails would not bring back a return letter for several weeks. Maybe even months, she told herself.

If and when it came, what would the reply be? Sarah wondered what she really wanted it to be. Of course, she longed to give Rebecca a good education. But could she bear to be all alone, with Rebecca miles away becoming a proper young lady? There would not even be the welcomed few hours at the end of each day and the precious Sundays when they had the entire afternoon together.

Sarah cherished those times with Rebecca. She longed for them throughout the working hours—and then often felt bad when they were together as she watched her young daughter become more and more like the frontier people around her. Was that what Michael had expected for his daughter? Of course he had thought that she, Sarah, would be nurturing and training their daughter—not running a business and turning over the main portion of Rebecca's care to another. Tears of frustration and sorrow filled her eyes.

Was she letting Rebecca down? Was she letting Michael down? Was there something more she should be doing? Was there any way that she could stretch the monthly earnings to cover a school bill? Was there any way that she could add to her income?

Then Sarah remembered that the debt at the bank was almost paid up. Soon the team, the wagon, the whole business would be hers, debt free. She would not have to make the hated trip to the sturdy brick building and count out her hard-earned bills and coins into the eager hand that stretched for them.

No. She would soon be her own boss and perhaps—

just perhaps—the extra money would cover the costs of a young daughter at boarding school. Sarah felt slightly comforted as she laid the letter on the table so she would not forget it the next morning.

Chapter Nine

Sharing the Plan

Was it a miracle or just coincidence, Sarah wondered as she fingered the letter she held in her hands, *that the reply to her letter arrived the very day she had counted out the last payment to the banker?* Whatever the case, she could hardly wait to get home to read the contents.

After she had cared for her team she hurried into the coolness of her kitchen and lowered herself to one of the painted chairs. Her hand trembled as she tore open the envelope and lifted the pages to catch the light from the window.

It was a long letter, bearing the signature of Miss Nola Ann Peabody with the interesting letters behind her name. Sarah scanned the first several paragraphs. She would read them in detail later. Her immediate question was if she could afford to send Rebecca.

The monthly cost nearly took her breath away. It was far more expensive than she had imagined. Mentally she began to calculate. It was impossible. She could never make it. It was a dream that couldn't ever come true. She simply wasn't able to make that much money with the freight run.

She stood to her feet, still trembling, and lifted a hand to brush back a wisp of hair. As she moved, she caught a glimpse of herself in the mirror on the wall. Even Sarah was shocked at how much she had changed since Michael's death.

"Look at me," she whispered to herself. "Just look at me. I'm a—a skeleton. I—I'm unkempt and—and old. Michael would—wouldn't even know me now."

Sarah wanted to return to the chair, lay her head on her arm and weep.

But she did not allow herself the comfort of tears. Instead, she straightened her tired back, lifted her chin, and stared back defiantly at the face in the mirror. "Well, I won't have this kind of life for Rebecca," she declared aloud with a voice remarkably calm. "She will be properly educated. She will be trained in—in something—so that should she ever be on her own she will not have to—to resort to any activity unbecoming to a—a lady. She will be one. Somehow. I'll do it— somehow. I will."

And Sarah forsook the woman in the mirror and crossed to her bedroom to improve her appearance before the little trip to the Galvans for Rebecca. She still had several months before Rebecca would be ready for her first year. Sarah would spend those months saving. She would have the equivalent of the bank payment as additional income now. And she could find other ways to cut corners. By the time Rebecca had to leave for school, Sarah should have been able to save up for the initial expenses, she reasoned. From then on—well, she would cross that bridge when the time came.

————

"Why don't we marry Uncle Boyd?" asked Rebecca at the supper table.

Sarah had assumed that the child had forgotten the foolish gossip of the town's busybodies, and she looked at her daughter in alarm. Had the idle talk started again? She had been so careful. Even distant to the two men who had been so kind to her. She often felt ashamed of her own stiffness. She refused the cups of tea as much as she had looked forward to them. And she never even stopped to chat with Boyd if she could avoid it. She always found something pressing that needed to be done while he helped Newton unload the freight. She missed the chats, but she had no intention of feeding the town's gossip mill.

Here was Rebecca boldly bringing it up as though they were speaking of what they should have for lunch.

"What—what do you mean?" stammered Sarah.

"We should git married and—and be a fambly."

"Family," corrected Sarah. "We should be a family."

"Ya-ay," agreed Rebecca noisily, lifting her hands to clap them in the air. Sarah at once realized her misstatement.

"No. No, I didn't mean—that," Sarah quickly explained. "I just meant that—that was the proper way to say it—not that—that it was what I thought should be done. I mean—I have no intention—none whatever of—of marrying anyone, Rebecca. I—we—don't you understand?"

Rebecca looked crestfallen.

"You promised," she accused her mother.

"No. No, I certainly did not promise any such thing. I was—was simply correcting your—your word—fambly. I—I didn't mean—"

"But you said it," cut in Rebecca. "You said we

should be a—" She stopped and thought hard, then slowly and carefully pronounced the word, "fam-i-ly. You said so."

"Yes—I said it, but I didn't mean that we—" Sarah stopped and rose to her feet. She didn't wish to be involved in this ridiculous debate with her young daughter. It would spoil their whole evening together, and their time was limited at best.

"What should we do tonight?' she asked as brightly as she could. "Would you like to make cookies?"

"I already made cookies with Aunt Min," replied Rebecca a bit dourly.

"Well—then—we won't make cookies. We'll—play a game."

"I don't feel like playing a game," said Rebecca.

"Well—what do you feel like doing?"

Too late Sarah realized her mistake. Rebecca looked at her calmly and then replied, "I feel like being a fam-i-ly. I hate always having to come home just when it's time for Uncle Boyd to come home from work. I hardly get to see him anymore."

Sarah drew in her breath. She felt the sting of tears behind her eyelids. She would not allow herself to cry—especially not in front of Rebecca. But it didn't seem fair that Rebecca should care more about her personally adopted Uncle Boyd than she did about her own mother. It just didn't seem fair. It was she, Sarah, who filled her days with back-breaking work to care for her young child. Boyd just pampered and spoiled her—had fun with her. Why should he be the one to receive her love and devotion?

But as quickly as Sarah's hurt and anger washed over her, it also drained away.

It's not the child's fault, she told herself firmly. *Boyd has been good to her. She misses her father. She misses me. I should—as her mother, be caring for her myself. Then there wouldn't be this—this wrenching of loyalties. She would have a home. A constant. She wouldn't be shuttled back and forth between people. No wonder she is confused and—and longing for a real home. No wonder.*

Sarah reached out a hand and pushed back Rebecca's soft hair. "This has been hard for you," she wished to say, but she knew if she tried to speak, the tears would fall, so she said nothing, just stroked the child's hair and longed with all of her heart to be able to stay at home—as a real mother.

"How would you like to go to school?" she asked at length.

Rebecca clapped her hands. She had begged to go to school with the other kids in the small town. Ever since she had turned four, she had been asking when she would be able to go.

"Not—not right away," hurried on Sarah, lest Rebecca run and change her clothes for the upcoming event. "Not until next fall—when you are six. Past six."

For a moment the eyes clouded.

"It will be for the fall term," went on Sarah, "the next school year."

It began to sound better to Rebecca. She had never been promised any school before. Maybe "next year" wouldn't be so long after all.

"I need to tell Mary," she said with excitement. "She's been waiting for me for a long, long time."

Not such a long time, thought Sarah. Mary, from across the street, was only a year older than Rebecca.

"Can I go tell her?" coaxed Rebecca.

"Not—not tonight," said Sarah firmly. "You see— I've—I've been doing a lot of thinking—and praying about—about school—for you. I—I've thought that maybe—maybe we would let you go to—to a special school."

Rebecca's eyes grew wide. One emotion after another seemed to move across her face. Sarah wondered just where they would lead her. At last Rebecca spoke. "What special school?" she asked directly, her eyes showing her doubts.

"Well it's a—a special school for—for girls. They teach you all sorts of—of special things like—like how to—to ride horses and care for them—how to play the piano—how to—"

But Sarah got no further. It seemed that she had just named two of Rebecca's favorite dreams.

"Really?" she said, her eyes shining.

"Really," replied Sarah, her eyes shining to match her daughter's.

"When can I go?" asked Rebecca eagerly.

"Well—not until next school term."

For a moment Rebecca looked disappointed; then she seemed to regain her enthusiasm. "Next term—that's not too long, is it, Mama?"

"No. Not too long at all," responded Sarah.

"Where is the school?" asked Rebecca. "Is it very far away?"

Sarah nodded. That was the hard part.

"Yes," she answered truthfully. "Yes, it is rather far away."

"As far as the train depot in West Morin?" asked Rebecca.

"Oh—even farther than that," said Sarah sadly.

"Then how do I get home each night?" asked Rebecca.

"Well—I'm afraid that—that you wouldn't come home each night. You'd—you'd stay. Have your own room—with a roommate or maybe more than one roommate. Other girls. Your age. I'm sure you would like them."

As Sarah talked hurriedly she watched the changes in Rebecca's eyes. They mirrored her every emotion, and now, as the child listened to her mother, her eyes showed excitement, fear, concern, eagerness, and doubt.

"I don't think I want to go," she said when Sarah stopped.

"But you have no—" began Sarah.

"I wouldn't get to see Uncle Boyd, would I?" said Rebecca. "And Aunt Min—I wouldn't get to see her either. And you. I wouldn't even get to have visits with you, would I?"

"No-o," agreed Sarah slowly, her own eyes clouding with the thought.

"I don't think I'll go," repeated Rebecca firmly.

"You don't want to learn to play the piano?" Sarah wondered if she was being fair. Was this too much pressure, too big a decision, for the little girl?

Rebecca looked caught between two desires. She shook her head sadly, then nodded it instead. "I'd like to play the piano," she admitted, "but I'd get lonesome."

"I—I think that you might—well, rather enjoy it— once you made friends with the other girls," continued Sarah.

Rebecca looked doubtful.

"Well—we don't have to decide now," went on Sarah. "We'll just think about it and make up our mind later."

"I'll ask Mary," Rebecca said simply.

"No. No, I don't think that we'll—" She stopped, then went on. "Let's not talk about this to anyone until—until we have made up our minds what we plan to do," cautioned Sarah. She didn't wish to get the gossipers started on something else that was none of their business.

Rebecca nodded slowly, but she did look disappointed.

"Do we have to decide—all by ourselves?" she asked her mother.

"I think—I think that you and I are quite capable of deciding ourselves," Sarah assured her.

"I—I guess," said Rebecca, and she sighed deeply.

"But we don't have to decide right now," Sarah reminded her. "We have lots of time."

The thought seemed to please Rebecca. She nodded. She could put off the weighty decision and concentrate on things at hand.

"Is it time to go to Aunt Min's now?" she asked Sarah.

Sarah was about to reply that they still had some time to play a game or do something fun together, but she bit her lip. Rebecca seemed anxious to leave her mother's company.

"Uncle Boyd is making me my own table and chair—just for me. He might have it finished now," Rebecca continued, reminding Sarah again of how their conversation had started.

She nodded reluctantly. "If you wish to go right away, I guess we can go," she said. Mentally she was thinking ahead to the extra time it would give her to finish some of her household chores.

Rebecca ran for her cape and bonnet.

"I hope he made a red one," she called. "He knows I like red best."

The table and chair were finished and they were red. Rebecca beamed her pleasure, though Sarah could not help but wince at the bright, bright color that rather clashed with Mrs. Galvan's kitchen.

"You remembered," squealed the little girl. "You remembered I like red."

Boyd just smiled, happy with her excitement over the simple homemade gift.

After giving Boyd a big hug, Rebecca set about playing with her new possession while Mrs. Galvan went to fill the teapot to prepare a cup of tea.

Mr. Galvan laid aside his paper and pulled his chair up to the table, and Boyd took a seat opposite him. Adult talk. Sarah often longed for it. She prepared herself for enjoyment now. It was so good to have a real conversation with something other than her horses.

They talked of local affairs. Plans for a new store. The sale of the livery stable. The move to try to bring water from the nearby spring into the town. The recent accident of Widow Harlow while doing her window washing. Little things. Really of no import. Yet important to the life of the town, part of the fabric of everyday life.

Sarah could scarcely believe how quickly the time passed. As she glanced at the clock, she found that she had already squandered the extra time she had promised herself.

Sarah turned to interrupt Rebecca's playing. "You'd better get ready for bed, Rebecca," she told the child, "so Mama can kiss you good-night and hear your prayers."

The child opened her mouth as though to protest but then cast a glance at Boyd. Sarah wasn't sure just what transpired between the two, but Rebecca said no more, just went to do as bidden.

When Rebecca returned to announce that she was ready for bed, she made her rounds to say her good-nights.

"Good-night, Mr. Galvan," she said, giving him a quick hug. "Good-night, Aunt Min." The hug was much longer and with more warmth.

"Good-night, Uncle Boyd," she said, reaching up to encircle his neck with her arms. She lingered there, Sarah noticed, as though she hated to leave him behind.

"Good-night, Becky," he said to the top of her head. "Sleep tight."

And he kissed her forehead.

"When I go away to school—" began Rebecca and then caught herself and cast a quick look at her mother.

Three pairs of adult eyes looked from Sarah to Rebecca and back again.

"I didn't mean to—" began Rebecca again, drawing more attention to her error.

"That's okay," said Sarah in an effort to downplay the little slip. She looked at the three people around the table. "Rebecca and I have been discussing some possibilities," she said in what she hoped was a casual manner and then went on lightly, "Time for your prayers now. Come—I'll tuck you in."

When Sarah returned to the kitchen, it was painfully quiet. She wanted to discuss the inadvertent announcement of family plans, but she didn't know where to start. Besides, it was all so unsettled. And the three around the table looked so glum. What were they thinking? Didn't she, as Rebecca's mother, have the right to plan for her daughter's future?

"I—I think I should be going home," she said as

naturally as she could. "I have all sorts of things to get done tonight."

Mrs. Galvan nodded. Mr. Galvan did not even look her way. He fidgeted with a corner of the paper.

Boyd met her eyes squarely. "So when is this to take place?" he asked directly. There was no condemnation in his voice, simply interest.

"Well—I—I don't know. It is—as I said—just something I am looking into—at this point," Sarah said defensively.

"You don't like Kenville's school?" put in Mrs. Galvan, a bit of an edge to her voice.

"Oh—I've—I've nothing—nothing personal against the school. No. It's—it's not like that. I mean—I just think that Rebecca could—should have some—some things I'm not able to give her."

"Like?" prompted Mrs. Galvan with a shrug.

"Like—like—piano. She'd like to learn to play the piano."

"Maybe the preacher's wife would teach her," put in Boyd.

The preacher's wife played the church pump organ to accompany the Sunday hymns. She wasn't an expert, by any means. In fact, her mistakes often grated on Sarah's ears and nerves.

"She is very busy—with her family and all," Sarah said softly in answer.

Mrs. Galvan nodded.

"Well—anyway—I am—am just thinking about—about possibilities," went on Sarah lamely. "She won't be ready for school until next fall term anyway. No hurry. I'm—I'm just thinking."

She nodded her good-night to the three, mumbled her thanks for the refreshments, and hurried from the house.

Chapter Ten

Plans and Parting

"Do you really think you're doin' the right thing?" Mrs. Galvan asked Sarah as they shared a cup of coffee at her kitchen table.

Sarah was slow to answer. When she did she was still a bit hesitant.

"I've prayed about it. I—I'm—well, I think it would be best for Rebecca. There is—so much that she could learn at this girl's school that she would never get here. She has always been interested in music, in the piano. She loves books. She needs to learn how to sew—"

Sarah stopped, remembering that Mrs. Galvan had expressed the desire to teach Rebecca how to sew.

"You don't think she can get those things here?" asked the older woman.

"Look at me," said Sarah. "Here I am with no training—in anything. Well, in anything but piano—and I don't have a piano. When Michael died—well—I had to try to learn a man's job. Look at my hands. They certainly don't look like the hands of a lady."

"But you went to a fine school," Mrs. Galvan reminded her gently.

For a moment Sarah was shocked and then embarrassed. It was so. She had gone to a fine school. She had learned to be a lady. It had not helped her when it came to finding her way in this western town. *If Father had been content to stay in the East,* she found herself thinking, *I would have managed much better.*

But you wouldn't have met Michael, and you wouldn't have Rebecca now, her heart quickly answered.

But even with her enviable education, she was trained for very little that was of practical help when it came to supporting both her and Rebecca.

"Well—this school is different. I've read all about it. It does teach the girls much more than—than social graces. It teaches them practical things as well. They can even become a—a teacher or a—a seamstress. Lots of things. My school wasn't like that."

Mrs. Galvan nodded.

Silence hung in the room. Sarah found herself fidgeting uncomfortably.

Mrs. Galvan sat staring into her cup of steaming coffee. "It must be expensive," she said at last.

"Yes—yes, it is," Sarah admitted. "I did lots of figuring and I think I can make it."

"Can we help?"

The question caught Sarah totally by surprise.

"You? Why—why, I wouldn't think—I mean—you've already done so much. I—I couldn't ask—"

"I haven't heard you askin'. We've—discussed it—and we'd like to help."

Sarah stumbled for words. "I—I do appreciate the offer. Really—it is much more than—" She stopped. "But—no—I couldn't let you do that. She's my daughter. It's my notion. I—I'll manage—just fine."

Mrs. Galvan looked doubtful. "Well—if you ever

find yerself—well—short—please, don't be afraid to ask."

Sarah felt chastened. Here she had been set to fight to send Rebecca away from the Galvans, knowing full well that they thought Sarah's notion a foolish one, and they were asking to help with the expense. They were very special people.

"I thank you. Sincerely," replied Sarah. "I really can't say how much. You have been so good. To Rebecca—and me. I thank God for you every day."

And with those words Sarah stood, smoothed her skirt, and prepared to take her daughter home.

The night was cold and very dark in spite of the winter snow that should have brightened the world. But Sarah felt as if she had never seen a more dismal winter evening.

"Looks like it plans to storm again," noted Boyd, who was walking her home after she had returned Rebecca to the Galvans for her overnight stay.

Sarah let her eyes lift to the sky. It certainly looked dark and gloomy. No stars showed in the dense curtain overhead. No Northern Lights danced on the northern stage. There was nothing but blackness. Deep and foreboding.

With her eyes on the sky overhead, Sarah tripped on the rutted road they were traversing. Boyd reached out a hand quickly to keep her from falling.

"Best take my arm," he offered when he released his hold of her.

"If I'd pay attention to where I was putting my foot instead of stargazing," said Sarah with a bit of a laugh at herself. But she accepted the offered arm.

They continued on in silence. In the distance a dog barked. Another answered from its own yard. It was the only sound in the silent world.

"Becky is quite excited about goin' away to school," remarked Boyd.

"Yes. Yes—she is—now," answered Sarah. It had taken a while for Rebecca to be convinced that it would be fun to go.

"Sure goin' to miss her," admitted Boyd slowly. "I can't imagine what yer feelin'," he said, looking at her through the darkness.

Sarah nodded. She didn't trust her voice to answer. Sarah still lived in dread of the day when Rebecca would actually be placed on the outgoing stage.

They continued in silence. Sarah could just make out her own gate in the darkness ahead.

"My—it seems so late when it gets so—so dark," she said, fumbling for something neutral to talk about. "It seems like—like another world from the one we see in the light."

Boyd nodded. Even at close range Sarah had difficulty catching the slight motion.

He opened the gate in the picket fence and they moved up the boarded walk together. It had been cleared of the snow from the last storm. Someone— Sarah guessed it to be Boyd—always cared for the snow.

When they reached the back door, Sarah moved to withdraw her hand from Boyd's arm, but he surprised her by reaching his other hand to clasp hers and hold it in place.

"Will you stay on here—once Becky goes?" he asked, seriousness deepening his voice.

Sarah had not even thought of leaving. "Of—

course. Where would I go? I mean—I've no family left.
I—"

"I thought you might settle somewhere in the
East."

"But I have to pay for Rebecca's schooling."

"I know," he acknowledged. "I thought you might
like to find—to find—work that is easier."

Sarah was ashamed. "I—I've been trained for—for
nothing else," she admitted. "The fact is—" She lowered her head. Even in the darkness she did not feel
safe from observant eyes. "I really know very little—
about—about earning my way. I could teach piano, but
even if I had the money to buy one, I wouldn't be able
to support Rebecca and me on the little that piano lessons would bring in. I—I have thought about moving—
closer to the school. Back East. Back to a—a city. But
I—I haven't been able to come up with one skill that
would help me to get a job—to—to see us through."

There was a pause. To Sarah the silence seemed as
deep and as dark as the night around them.

"Have you—ever thought of remarrying?" Boyd
asked her softly.

Sarah's head begin to whirl. What was he asking?
Did he think she would look for someone to marry just
so she wouldn't have the difficult task of providing for
herself and her daughter?

Sarah pulled her hand free and stepped back.

"No," she said with a bit of emphasis. "No—I have
not. I—I am quite willing to accept responsibility for
me—and my daughter. I would not—marry—any man
just to—to take advantage of—"

"I didn't mean that," Boyd stopped her gently. "I
know you better than that."

He reached out and reclaimed her hand, trying to
draw her closer. Sarah resisted.

"I just meant—you're young. You're very—attractive and—pleasant. You—you must get lonely. I wouldn't think—"

Sarah tried to pull her hand away again. She looked away from Boyd. Her shoulders shook slightly. Her chin lifted.

"I loved Michael—very much," she said, her voice trembling. "I—I miss him—more each day—in—in a different way than I did at first. I—I— But I would never remarry to—to fulfill my emotional needs any more than I would remarry just to fulfill my financial needs," she said with deep conviction.

Boyd nodded slowly and Sarah felt his hold gently release hers.

"I—I see," he whispered into the darkness.

Sarah stirred herself.

"Well—I must get in. I have laundry to do and—"

Boyd turned to go. "Good-night then," he said.

Sarah watched as he walked back down her sidewalk, his broad shoulders hunched against the cold of the night. For some reason it was hard for her to see him go. She felt troubled, uneasy.

"Boyd," she called after a moment of hesitation.

He turned. She could just make out his outline in the blackness.

"Thanks," she said, and hoped that her voice, soft with emotion, would reach him in the darkness. "Thanks."

"Anytime," came his reply. That was all, just, "Anytime."

Sarah waited until his form disappeared from her sight; then she pushed her door open and went in to refuel the fire and get started on her evening tasks.

She was still troubled by the exchange with Boyd. Just what had he meant? Just what did he feel? What

did she, Sarah, feel? Her emotions had been so raw—
so vulnerable—for what seemed forever. Sarah wondered if she honestly felt anything anymore. Anything
but love and devotion to Rebecca—Michael's child.

She hoped that Boyd understood her simple
thanks. She felt so inadequate in expressing her gratitude for all he did on her behalf. How could she show
him that she appreciated the many things he did to
make her life and Rebecca's easier?

Thanks. It sounded so—so empty—so sterile—so
void of all the true gratitude she felt.

"Anytime."

Sarah knew that the one word conveyed so much
as it had come to her through the darkness of the night.
Anytime. Boyd would be there. For her. For Rebecca.
Assisting. Supporting. Perhaps—perhaps even lov-
ing—Sarah wasn't sure.

But suddenly she knew just how much she had been
depending on Boyd. Even leaning on him. For Rebecca.
Maybe even for herself, without realizing it.

From past experience Sarah had learned that with
dependence, one was vulnerable. With dependence
could come the pain of loss. The chill of fear crept
through her body, making her tremble.

"I—I must—must learn to be more independent,"
she scolded herself. "I mustn't—"

Sarah stopped. She tried to get control of her troubled feelings.

"That is another reason Rebecca must go away for
school," she told herself. "If—if she doesn't need Boyd
Galvan anymore—then—then I won't need him either.
I—I won't even see him—much."

And the thought brought both pain and relief. She
was going to miss the Galvans. All of them. They had
become like family. But with Rebecca gone, there

would be no reason for her to visit their house each day. There would be no reason to keep such close company with the family that had given so much of themselves to meet the needs of the young woman and her small child.

"I'm sure they will miss Rebecca," Sarah said to herself, "but it—it may be a great relief to them too. They—they have been raising her for—for four years already. They need to—to have things back to—to normal again."

But Sarah still felt troubled as she went to gather up the laundry.

———

Sarah spent her last summer with Rebecca, crowding in all the "together times" she could make fit. She sometimes wondered if her business would suffer because of it, but things seemed to continue on as before. She needed that business. She needed it more than ever if she were to keep up with the stiff school tuition.

But Sarah wanted to store all the memories of Rebecca's childhood that she could. Both for her sake and for the sake of Rebecca. There would be so many months, many years when they would be apart.

As the summer lazily rolled toward its end, Sarah felt almost panicky. Rebecca would soon be gone and she would be alone. Was Rebecca prepared? Was *she* prepared?

Was Sarah really making the right choice? Would she live to regret her decision? Did the child need the love and stability of herself and the Galvans more than she needed the training of the special school?

Sarah fretted even more and prayed harder. She worked with agitated fury. She lost even more weight.

"Can you come to school with me?" Rebecca asked one day.

Sarah caught her breath and then looked at her daughter with longing.

"Oh—I wish I could," she replied with honesty. "I—I hate to see you go. I hate to have you travel all alone. But I—I—Mama just doesn't have the money to buy a second ticket." She paused and then went on with as much reassurance as she could muster. "The stage driver will look out for you. He promised me. I talked with him. He will see that you are properly settled on the train. He will talk to the conductor—he told me. The conductor will be with you all the way to the station where you will be met by someone from the school. I wrote them. They promised. And—I'll bring you home—for summer—maybe even for Christmas— whenever—whenever I can. I'll start to save money for your ticket and—and it won't seem long."

Rebecca still looked doubtful.

Sarah crossed the room to gather the child into her arms and held her for a long, long time. Rebecca finally squirmed. Sarah released her. Oh, she was going to miss her. There just wouldn't seem to be a reason to come home at night.

———

Rebecca came hippity-hopping into the yard where Sarah was unhitching the team. Another long, hot day of hauling freight had ended, and Sarah had been anxious to get cleaned up and hurry off to pick up her daughter. Instead, Rebecca was already home.

"Aunt Min said I could walk home by myself," she informed her mother.

Sarah felt a pang of apprehension. She knew that

neighbor children ran about the town freely, but she had never allowed Rebecca to do so.

"Aunt Min said if I am to travel halfway around the world on my own, then I'd best learn how to walk down my own street."

Sarah shivered with the reminder that she was sending her small daughter off all alone.

But Rebecca interrupted her thoughts.

"It's okay that you can't come with me, Mama," Rebecca assured her. "I'm not scared anymore. I won't be alone."

Sarah felt relief wash over her. Maybe Rebecca was finally understanding their little talks when Sarah tried to reassure her over and over that as a child of God, she would never be alone. God would be with her wherever she went.

Sarah smiled. "Jesus will be with you," she said again to her daughter.

"I won't need Him, either," said Rebecca with quiet confidence. "Uncle Boyd's going with me."

Sarah dropped her currycomb and stared with open mouth.

"What?"

"Uncle Boyd is coming. He showed me his ticket. He says he's goin' to make good and sure that I git there 'safe an' sound.' That's what he said."

For one moment Sarah felt resentment. Would Boyd *never* let Rebecca go? After all, she wasn't his child. She belonged to Sarah. Rebecca was hers. Hers and Michael's. If anyone traveled with Rebecca it should be her. Rebecca's mother. Boyd had no business butting in.

"Uncle Boyd said he didn't want you worryin' that I might not get there safe an' sound," went on Rebecca hurriedly. "He said you get precious little sleep as it is—you couldn't afford to have days and nights of worry before they sent a wire that I was there safe and sound—that's what Uncle Boyd said."

Sarah felt ashamed of her resentment. So it wasn't just Rebecca Boyd was protecting. He was still trying to shield her as well.

She swallowed hard, blinking back tears that threatened to spill.

"That's—that's nice," she managed to say to her daughter as she stooped to pick up the currycomb to stroke the broad side of Ginger. "That's nice. I—I won't worry with—with Uncle Boyd traveling with you, will I?"

Rebecca did not stop to answer. "I'm gonna go find Cat," she flung over her shoulder.

Rebecca had changed the name of her cat from Unca Boy to Cat after the pet had produced a litter of five fluffy kittens.

"Uncle Boyd says he will take care of Cat and her last babies for me when I'm gone," she called back to her mother. "He says you are too busy to worry about cats all over the house."

Sarah smiled. She had wondered what she would do with Cat and her penchant for motherhood. She was glad to turn that problem over to Boyd.

———

On the day that Rebecca was to be boarding on the outgoing stage, Sarah literally felt ill. Her stomach churned and she felt faint. She wondered if she would be able to make it through the ordeal of saying good-bye.

There was a knock at the door. Rebecca ran to answer it. Boyd stood there, hat in hand.

"Uncle Boyd!" squealed Rebecca, opening wide the door so he might enter. Then she took another look and anxiety showed in her face.

"We need to go soon. It's almost time. Where's yer bag?"

Boyd grinned an easy grin. "Oh, don't worry. I'm ready to go. I already dropped my bag off. Cice says he will pull out in twenty minutes."

Sarah felt about to faint.

"I better get my things," said Rebecca with alarm and ran toward her bedroom.

Boyd lifted his eyes to Sarah. "Are you okay?" he asked with deep concern.

"I—I'll be fine," she tried to assure him, but she knew that her face must have given away her true condition.

"I—I wondered if you might like to—to say goodbye to Rebecca here at home—instead of—of coming to the stage," he went on gently.

Sarah was torn, wanting to be with her Rebecca every possible minute. On the other hand—she knew she would dissolve into tears once the stagecoach door closed on her child. She wavered. Should she crowd in that extra minute and risk a public display of emotion or should she say goodbye at their own door and be free to weep for the child she was losing?

"Maybe—maybe you're right," she said at last. "Maybe I will just—just say goodbye here."

"I think you should sit down," Boyd advised, studying her pale face.

Sarah dropped to the chair he held for her.

"I'd best help her with her luggage before she tries to tote it all herself," he said lightly and grinned at Sarah. She tried very hard to smile in return.

And before Sarah had a chance to sort it all out,

she was saying goodbye to a bubbling Rebecca who was going on a wonderful journey with her Uncle Boyd.

"I'll look after her," the man whispered to Sarah.

"I know you will," she replied through her tears.

"I won't come back until I'm sure she's settled," he went on.

Sarah could not speak again, so merely nodded.

"You take care," said Boyd and surprised Sarah by drawing her close and holding her. For a moment Sarah longed to lean on him—to be comforted by the strong arms that held her.

"Uncle Boyd—hurry," called Rebecca. "We might miss the stage."

Sarah pulled back. She managed to look up into Boyd's eyes. The two did not speak again. What could they say to each other?

He released her and turned to follow Rebecca down the boardwalk, the child's luggage in his hands.

Sarah thought of that previous time she had watched him go. The night had been black and wintry. Much as she felt today. And he had called back to her in the darkness, "Anytime." Anytime. She knew that he had meant it then. She knew that he meant it now as he shepherded her child safely off to school.

Her Rebecca. Her little baby. So far away—for such a long, long time. Sarah turned back to her quiet little home. She groped her way toward her bedroom. She was glad she had hired someone to take the daily freight run for her today. She was in for a very long cry.

Chapter Eleven

Moving On in Faith

Even though Sarah felt very relieved to have Boyd accompany Rebecca to her new school, she still found herself fretting as the days slowly dragged by. She would be so glad when Boyd returned and she could hear firsthand the account of their travels and Rebecca's adjustment.

There was no time to sit around and mope. Sarah had to get back to work. She needed every penny she could scrape together to see her way through the expensive school years that lay ahead.

She tried to turn her attention to her business. Was there a way that she might increase her earnings? Could she load and unload by herself and save the money she had been paying for help? No, it didn't seem plausible. She simply was too small to have the strength the job required.

Then, could she increase the amount of freight she hauled? No. She was already hauling all that came into the town. Could she raise her prices? Perhaps—minimally. But Sarah was reluctant to ask her patrons for more money. They could not afford to pay higher delivery costs and, for the most part, they had been so kind in staying with her when she had been given competition by the man who had tried so hard to destroy her business. And she couldn't have a double rate, penalizing those who had switched to the competition and then back again.

No, it seemed that the only way to increase her income for school expenses was to cut back on her own expenses. With Rebecca gone she wouldn't need to spend quite as much on food costs. But that wouldn't save her much. Rebecca had already taken most of her meals with the Galvans.

She would just have to struggle along as best she could—and trust in God to provide for her inadequacy.

She had prayed for God's leading. Now she simply had to take the provisions for the future, for both herself and her daughter, by faith. Somehow, God would provide.

———

It seemed forever as Sarah waited for Boyd's return. Day by day as she made her Kenville deliveries, her eyes sought out the incoming stagecoach, hoping to see a broad-shouldered man in a dusty black Stetson step from the conveyance. Day by day she was disappointed.

"Would you care for a cup of hot tea?" Alex Murray surprised her by asking as he came down the steps from his building to help the young lad unload his freight.

It was the first time he had asked the question for many months. Sarah could not remember the last time. She had started turning down the cups of tea in her effort to stop the town gossips. She hadn't wanted Rebecca hearing whispers that might cause confusion. After a number of refusals, Alex had stopped extending the invitation. Now he was again offering the bit of refreshment.

"I've just brewed a fresh pot," he went on. "It's in there on the table."

Sarah sighed and wiped her hand across her brow. With no Rebecca to go home to, she was in no hurry.

"I'd—I'd like that," she replied and managed a bit of a smile.

Alex just nodded toward a door at the back of his shop.

Sarah entered the neat, simple kitchen. She noted that the table was set with much more than just tea. Buttered bread was placed on a plate, the jam jar open beside it. Two thick slices of fresh banana bread rested on another small plate.

Sarah had not realized how hungry she was.

She lowered herself to a chair, then took a look at her hands. She was appalled at what she saw and wearily lifted herself up again. She crossed to the corner basin and washed her hands thoroughly with the fragrant soap. Then she splashed water over her hot, dusty face, rinsed, and wiped it on the towel.

While she stood before the basin, she took the time to glance in the mirror and tidy her hair, clasping it more firmly with the pins that had worked loose with the rumbling of the wagon.

Already she felt better. Now she would be able to thoroughly enjoy her tea.

Alex Murray's was the last stop of the day. She had no laundry that needed her care when she arrived home. In fact, there was no heavy task waiting for her. She would simply care for the team, fix herself a light supper, and then—then what? She wasn't sure what she would do with her evening. It was so lonely in the house with no Rebecca. She would need something to fill her mind and her hours.

She poured some of the pungent, hot liquid for herself, still puzzling over how she might fill the empty void that Rebecca had occupied. She didn't even have an excuse to visit Mrs. Galvan anymore.

Sarah reached for a slice of the buttered bread and spread over it a generous supply of the berry jam. She hadn't eaten anything that had really tasted this delicious since—since Rebecca had left.

She ate the second piece, serving herself more tea to go with it.

She was enjoying another cup of tea and the last bit of banana bread when Alex Murray joined her. He was rubbing his hands on his pants as he entered, then reached up and brushed back the lock of brown hair that had fallen over his forehead.

He looked pleased. Sarah smiled, pointed to the empty plates before her, and flushed a bit.

"I do hope you weren't counting on joining me for tea," she managed with an embarrassed laugh. "I fear I've eaten the whole thing."

The man did not even reply. Just grinned at Sarah.

He stroked back his hair again and reached to loosen his tie from where he had tucked it in his shirt to keep it out of the way of the freight boxes.

He didn't ask her how things were going or if she was missing her daughter. Instead, he pulled out the chair across from her and sat down backward, straddling the seat and resting his arms on the chair back.

"Thought you might have some time on your hands with Rebecca and Boyd—" He stopped. He brushed at his hair again, then lowered his chin to rest it on his hands.

Sarah was suddenly impressed with how young Alex really was. He didn't have much in years on her Michael. For some reason she had always considered him to be older than that.

She finished her last sip of tea and lowered the cup slowly to the saucer.

"There is a play over at the school tonight. Mrs. Brady was telling me about it. Her Bud has one of the main parts. She says it's worth seeing. Would you care to go?" His words surprised her.

It would be her answer to a long, lonely evening. Before Sarah even stopped to think, she had replied, "I'd like that."

Alex was smiling. "I'll pick you up at seven-thirty," he said and unstraddled the chair.

Sarah stood up and shook her skirts. For some reason she felt a little more like a lady.

She smiled softly. It would be good to get out. She couldn't remember the last time she had done something for sheer enjoyment.

"I'll be ready," she promised as she paused in the kitchen door.

"Seven-thirty," Alex repeated.

————

"What in the world have I gone and done?" Sarah asked herself later as she brushed down the team. "It—it might look to others like—like I am *keeping company* with Mr. Murray."

The thought brought horror to her thinking and a flush to her cheeks.

"Well—I can't back out now. I—really must go through with this—I guess. But I certainly—certainly will guard my tongue in the future. I've no wish to start rumors circulating again."

Sarah brushed so energetically that Gyp turned his head and studied her, then shifted uncomfortably from one big foot to the other.

"Well—I needn't take my stupidity out on you," Sarah rebuked herself and slowed down her efforts.

Once the team had been settled in the barn, Sarah set out making her plans for the evening. In spite of herself, her pulse quickened. She didn't know if it was excitement, nerves, or remorse.

"This is so—so frivolous," she scolded herself. "I should have stopped and thought before answering."

Sarah's hand trembled as she looked at the gowns in her closet. Many of them she had not worn since Michael had died. She no longer wore the black of mourning, but she had been wearing simpler things for Sunday morning worship, and besides her freight route, that was the only place Sarah had been going over the past five years.

"This was Michael's favorite," she whispered, her hand resting on a pale blue organdie with a flounced skirt and puffed sleeves. "Well, I'll not wear it—that's certain. This is just an evening out—with a long-time friend—to fill the hours."

She wasn't sure if she was speaking to herself or the memory of Michael.

She looked at another gown. "This is the one Michael bought for me when we learned that Rebecca was on the way," Sarah remembered with tears in her eyes. "He said he wanted me to always remember what a lovely mother his son would have—Michael was sure it would be a boy. Later he—he said that Rebecca was—was even better than a boy."

Sarah smiled through her tears and studied another gown.

"That one I bought for our first anniversary. Michael always teased about the sash. He said it made me look like a little girl playing house."

Her hand caressed the dress before she moved on.

"He said this one made my eyes look even bluer."

At last Sarah was able to select a gown with no special memories attached. It was rather a simple flowered frock, unextravagant in style. Sarah felt that it would be appropriate for an evening out among town folk at the community school.

She poured herself a bath from the reservoir of hot water on her kitchen stove, and immersed herself for a lingering soak. It had been months since she had enjoyed the luxury of *time*. It felt so good to just relax. She closed her eyes and felt that with the least opportunity she could nod off to sleep.

She couldn't do that. She had to be ready by seven-thirty.

———

Sarah could not deny that she enjoyed the evening. The Kenville school had worked hard to put on the play to raise funds for some new sporting equipment. The cover had come off their last softball, and there wasn't a single bat without a crack being held together with twine and binding tape.

After the play ended, refreshments were available for purchase. Alex was one of the first in line.

Sarah had opportunity to chat and laugh with neighbors. She felt like a different person than the small, determined woman who had been riding the delivery wagon for the past several years. Her dress softly rustled when she moved and her hair was fashionably secure. She even smelled like the lady she used to be, thanks to the luxury of the bottle of cologne Michael had purchased for her on one of his rare trips to the city.

But anytime that Sarah glanced down at her hands, the feminine illusion quickly left. There had been nothing that she could do about her calloused and chapped brown hands. She had rubbed lard into them. It just made them greasy. She cleaned it off and tried the cream from the top of the milk bottle supplied by farmer Tarkington. The cream wasn't that much better. She wiped it off as well.

The nails were short and uneven, broken by moving crates and harnessing horses. She hated the look of her hands.

"Rebecca's hands will never need to look so—so neglected," she had told herself. At least that was some consolation. Though it was fashionable to wear gloves, no other woman in the room was wearing them while partaking of the refreshments. Sarah looked longingly at her gloves in her lap and tried to hide the worst of her hands beneath the plate of small sandwiches and squares of cake that Alex had bought for her.

But no one seemed to pay much attention to her hands. There were many warm greetings and a few well-meaning remarks about her weight loss. Sarah was aware that her dress hung on her rather than fitting well-rounded, feminine contours. She didn't need to be reminded of her weight, either by meddling comment or sidelong glance.

But for all that, Alex did not seem embarrassed to be seen in her company. In fact, his eyes seemed to twinkle with pleasure at having her by his side. Sarah found that fact a relief.

Before Sarah was ready, the evening ended and it seemed there was nothing to do but to leave the schoolhouse and start the walk home through the autumn evening.

"That was fun," Sarah said as they slowly ambled down the wooden sidewalk, the dust lifting gently to brush the edges of her trailing gown.

"It was," agreed Alex.

They walked on in silence, listening to voices of the townsfolk calling good-naturedly to one another as they left the school premises.

"We must do it again—soon," continued Alex.

Sarah looked at him. "Are they doing another play?" she asked.

"No. No—not that I've heard. Mr. Holmes said he'd never get talked into *that* again." Alex laughed at the thought of the teacher and his emphatic little speech.

"Then what—?"

"We'll think of something," Alex stopped her.

Sarah half turned to look at him. He met her eyes, his own undeniably sparkling.

Sarah felt concern wash through her whole being. Was this evening as harmless as she had tried to convince herself? Did Alex see it as something that she did not? It frightened her. Surely—surely he didn't think that they were—were stepping out or anything. Was that what the town folk would think? Was it what Michael would have concluded about the evening?

Sarah was very quiet for the remainder of the walk home. They had reached her gate before Alex asked gently, "Tired?"

Sarah nodded. She was tired. Now.

"I have to be up early for the freight run," she admitted.

"I know," he answered. "I'm sorry."

"I really don't mind it," responded Sarah. She was not looking for pity.

"It shortens our evening," he replied, then chuckled to soften the words.

"Our evening." The words hung in the air to haunt Sarah. He had totally misconstrued the outing. She felt panic.

"I really must get in," she said too quickly. They had not even reached her door.

"I know." He sighed now, entirely serious. "But it's been—been—"

Sarah did not let him finish. "Great fun. The play. The chance to see neighbors. The lunch. It was all—all a very nice change and I thank you. Now it is back to business for me. I have freight to haul in the morning. But thank you for—for inviting me along. I enjoyed it."

And Sarah managed a smile, then let herself in at her door.

She closed the door behind her and leaned back against it, shutting her eyes and breathing deeply. Then she opened them and gazed at her gown.

She had made a terrible mistake. She had been dreadfully wrong to accept the invitation of Mr. Murray. She would never be caught so totally off guard again. She had no business going out for an evening with a man. What would Michael think?

Guilt washed through Sarah, making her cheeks burn and her eyes fill with unbidden tears.

"I will never, never do that again," she promised herself. But even then her tender, painful memories would not let her quit condemning herself.

———

Three days later Sarah saw a tall figure climb down

from the stagecoach and survey the streets of the familiar town. Then he lifted a hand and greeted her with a wave. Boyd was finally home. Sarah could hardly contain her eagerness. How had the trip gone? Was Rebecca safely and happily settled in the new school? What was it like? Was he sure that the young child would be well cared for? That she wouldn't be lonely?

She had so many questions—and she still had freight to unload.

But he was walking toward her, his small bag in his hand and a bundle on his shoulder.

"Howdy," he called before he even reached her. Sarah wished to run to meet him but she held her place, her feet shuffling agitatedly in the dust of the trampled street.

"Hello," she managed in reply. She waited for him to come closer, then asked in a husky voice, "How is she?"

"Took to the school like a duck to water," he offered, giving Sarah a big smile. "I think you were quite right. She will do well at the school. Already she has made some friends. She just bubbles—about everything."

Sarah felt her eyes filling with tears. She blinked quickly to try to remove them. She managed to give Boyd a nod. "I'm—I'm glad," she said under her breath.

"Why don't you come for supper tonight and I'll tell you all about it?" he offered.

"But—"

"Ma will be glad to have you. I'll need to give her and Pa a full report of everything anyway. It'll save me goin' over it twice."

"If you're sure."

"I am."

Then he looked at her closely. "How have you been?" he asked quietly, seeming to study her very thoughts.

"I'm—I'm fine," she answered and tried a smile to prove her declaration.

He nodded. She wasn't sure if he was accepting her acclaim or vowing to discover things for himself, but he dropped the subject.

"Need a hand with the deliveries?" he asked instead.

"No—No, we're almost done. This is the last of it and Newton is doing most of the unloading."

"Guess I'll git on home then and git cleaned up from the trip. I sorta feel like I'm dusty all the way through to my soul."

Sarah laughed softly at Boyd's declaration.

"See you soon then," he said as he hoisted up his bundle. "I'll tell Ma to set an extra plate."

Sarah nodded. It was nice to have an excuse to eat with the Galvans. She could hardly wait to hear a full report on Rebecca. She would hurry with her deliveries and stabling the horses.

As she moved toward Newton, who was lifting the last crate, her mind was saying its own little prayer of thanks.

"Thank you, Lord. Thank you. Boyd says she's settled. He says I did right. Thank you, Lord. Now I—I know that if this is where Rebecca is supposed to be, then you'll help me with the expenses of keeping her there."

And for the first time Sarah felt confident that she had made the right move.

Chapter Twelve

Rebecca

The supper hour was pleasant, with Boyd telling story after story of his trip and Rebecca's reaction to all she experienced. He had not left the city to return home until he was sure she was well settled and content to be on her own. Sarah was more grateful than she could express for Boyd's care of her daughter.

"I'm sure she'll do well," he proudly informed the table of interested people. "They did some testin' of some sort, and the teacher said thet she is more than ready for the first year. 'Very mature and advanced fer her age' was the way she put it. She said thet Becky was bound to make the school proud."

Sarah beamed. She was sure that her little girl would do well.

"There are three other girls in her room. Two are from the South. The other from the city. Becky and Annabelle—thet's one of the girls' names—took to one another right away. Declared immediately that they would be best friends. Different as night and day, they are. The other girl is taller than Becky and thin as a pole, with hair so fair it looks white, and pale blue eyes and the palest of skins. Looks almost sick—but Becky told me Annabelle's mama wouldn't let her in the sun at all and should she be out she had to always wear a bonnet and carry a parasol.

"This new friend of Becky's, Annabelle, she's already lost her two front teeth. Becky figured Annabelle quite grownup. By the time I left she was pesterin' me to see if her teeth were gettin' loose yet." Boyd stopped to chuckle and Mrs. Galvan laughed outright. Even Sarah smiled at Rebecca's attempt to hurry growing up.

"Becky and I were invited to the Fosters. That's Annabelle's folks. They're a fine family. Annabelle is the middle of five children. The two boys are the oldest. They are at an—Academy, I think they called it— somewhere in the East. The two younger ones are both girls. They are too young yet fer schoolin'. He's a lawyer with a big firm in the city. The mother is a woman from the South with a soft voice and fine manners. They have strong Christian principles. Annabelle will be a good friend for Becky.

"They have devotions each day at the little school chapel. Then on Sunday the staff takes all the girls to a large church in the town. It's within walking distance so they get 'exercise for the body and food for the soul,' according to Miss Peabody.

"Miss Peabody—now that is some woman." Boyd paused to consider his description. "She's a typical boarding-school matron, to my way of thinkin'. She's as stiff and starched as a fresh-ironed shirt, with her hair pulled back real tight in a biscuit—no, a bun at her neck, high-standin' collars, and eyes that would make a grown man squirm. I don't think one would do much of questioning Miss Peabody. A teacher I talked with said she's strict but fair—and the girls soon learn thet they are there to study, not to be pampered. 'Good for 'em,' says the teacher, and they don't really have thet much to do with Miss Peabody 'less they misbehave. I could guess by her bearin' thet she runs a tight ship.

"Teacher of the first grades seems kind. And they have a school nurse—right there, should they need her. An' a woman in the living quarters, 'Dorm Mother' they call her, to sort of care for the needs of the girls."

Sarah was delighted with all she was hearing. Her sacrifice on behalf of her daughter was more than worth it. Rebecca would get a good education and excellent training in her faith.

Sarah had never heard Boyd talk so much. She wondered if he really enjoyed it or if he was simply going on and on because he knew the two women at the table would give him no rest until he had told them everything he had learned of the school where Rebecca would be.

At length he stopped and looked around the table. "An' I reckon thet's about the sum of it," he said, and Sarah wondered if she detected a bit of relief in his voice.

Mrs. Galvan relaxed in her chair and took a deep breath. Even Mr. Galvan had been listening to every word as though the fate of the world rested on Boyd's report.

Sarah stirred restlessly in her chair. She was so thankful for the good news Boyd brought back to them. Had he not gone with Rebecca, they all would still be wondering about the young girl. Now Sarah felt she could relax and get on with the business of earning the funds that would keep Rebecca in the school.

"I see you glancin' at the clock," Mrs. Galvan observed. Sarah didn't realize it had been noticed. "I know you have lots to do. You run along now. I guess we've heard all we're gonna hear."

"Let me help with the dishes," said Sarah, quickly getting to her feet and beginning to stack plates.

"No—no. You've enough to do before bedtime. Now run on home. It was good to have ya visit. Seems a long time since you've been here. I've been missin' our little chats."

And Sarah was handed her cape and bonnet and gently pressed from the room.

"I'll walk along," said Boyd, reaching for his hat and falling into step beside Sarah.

The lovely fall evening was crisp and clear. The fragrance of burning leaves reached to them, seeming to curl warm and comforting fingers around Sarah's very soul. She loved the fall. God always seemed so close. So faithful in His provisions. The harvest grains and bountiful gardens were a reminder that He was always at work on behalf of His creation. Beneath their feet the fallen leaves rustled and a gentle breeze brought the perfume of late-blooming roses.

They did not speak. Boyd probably was already talked out, and Sarah was much too busy with thoughts of her own.

When they reached her gate, they stopped and Boyd opened it to allow her to enter. Sarah said, "Thank you." But she was not speaking of the courtesy of opening the gate. She was speaking of other things. So many things. She didn't suppose she would ever be able to put them into words.

"Ma says you been seein' Alex Murray," Boyd said when they were almost to the back door. His candid comment was neither condemning nor prying.

Sarah turned to face him. Her eyes grew big. "Is

that what folks are—the way they see it?" she queried, concern in her face.

"Isn't thet the way it is?" he asked gently.

"No. No," said Sarah a bit too forcefully. "No—we—I just—just went with him to the school play to—to—I was finished with work and had nothing to do and didn't want to be all alone—all evening, and he asked if I'd like to see the play at the school and I said yes and . . ." Her voice trailed off. What difference did it make? Why did she feel that she had to defend her actions?

She looked up at Boyd in silence, wondering if he understood what she was trying to say. She saw no condemnation in his eyes.

"I—I was foolish," she added lamely, dropping her gaze. "I didn't think. Afterward, I—I was afraid that folks might think that—well, that I—"

She couldn't finish that sentence either.

"Look," said Boyd gently. "You've got every right in the world to step out with a gentleman if you want to. No busy tongues should stop you. It's been five years. Five years already. You don't have a need to apologize—or—or make excuses."

"Oh, but I—it's not like that," insisted Sarah.

"I—I'm sorry," said the man, reaching out to touch her arm. "I had no right to pry like thet. It's jest—jest—I felt I had to know—how—how things stood. I mean—I didn't want to—"

It was his turn to stop without finishing his thoughts.

"Well," said Sarah, straightening herself to her full height. "If you wish to know—then I'll tell you. I have no secrets. My act was impulsive—foolish. I was lonely and I acted without thinking. But I wished later that I had not. I still love Michael. I felt—wrong—in doing what I did. Alex—Mr. Murray—is a fine gentleman. I will not deny that I had a good time. The best time that I have had since—for a long time.

"But I've no notion of repeating the mistake." She went on, her voice firm. "I will not be keeping company with Mr. Murray—or any other man again. I've made the promise to myself—and I intend to keep it."

Sarah may have expected to see relief in the eyes of the man before her, but it was something else that showed there. She wasn't sure just what it was. Pain? Regret? Disappointment?

Boyd said nothing, just reached in his shirt pocket and withdrew a crumpled and dirtied envelope.

"I have something for you," he said. His voice sounded low and strained. "I tried to keep it clean and unwrinkled, but a long trip doesn't make it too easy.

"It's from Rebecca. She told me what to write and I wrote down what she said—word for word. I think it will say more than all my stories. I thought you might like to get it when you could read it all alone. Uninterrupted."

He handed the envelope to Sarah, tipped his hat, turned, and was gone.

Sarah did not wait to watch him go. She hastened into her kitchen, threw her hat and cape on a chair, and settled herself to read Rebecca's letter.

Dear Mama,

The Tall Elms school is nice. They have a swing with a seat that moves. They even have tables for an outside picnic but we have to eat in the big room indoors. There are lots of girls but some of them are big.

I like Miss Brooker. She will be my first teacher. She has red hair and wears funny shoes.

I have a friend. Her name is Annabelle. She is

bigger than me and has her teeth gone. I like her. She showed me a picture of her family. She gots two big boy brothers and two little girl sisters and a dog.

We have four beds in our room. One is for Annabelle, one is for Priscilla, one is for Jo, and one is for me. My bed is by the door.

I get to learn the piano. I can hardly wait. It has lots of keys all up and down. I didn't know that pianos had so many keys. I get to play them all but now I just get to play on a few in the middle.

It was fun riding in the stagecoach, but I got hot and tired. Then one horse hurt his leg in a hole and we had to wait for another horse. Uncle Boyd lifted me up on a high rock in the shade while we waited.

It was dark when we got to the town where the train was. Only the train wasn't there anymore. It already went away without us, so Uncle Boyd made a bed for me with coats and I slept pretty good. The next day we had to wait, too. We waited three days before the train came to get us. Then we went on the train to the school.

Sarah stopped reading, her eyes filled with horror. What if Rebecca had been all alone? What could she have done? Sarah had not even considered problems like horses with broken legs and missing the scheduled train.

We saw lots of things in the town while we waited for the train. Uncle Boyd got me a room with a boardinghouse lady. She was nice and made good cookies. We looked at houses and stores and things. I even saw a goat. And when we were on the train I saw buffaloes and deer and even a coyote. And lots of birds and prairie dogs too.

And that's all I seen. And some rabbits.

Uncle Boyd says that if I work hard I will soon be able to write you letters all by myself. I will work hard.

This is a real long letter. Uncle Boyd says that if I don't soon stop he will run out of paper and you will be up all night reading and your lamp will go out.

Sarah could almost hear Rebecca's childish giggle. She blinked away tears and continued her reading.

And I need to tell you about Miss Peabody. She is big and wears her hair back tight and looks at you like she's cross when you haven't done anything bad yet. But Uncle Boyd says I don't need to be afraid. I just need to be good.

There are lots of books here. I like them. Some have pictures. I looked at a picture book today and Annabelle has a picture book too that she let me see.

We all wear the same clothes here. Even the big girls have to share the clothes. Not share the clothes 'cause we each have our own dress but the dresses all look just the same except Priscilla got a tear in hers and Jo has a spot that won't come out on her collar. My dress is just fine but a little big and I have another one just like it in the drawer by my bed.

They have big trees here and they have squirrels that live in them and eat the things that fall on the ground and bury them in holes. I like the squirrels. They have funny tails. Not like Cat. Please take good care of Cat until Uncle Boyd gets home to take care of her. Don't let her kittens play in the street where they might get runned over by a wagon or boys running.

I love you. I will miss you but I promise to be
a good girl.

Rebecca

By the time she finished the lengthy letter, Sarah
was weeping so that the words on the pages blurred
before her eyes. Oh, how she missed her. Her little girl.
The hand that held the letter trembled. How long
would it be before she saw her little girl again, she wondered. It was all she could do to pay the school fees.
How would she ever save money for a ticket so that
Rebecca might make a trip home? Sarah feared that by
the time Rebecca returned, she would not be a child
any longer. Sarah would have to content herself with
little scraps of sharing on sheets of stiff paper. It was
not easy for Sarah to face the fact that Rebecca might
not come home for Christmas—for the summer. Would
they both need to go on and on—alone? It would not
be easy living the empty years without her—waiting—
ever waiting—for the day when there finally would be
enough money for the train fare. Sarah prayed that the
day might come soon. That God might work a miracle.
She needed her little girl.

———

With little change in the routine, the days that followed seemed to slide from one to another. Only the
weather fluctuated. The freight was hauled. On some
days Sarah was so weary when she reached home that
it was all she could do to care for the horses.

Week by week she carefully counted up her earnings. There never seemed to be quite enough. Week by
week she denied herself one more thing to make the
pennies stretch further. Soon her diet consisted of bare

necessities, mostly garden vegetables taken from her cellar. Now and then she was invited to a church home for a meal. Sarah feared that her eagerness might show as she devoured the meat and fresh bread. Occasionally someone sent something home with her or brought it to her house. These were welcome gifts, and she made them last as long as she could.

Each Sunday Sarah sat at her small writing desk in the corner of her living room and wrote a long, long letter to Rebecca. There really wasn't much news from the town, so Sarah filled the letters with her own thoughts and feelings, and encouraged Rebecca to listen well to her teachers and follow closely the promptings of her God.

Alex Murray suggested evening outings on three occasions. Sarah always found some excuse to decline, though she longed for adult company. Yet she had no intention of giving reason for further speculation. Had she known that one town matron had suggested that Sarah had sent Rebecca off to school so she might accept the attention of gentlemen callers, Sarah would have been mortified. But Sarah was protected from the ugly comments and never suffered from the sting of those words.

That first winter without Rebecca to gladden her heart and bring a ray of sunshine to her day was long and lonely for Sarah. As spring neared, she realized that it would be impossible to bring Rebecca home. There had been no miracle. With a heavy heart she wrote to the school, asking them if they knew of a home willing to take Rebecca in for the summer. She knew with her tight money situation, she could not afford the ticket home. Besides, she now feared to let Rebecca travel so far alone. There would be no Uncle Boyd to see to her well-being should something unforeseen happen.

The letter that Sarah received in return informed her that the Fosters would be happy to have Rebecca join their family for the summer months. Sarah was more than relieved. She was ecstatic. She rushed to the Galvans, letter in hand, her cheeks flushed with her good news.

But even though she rejoiced, she still felt sadness. Oh, how she missed her precious daughter! It would be so wonderful if she could have Rebecca home with her for the summer months. It would be so wonderful to see in person how Rebecca was growing and maturing instead of reading between the lines of Rebecca's first attempts at letter writing or the reports of the school officials.

But Sarah brushed all of that aside and concentrated on adding up the bills and coins that would keep her young daughter in the school for "proper young ladies."

Chapter Thirteen

Changes and Chances

Sarah felt that she was always counting money. Over and over, week by week she counted and recounted, scheming and figuring and working toward the next payment due for Rebecca's schooling.

For many months there simply was not enough. If the funds were short a small amount, Sarah found ways to deny herself so she could make up the difference in time. Other times she had to devise ways of making up larger amounts.

One month she found a buyer for the mantel clock, on another the pin her mother had given to her, and on another the pocket watch that had been passed on to Michael by his grandfather. And so it went—whenever Sarah needed additional money she looked to her possessions for something else that might bring the needed dollars. Each time she had to sell one of her few dear possessions, her heart broke a little bit more, but each time she reminded herself that it was for Rebecca's future. That made it easier to bear.

Sarah treasured each of the letters that came from Rebecca. That first one had been written in a child's beginning script, short and obviously copied.

"Dear Mother," she wrote. (Rebecca had never called Sarah "mother" before.)

"I am fine. I like school. I am learning to read. With regards, Rebecca."

Sarah smiled at the stiffness of the letter. It was so unlike her bubbly, expressive child.

As the months passed and the letters continued to arrive, Sarah was able to watch the development of her only child. She wept the first time one arrived that sounded like the little girl had written her own thoughts. Rebecca was now in her third year and able to write letters on her own.

Dear Mama,

How is Cat. I think about her a lot. Has she had more kittens. I had a leter from Uncle Boyd but he forgot to talk about Cat.

I miss you all but I like it hear at schol. Annabelle is my best frend. I like going to her house. Thank you for letting me go to her house in the somer. I pray for you and Aunt Min and Uncle Boyd and Mr. Galvan to sometime. and I pray for Cat to.

Love,
Rebecca Marie Perry

There was no longer reason to rush home and change garments and tidy her hair to go pick up Rebecca. At first Sarah had followed the old pattern of cleaning up and changing her work clothes when she came home from the freight run. But as the deliveries had increased and her energy had depleted, she eventually decided that it was unnecessary. She could save time by going directly to her home chores.

She dressed in simple skirts and shirtwaists. Frills

were costly and too hard to keep clean and pressed. Only on Sundays did Sarah make the attempt to look feminine and ladylike. Sarah would have looked forward to Sundays—had they not been so lonely. That one brief day of rest certainly was a respite from heavy boxes and endless, backbreaking labor, but she also found herself restless and at loose ends on Sunday afternoons. After the morning service, a quick bite to eat, and a nap, there was nothing with which to fill the rest of the long day. She wished there were services in the evening. She longed for a friend to share a long walk or a drive in the country. As inviting as it could have been, she would not accept the invitations of her single male friends, and all the women her own age were busy caring for their own families.

Sarah did accept invitations to the homes of church friends, but they didn't come often. Families were too busy with those of their own to think of the young widow down at the end of the street.

So on Sunday evenings Sarah often paced her small rooms or fidgeted in her kitchen. She tried to read, but she often found it difficult to concentrate. Her letters to Rebecca gave her mind and hands something to do, so she gave a great deal of time and attention to these links to her daughter. Sarah was never sure just what filled all those pages. Sometimes she wrote lessons from Bible stories in a folksy, motherly way. At times she wrote other little stories, just as she used to tell them to a young Rebecca at bedtime. Even at the distance between them, Rebecca became her chief companion. Rebecca, the child she had borne and loved with all her heart, was her reason for living.

"Is Boyd in?"

Sarah had never taken the liberty of calling on a gentleman before—but she needed a man to talk to, and Boyd seemed the logical one.

Mrs. Galvan did not so much as raise an eyebrow. "He's writing his weekly letter to Becky. Come in. I'll tell 'im yer here."

"I hate to bother him but—"

"No bother. How ya been? Sit down. Just made a fresh pot of coffee. Ya can pour yerself a cup whilst I fetch Boyd."

Sarah went to the cupboard and lifted down a heavy mug from the shelf. She could use a cup of coffee. It might clear her head and help her thinking.

Boyd soon walked through the door, his broad shoulders reminding Sarah that here was someone she could lean on.

His eyes showed concern, and Sarah felt them studying her carefully. She smiled a tentative smile and broke the tension in the room. "I'm fine. I'm all in one piece. I just need a bit of advice."

He nodded, smiled in a relieved way, and moved to the cupboard to retrieve a cup, which he filled from the pot at the stove.

"Haven't seen much of you lately," he observed. "How's everything?"

"Fine," answered Sarah.

She shifted her weight in her chair. She wasn't sure whether to make small talk and ease her way into the topic on her mind or just plunge right in.

She decided on the latter.

"I hear a rumor that another freight run is to open up—to High Springs," she said.

Boyd nodded. He sat down at the table across from her and took a sip from the scalding coffee.

"Heard the same," he said with another quick nod.

Sarah leaned forward and tapped her fingers impatiently on the table.

"It shouldn't affect you none," Boyd said, setting his cup back on the table.

"I want it," said Sarah.

Boyd looked puzzled.

"I want it," Sarah repeated. "Do you know how I go about getting it?"

Boyd set down his cup and stirred in his chair. He leaned slightly toward Sarah. "From what I've heard," he began slowly, "you already have the bigger of the two runs. If it's smaller ya want—"

"I don't want smaller," said Sarah quickly. "I couldn't afford smaller."

"Then you're best to jest stay with yer present—"

"I plan to," cut in Sarah, pushing restlessly at her coffee cup without even looking at it.

"I don't figure—" began Boyd.

"I want them both," said Sarah.

"Both?"

Sarah nodded and pushed her cup to the side, leaning toward Boyd.

"The way I have it figured," she told him with animation, "if I had both of them I would do just fine in—in paying for Rebecca. I—I would even have some left over for—for whatever. It would—"

Boyd held up his hand to wave Sarah to a stop. "It sounds good, Sarah, but your team could never cover that many more miles in a day. They are plodders. This isn't a stagecoach run we're talking here. This is freight—heavy, and lots of it."

"I know," said Sarah, moving to the edge of her chair. "I have thought of that. I know my team couldn't do it. But faster horses could."

"Faster horses?"

"If I had faster horses—say a couple of teams—then I could make an early morning run from West Morin, as I do now, deliver Kenville's freight, and still have time to get back to West Morin to pick up High Spring's freight for an afternoon run. There would be time—with faster horses."

Boyd leaned back in his chair and studied her face.

"I could switch teams and give them a rest—if I had the two," went on Sarah.

He shook his head.

"And how do *you* get a rest, Sarah?" he asked slowly. "The High Springs run is a much longer run. And if you cut across country on the return trip, the road is even rougher. When do you rest?"

Sarah did not want to address his question. She felt it unfair of him to ask it. Yet she knew Boyd well enough to know he would press until he had the answer.

"It's not like—like it was when I first started," she began her argument. "I've—I've toughened up. I'm used to it now. I'm—I'm sure I can handle it."

His expression showed he was not in agreement, but he asked simply, "What do you plan?"

"Well—I thought I would sell Gyp and Ginger. They should bring a fair price. I've had—had offers in the past. They are—good horses. Then I'll buy four lighter horses and—do both runs." Sarah was out of breath by the time she had finished her speech. She didn't know if it was because of her excitement or her forcefulness.

Boyd just nodded, then said, "And what if the lighter horses can't stand up to the haulin' of freight?" He was twisting his cup back and forth by its handle.

"They will—won't they?" Sarah sat back into her chair. For the first time she was feeling some doubts.

Boyd shook his head. He seemed to be studying on

it. "I don't know," he said at last. "That's a pretty mean road. Particularly in the winter and after the spring thaw."

Sarah knew his words were true. But she hated to hear them. She stirred impatiently. One hand came up and brushed restlessly at the hair that insisted on curling about her face.

"I need that High Springs run," she said with emphasis.

Boyd looked at her—fully—evenly. After some minutes he spoke.

"So why don't you let me help with Rebecca's schooling? She's—she's special to me too, you know."

Sarah felt rebuked—much as she had as a little girl when her strict father had spoken firmly to her. But how could she let another man help pay for the education of Michael's daughter? No, she had to do it alone. Her chin came up.

"I'm responsible for it," she said with more strength than she felt. "I—it would just be—be easier if I—if I had that other freight run. If you wish to help—then I am asking—for your help now. I need to know how to go about getting that business—I need help choosing some horses."

There, she had spoken her piece. She had poured out all of her dependency. She needed a man. She needed Boyd. It had been hard for her to admit her need, but she had swallowed her pride for Rebecca's sake. Now it was up to him whether he would choose to help her—or refuse.

She didn't know if she dared to lift her eyes to look at him. She studied her hands that clasped together on the table before her, twisting and untwisting in their agitation.

Suddenly she felt her small, work-darkened hands

gathered into two stronger, larger ones. She lifted her eyes then. Boyd was leaning toward her, his coffee cup pushed aside.

"Sarah," he said gently, "you'll never know how I have longed to help you—how I have longed to take care of you. I'll do anything that I can. Anything."

Sarah was unprepared for his answer. This huskiness in his voice. This promise with his eyes as well as his lips. It would have been so easy to move toward him, lean her head on his shoulder, and release all her burden to him in tears and commitment. For a moment Sarah struggled. She remembered the words spoken long ago as he had left her on her step one dark night. "Anytime." She knew that promise still held true.

Then Sarah stirred. That wouldn't be fair. Wouldn't be fair to take advantage of this man in his kindness. She pulled her hands gently from his, blinked dampened dark lashes, and whispered softly, "Thanks. Thanks, Boyd—I—I really do need your help. I want that extra freight run. I need someone to choose my horses."

The spell was broken. He studied her, a look of sadness filling his eyes; then he cleared his throat, nodded, and reached a hand to pass it through his hair.

"What do you want me to do?" he asked, his voice sounding dull and defeated.

"I—I'll need to sell the bays. What's a fair price? I've no idea. Then I'll need two teams to replace them. I'll—I'll likely need to get a bank loan for the purchase but—" Sarah hated the thought of dealing with the banker, although it seemed to be the only thing she could do.

He rubbed his chin thoughtfully. Then he looked at her with directness. "Trust me?" he asked frankly. "Do you mind if I speak my feelin's?"

Sarah nodded her head.

"I'm not sure you should sell the bays," he began frankly and waited for her response. It was not long in coming.

"But I *have* to sell them to get the money for—"

"I understand that," he interrupted, "but if this plan doesn't work, you've nothin' to fall back on."

Sarah slumped in her chair and thought about his words. It was true. But it had to work. It just *had* to.

"And when it comes to buying lighter horses—I'd say a minimum would be five. Six'd be better—but ya might do with five."

Sarah gasped and he quickly went on. "It's not at all uncommon for a lighter horse to go lame—or get harness sores or just quit pullin' when pushed hard. Stage drivers have to have several spares. They change teams often. Now you—with hauling every day—you'll need more than just the four to count on."

Sarah sat mulling over his words. They weren't what she had wanted to hear.

"Now I've got a team of blacks I could lend ya until ya get started," he went on, and Sarah drew in a quick breath. Everyone in the county knew his blacks. They were a beautiful team—but spirited. She wasn't sure she could handle them even with her years of driving experience.

"I—I couldn't use your blacks," she said, shaking her head. "I couldn't. Hauling freight would ruin them."

He didn't argue with her. "Well—they're there if ya need 'em," he said instead.

Sarah nodded. It was nice to know.

"Guess the first chore is to see if we can git ya the run," Boyd observed. "No use changin' horses if the new run is already spoken for."

Sarah nodded. It was so.

"Well—I'll nose around some an' see what I can find out," he promised. Sarah knew he would keep his word.

————

Sarah was never sure just how he managed it, but he called on her three days later to tell her that the additional business was hers. It was to start in a week's time. She would need to have her plans made, her horses purchased, and her customers on line.

She felt both excited and frightened. What if it didn't work? What if she ended up losing both runs? It could happen. It had happened to others in the past. They had become too greedy, too aggressive, had spread their resources too thin and lost everything. Sarah prayed that wouldn't happen to her.

"Will you help me with the horses?" she asked Boyd humbly.

He nodded.

"I heard of some that might be got cheap," he told her. Before Sarah could exclaim her joy he went on hurriedly, "But they're just green broke. Hardly what a lady—what a person would be wantin' fer haulin' freight."

Sarah nodded, but she did so wish that she could find horses at a reasonable price.

"You gonna git a lighter wagon?" was his next question.

"I don't know," she answered honestly, remembering what had happened to her former competition. "It didn't work well for Fast Freight Lines."

"Well—he went far too light. There should be something in between what ya got now and what he went for. I'll do some lookin' around."

Sarah nodded and smiled her appreciation.

He found her a lighter wagon that seemed to be sturdy enough to take the shaking of the rough roads it would be traveling. He also found some horses, reasonably priced, that seemed as if they would behave fairly well in harness.

The price still was frighteningly high to Sarah. She swallowed several times at the thought of needing to pay off another bank loan. But she decided she would do her best to make it work. With that settled firmly in her mind, she approached the town banker. She was surprised that he agreed to lend her the money. "Of course," he explained carefully to be sure she was perfectly clear, "if anything happens that you are unable to repay, the assets belong to the bank."

Sarah swallowed hard. She had no intention for her assets to go to the local bank. Her hand trembled slightly as she accepted the bank note along with the challenge. Then she left with the money to take it to Boyd so he could pay for the purchases.

With the lighter wagon and the extra horses, Sarah's days were longer than ever. From early morning until sundown, she urged her teams over the rough roads to pick up the two freight runs at the depot and deliver them to Kenville's businesses as well as High Springs. By the end of the day she was so weary and aching from all the jostling and lifting that she wished only to fall into her bed.

Even her letters to Rebecca were shorter now. There was simply no time during the week, and by Sunday she was so exhausted that it was hard for her to even make it to church. By the afternoon she just wanted to be left alone to catch up on much-needed sleep.

If she had been so inclined, now there simply was no time to come home and change garments and tidy her hair so she might feel more like a lady. She dressed more plainly than ever in simple heavy skirts and ribbonless shirtwaists. Her hair was brushed and knotted to be pinned out of her face and tight to her head.

Her whole existence was tied to those horses and wagon. She came to think of herself not as Sarah, a woman, but as Sarah, the driver of the town drayage.

———

Boyd had been right. She did need the extra horse. She had operated for less than two weeks when one of her morning team went lame. It was all she could do to make it back with the wagon of loaded freight.

After a number of days of rest and some administration by Boyd, the horse seemed fine again and ready for harness, but then a second horse began to limp. Sarah had to rotate the team once again.

And so it went all through the long winter and into the spring. Sarah dreaded the soggy, rutted roads during the spring thaw. It made the wagon harder for pulling. At times she was afraid her lighter team would not be able to make it through. Once she had to unload part of the delivery, take half a load through the muskeggy section of road, and return to bring the other half. It slowed her down dreadfully, and by the day's end her back and shoulders ached until she was unable to sleep in spite of her weariness.

But summer came again—and with it better weather and better traveling. Each month Sarah was able to make the payment on her loan. Each month there were enough funds for Rebecca's schooling. In spite of her tiredness, Sarah felt that things were going well.

Chapter Fourteen

Growing Up

"How do you like it?" It was Annabelle who asked the question. She twirled in a circle, making the skirt of the flowing dress swirl about her ankles.

"It's lovely," Rebecca said enthusiastically. "It's the prettiest dress I've ever seen."

Annabelle's smile acknowledged that the dress was pretty.

"Well—" she said, her head tipped to the side, "it's better than those old navy-and-white uniforms anyway."

Rebecca agreed. She thought she had never seen anything so beautiful.

"What will you wear for the party?" asked Annabelle.

The question brought a furrow to Rebecca's brow. What would she wear? She had almost outgrown her dresses—again. It seemed that each time there was an end of term and they moved back to Annabelle's house, the dresses that had remained behind in the dorm closet were too short and too tight when they returned.

"Mother Perry hasn't sent money for new ones

yet," said Rebecca slowly. "Perhaps it has been held up in the mail."

"I s'pose you could wear one of my old ones," offered Annabelle generously. "Maybe Mother could alter it some. She's very good at that."

Rebecca nodded. Mrs. Foster was a skilled seamstress—though she scarcely ever sewed for her daughters. Usually she had the sewing done by a woman who came to the house.

At eleven, Rebecca still had not caught up to her roommate in height. She was beginning to think she never would. At one time it had bothered her. Now she wasn't sure. Annabelle had grown quite tall. Rebecca had noticed that the boys at church seemed to ignore her. She was taller than most of them.

Rebecca, on the other hand, got plenty of attention from the young lads. Untied sashes, pulled ribbons, and chases with frogs or spiders seemed to be a Sunday occurrence. Annabelle pretended she was glad that it was Rebecca getting the teasing and attention, but at times Rebecca wondered if that was really so.

There were other differences. Both girls were studying piano, but Rebecca played with a natural talent, while Annabelle had to work hard at it.

When it came to singing, Annabelle was ahead of Rebecca. She had a clear, bell-like soprano, surprisingly vibrant and mature for a child so young. Many people remarked on young Annabelle's singing talent, and the local pastor liked to use her in the service whenever she was home from her school.

Although the girls were so different in size, in temperaments, and in aptitudes, they got along well. They never seemed to tire of spending time together. Annabelle would have been lost at home had Rebecca not accompanied her for the summer months or holiday times, and Rebecca was so used to traveling to the Fosters at the end of each school term that she felt like one of the family.

So it was not an insult to Rebecca when Annabelle offered her one of her hand-me-down dresses. She began mentally reviewing Annabelle's closet, thinking which dress she would pick if allowed to choose.

"I think the green one might fit you," suggested Annabelle. Rebecca had never liked the green one—though she had never told her friend so.

She shook her head slowly now. "I think the money from Mother Perry will be here before the party," she said thoughtfully. "She knows I need it early summer so she always sends it along then."

"But what if she doesn't?" prompted Annabelle. "What will you do? You must have a dress for Carolyn's birthday party. You just *must*. You can't wear any of last year's. They don't fit and they make you look like a—a child. And you sure can't wear your school uniform. What will you do?"

"Mother Perry will send it. I'll write her a letter," insisted Rebecca, but her insides were twisting round and round, making her feel a bit sick.

"Well—if she doesn't, then you can wear my green," offered Annabelle with a toss of her light blond hair.

Her words did nothing to make Rebecca's stomach feel better. She didn't like the green. The shade reminded her of riding too long on the merry-go-round or eating too many candy apples—in Rebecca's opinion the color of the dress looked sick. She hoped with all her heart that she would not need to wear it.

Dear Mother,

(Rebecca consistently used that form of address now.)

One week from next Saturday is a very important birthday party. It is for Carolyn one of the girl's at church. She doesn't go to our school so we only see her when we come to the Fosters at end of term. Her Papa is a ~~polititien politision~~ politician. He is very important but he is never home so I don't know if I like him or not.

I have grown out of all my dresses again. I know that you just sent money for new ones at Christmas but they are already too small for me. Mother Foster says I am growing up. Annabelle says that I can wear her old green one but it really is an awful color. It makes my skin look yellow. I know because I held it up to my face one day. There are going to be boys at this party. It is the first time that I have gone to a party where there were both boys and girls. Of course you do not need to worry because it will be well ~~chaperooned~~ chaperowned. We are to play games and everything.

I hope you liked my last set of marks. Miss Peabody says that I am doing very well. I can play quite nicely now too. I still am not very good in ~~equestron equestrean eques~~ riding horses. I get a little scared when I know I have to go over a jump. I am learning tennis better and Annabelle says that I swim like a fish. I got 100% on my last Bible exam. I knew all my verses but I like to memorize things. I even memorized some poems by Tennyson. I hope you are doing quite well.

Affectionately,
Your daughter,
Rebecca Marie Perry

Sarah held the letter with trembling hand. Again she checked the date. It was too late. The party was in two days. There was no way to get the money there in time. Poor Rebecca. She had no new dress for the occasion. Would she need to wear the sickly green that she thought so ugly?

"I should have thought. I should have thought," Sarah scolded aloud. "I thought the Christmas dresses would still fit. I didn't realize how quickly young children grow. I should have sent money."

But where would she have found the extra money? It was all she could do to handle all her obligations. "Once I get the loan paid off—" she said to herself again. She had been living for that day. It would mean that money would be easier for her to come by. She was almost there. Almost. In a few months the profits from both freight runs would be hers. Hers for Rebecca. Then she would be able to send money for new dresses. New bonnets. Needed items. But what would Rebecca do about the party? *What?* Poor child. She would be so—so humiliated. And Sarah chastised herself over and over, feeling that she was a terrible mother for not fully supplying Rebecca's needs.

"I told you it might not come," said Annabelle, her tone a bit cocky.

It was the night before the big party, and no money for new clothes had arrived.

Rebecca said nothing. Inside she was churning again. *Why didn't she send it? Why?* she kept asking herself.

"Well—you can wear my green. You'd best try it on to see if Mother needs to have it shortened for tomorrow."

Rebecca nodded glumly. She hated the green dress. She looked woefully toward the closet where her own dresses hung. "Maybe I can still wear the white one with the pink ribbons," she said hopefully.

"I bet it's too small," was Annabelle's comment.

Rebecca did not answer. She crossed to her wardrobe, lifted out the white dress, and laid it on the bed while she slipped her everyday dress over her head.

The white dress with all the lace and the lovely pink bows slipped on easily. For one moment Rebecca dared to hope.

"Here—I'll do up the buttons," offered Annabelle companionably and came to give Rebecca a hand.

"Oh—oh," she said before she had scarcely begun. "They're not going to work. I can see it already."

Her voice was so singsongy that it angered Rebecca. She swung around to face her friend, jerking a button from her fingers.

"You haven't even tried yet," she accused.

"Did too," defended Annabelle.

"Did not."

"Did too. You're just mad 'cause it doesn't fit."

"Does too."

"Does not. You'd pop the buttons if you tried to wear it."

It was too much for Rebecca. She flung herself on the rose-colored spread and began to weep.

"Then I won't go," she said through her tears.

"You've got to go. Carolyn asked you."

"I don't care. I won't go."

"You can wear my green. I don't mind. Mother will—"

"I hate your green. I hate it. It's ugly. I'd never, never wear anything that ugly."

It was out. She had said it. She had told Annabelle exactly what she thought of the dress that Annabelle had worn so proudly.

For an awful moment there was silence, and then Annabelle stamped a foot. "Don't wear it then," she stormed. "Don't. Wear your ugly old school uniform—or—or your white with the buttons popped—or—or stay home and feel sorry for yourself. I don't care. I don't care!"

By the time she had finished her speech, she too was crying. She fled from the room, slamming the door behind her. Rebecca was left to herself, weeping over the fact that the party was the next day and she had no appropriate dress for the occasion. And it was to have been her first real party. The first time that she would share the games with boys. And now, to top things off, her best friend was mad at her.

She had one of two choices. She could wear the sickly green dress and look sick herself—maybe even be teased—or she could stay home and miss the most important event of her life. The very thought made Rebecca cry even harder. It wasn't fair. It just wasn't fair. Her mother should have sent the money. She should have. It was the first time that her far-off mother had let her down. But it was the first time that it really mattered. She should have known.

In the end Annabelle's mother had intervened in the situation, and Rebecca was allowed to wear another dress of Annabelle's in a soft lavender shade. She was much happier with the color. In fact, she felt quite grown-up and rather ladylike in the swirls of lavender lace. *If only I could wear my hair up,* she thought to herself as she studied her reflection in the mirror before leaving for the party.

"We should do our hair up," she said, turning to

Annabelle, who did not seem to be in nearly as much of a hurry to appear adult as Rebecca did.

But Annabelle, who thought the idea a splendid one, entreated her mother to let them, just this once, and Mrs. Foster had denied the request. "That will come soon enough," she said firmly. "There is no need to rush into things before you're ready." Both girls had been sorely disappointed, but Annabelle knew better than to press further. They pouted for a few minutes and then turned their attention back to guessing which of the boys would be invited to Carolyn's party.

"She's c-r-a-z-y over Daniel," said Annabelle, pretending to swoon. "I just know he will be there."

Rebecca turned up her nose. "Well, she is welcome to him. He's a show-off," she maintained.

Both girls giggled, the matter of pinning up their hair quite forgotten. After all, this was their first real party and both of them intended to make the most of it.

Chapter Fifteen

Passing Years

Carefully Sarah counted out her money. She had enough. Enough for the final payment to the bank. That meant there could easily be new dresses for Rebecca. Rebecca was thirteen now. Thirteen and "blossoming," according to Mrs. Foster's recent letter. She tried hard to picture her daughter, but in her mind she still saw a coming-on-six-year-old with big brown eyes and masses of curls tied up with a ribbon.

"What is she like now?" she asked herself often.

Over the years Rebecca's letters had changed, in tone and frequency. Sarah often had to wait weeks for one to come. Rebecca seemed to be terribly busy with her whirl of social activities, various lessons, sports, and school. She still loved the piano and had sent Sarah little clippings from the school news, telling of her accomplishments at various recitals and school programs. It made Sarah proud. Her struggle to earn the funds to send Rebecca off for her education seemed well worth all the long, trying days. Sarah couldn't believe that so many years had already slipped by. Years without Rebecca. But there had never been money to bring her little girl home for a visit.

And now the bank would be paid off—finally. Sarah
was back to receiving the full rewards of her work. She
could hardly wait to send the first generous sum to
Mrs. Foster to bring Rebecca's wardrobe up-to-date.
For the moment, Sarah felt that was more important
than putting aside money for a train ticket.

———

"You look lovely. Both of you," said Mrs. Foster,
beaming at the two girls. Rebecca had grown to be very
much a part of the Foster family. In fact, Mrs. Foster
often boasted that her family came in twos. First the
two fine sons—still at school at the Academy. Then Annabelle and Rebecca from the school for young ladies,
and then her two youngest, always thought of as the
babies of the family and treated accordingly.

Rebecca smiled demurely at Mrs. Foster's compliment, and Annabelle couldn't suppress a nervous giggle.

They were to participate in the morning church service, and Mrs. Foster had gone to great pains to make
sure that "her girls" were appropriately attired for the
occasion.

"Now remember to stand tall, Annabelle," she went
on. "Be proud of your height. You look—regal." And
Mrs. Foster gave her eldest daughter a smile of encouragement and placed a hand in the middle of her
back to urge her to straighten the slump in her stance.

The woman turned to Rebecca. "Make sure your
skirts cover your ankles when you seat yourself at the
piano," she reminded her.

Rebecca's feet were always being inhibited by the
mass of skirts. She wished she could just hoist them
up a little, out of the way of the feet that reached for

pedals. But she nodded her assent. She would do as
bidden—and likely pay the consequences with a few
errors in her presentation.

"You will both do fine. I know you will make us
proud," Mrs. Foster went on and gave each girl a little
hug.

Rebecca did not usually feel nervous when playing
in public. She loved it. But today was different. Today
Robert and Stanley Foster, home from school, would
be sitting with their parents.

Rebecca had never really thought of them as her
brothers, though Mrs. Foster had tried hard to en-
courage that kind of relationship. In the first years that
Rebecca had spent time in the home, the two older boys
were teases, their presence dreaded and avoided whenever possible. She and Annabelle, who took the brunt
of the teasing, stayed as far away from the boys as
their room would allow. Rebecca had come to think
that having brothers was a dreadful burden.

And then things changed. The boys seemed to avoid
the girls. When they were home from the Academy, all
they talked about, all they ever seemed to want to do
was sports, sports, sports. Rebecca got quite tired of
hearing of football games and soccer matches and tennis tournaments. She would have been happy to snub
the two growing sons—but it would have gone totally
unnoticed. They seemed to ignore her and Annabelle
with near contempt.

But this time—this time it was different somehow.
She had met Robert in the upstairs hall—quite by accident on his first morning home—and he had looked
at her. Looked at her as if he actually saw her there.
Then he had smiled and wished her a good morning.

It had taken Rebecca's breath away.

Later when they had been called to the noon meal,

Rebecca had seen Robert's elbow nudge his brother and clearly heard him whisper to Stanley, "See!" and Stanley had looked at her, swallowed, and his eyes widened and misted for a moment—as if he might choke.

Rebecca had not understood what the one word "see" might be meant to convey, but she felt two pairs of eyes turned upon her several times during the meal and found it hard not to squirm under the scrutiny.

They still talked of sports. They still talked a bit loud. They still drew critical comments from Annabelle, but Rebecca knew that somehow things had changed.

And now she was to play the piano before them in the morning service. She did hope her hands would not tremble—that she would not entangle her feet in the folds of her long skirt and do something dreadful with the foot pedals.

It was all so strange—this funny little nervousness that was so unwelcome—but it was also rather exciting. Rebecca tried to still the beating of her heart. She was *so* thankful that Mrs. Foster had finally allowed her to pin up her hair. She tossed her head slightly now just to get the feel of it. It held firmly in place. Pinning it up made her look so much taller—so much more a young woman. No—a lady, for at fourteen Rebecca felt that she was fast becoming a lady.

———

Sarah slumped into the chair near the kitchen door. It was as far as her weary body could go. It had been a particularly trying day. By now both freight loads had just grown and grown, and in spite of the help of the loaders Sarah was exhausted. She had even skimped on her brushing down of the horses. Something that normally she never did.

She put a hand to her forehead. She hoped she wasn't coming down with something. That would never do. In all the years she had been hauling the freight, she had been sick only twice. On the one occasion, Mr. Curtis had driven her team. On the other, she forced herself to carry on despite how she felt.

She detected no fever. For that Sarah was thankful. But she was so tired. So weary with all of the driving and hauling and bumping over the rough roads. If only she could sleep. Could just sleep and sleep and sleep.

But then Rebecca would never have the new things she needed. Rebecca would be forced to leave her school before graduation. Rebecca's most recent letter warmed Sarah's tired body with its presence in her pocket.

At the thought of the letter, Sarah reached in and drew it forth.

Dear Mother,

(Sarah thrilled to see the word mother, though she was bothered when Rebecca had used it in a previous letter to refer to Mrs. Foster.)

> Thank you for the last sum of money that you sent to Mother Foster.

(There it was again, and Sarah felt a twinge prick her heart.)

> She had two lovely dresses sewn for me. We also bought a pair of new slippers to wear with them. They are gorgeous. Even Annabelle envies me. I also had enough to buy some very nice under-things. I needed them badly.
>
> School starts again soon. It doesn't seem possible that I will soon graduate. Mother Foster is already planning a big party for Annabelle and me. It is fun to think about it.
>
> I plan to be on the honor role again. It seems

a bit harder each year because we are kept so busy with other activities during the school year. This year we are even to exchange parties with the young men from the nearby Academy. (It is not the same one that Stanley and Robert attend.) Miss Peabody says that it is important for us to learn how to "properly" conduct ourselves in the presence of gentlemen.

I must run as Annabelle is waiting on me to go play tennis. We are playing doubles with Stanley and his friend.

> Affectionately,
> Rebecca

P.S. I really do need a new bonnet. My last year's doesn't fit well at all, now that I am pinning up my hair.

I must get the money off to her, thought Sarah. And rubbed her hand over her forehead again. She was so weary. She wished she didn't face tubs of laundry. She hated washing the heavy, masculine trousers that now formed most of her wardrobe. But it just didn't make any sense to dress in any other fashion during the cold winter months.

"Where are you from?"

A new girl had come to share their dorm room, a girl full of uninhibited questions. Priscilla had graduated. Annabelle and Rebecca and Jo still had to finish the present term, plus one more year. The bed by the window now belonged to a girl named Peony. Rebecca and Annabelle had snickered over the name when they had first been informed by Miss Peabody who their new roommate would be, but as proper young women they did not laugh when introduced to its bearer.

"I am from the West," answered Rebecca a bit stiffly. "A town called Kenville."

"The West? What's it like? Oh, I've always wanted to go west," enthused the girl. "It's—it's so romantic."

Rebecca frowned. She had never thought of her little hometown in those kinds of terms.

"What's it like?" the girl prodded again.

Rebecca scrambled to remember the town that had been her home for her first years. She really couldn't remember much about it. She remembered her mother— vaguely. She remembered Aunt Min and Uncle Boyd— vaguely. Had it not been for letters that kept her in touch, she might well have forgotten that they existed.

"Well—I—I was quite young when I came back East to school," admitted Rebecca.

"How did you come?" asked the girl.

Rebecca sorted through her memories.

"By stagecoach—the first of the way. I remember it—something happened and we had to sit and wait and wait. Then we traveled by train."

"Oh-h," squealed Peony. "That is just so—so romantic."

It hadn't been very romantic, Rebecca remembered. It was hot and dusty and she had become so thirsty and hungry and tired. It hadn't been romantic at all.

"Did your mother and father—?"

"No," said Rebecca tersely. "My father is dead."

The girl looked a bit shocked. She even fell silent— but not for long.

"Where's your mother?"

"Back in Kenville."

"Do you have a—a stepfather?"

Rebecca in turn looked shocked. Of course she didn't have a stepfather. "No," she said firmly and turned away. She didn't like all the questions.

"What does your mother do?" Peony was not to be deterred.

"Do?" echoed Rebecca, wheeling around to face her.

"Yeah—if you don't have a stepfather, who cares for your mother?"

"She cares for herself," stated Rebecca simply.

"What does she do?"

Rebecca tried to think. What did her mother do? She had such vague recollections. She remembered far more about Aunt Min and Uncle Boyd—and even Mr. Galvan—than she did of her mother. Who was her mother? The lady who wrote letters—who sent money for her necessities. But who was her mother? Rebecca thought hard about the question. Slowly, little bits of memories took fuzzy shape.

Her mother. The lady who used to rush to meet her at the end of the day, almost breathless as she scurried up the board sidewalk to the Galvans. They used to play games. They used to sing together. Her mother taught her songs, told her stories, and heard her prayers. That was her mother. She was a smiling lady. A pretty lady with long dark hair that she used to unpin when they were alone and let tumble down her back and over her shoulders in soft curls. Rebecca could almost, almost see her face. Her eyes. But not quite. She couldn't quite remember. But she had loved her. She remembered that. They'd had fun together.

"What does she do?" the new roommate insisted.

"She—she—ah—" Rebecca thought hard. "She—drives horses—I think."

"Drives horses?" The new girl seemed horrified. "A lady?"

Rebecca jerked to attention at her own words. Her own admission. She had never thought of it before. It did seem strange. A mother who drove horses. She felt her cheeks begin to burn. She did turn her back on the girl now.

"Well—maybe she doesn't," she said, flinging her curls as she tossed her head. "I really don't remember much—it was all so long ago."

She turned to Annabelle. "Come on," she said impatiently. "It's time for choir rehearsal." And Rebecca stalked from the room, troubled deeply by her own thoughts. Was it really true? Did her mother drive horses? Rebecca resolved never to mention the fact again.

"You look tired," Boyd commented as they walked the short distance from the little church to the Galvan home, where Sarah was to join them for Sunday dinner.

"I am," Sarah said. It was the first time that she had admitted that fact to Boyd or anyone else.

"You're pushing yourself too hard." There was concern in his voice.

Sarah turned to him and a weary smile played across her face. "I've paid off the note at the bank," she announced with some enthusiasm.

"That's great!" His tone indicated genuine joy.

"It is so good to be free of debt," she told him.

"Now maybe you can slow down. Catch yer breath," he pressed on.

Sarah shook her head. "There seems to be more freight coming in all the time," she acknowledged. "On both runs. I hardly have time to fit it all into the day."

"I've been thinking about that," he said, reaching for her elbow to guide her across a muddy spot in the road. "Have you ever thought of hiring someone for that second run?"

Sarah looked at him. "Hiring someone?" she repeated, surprise in her voice.

"As driver. You'd still get the profit from the run—but only have to make one trip a day."

Sarah thought about his words.

"I don't know," she responded at last. "Rebecca only has a little more than a year left. But the older she gets—the more she needs. You know? Church functions and parties and—"

"I wish you would let me—"

"No. No," said Sarah firmly, waving a gloved hand. "She's my daughter. I'll—do the caring of her. I've managed fine—and now—now things are—are much better. There's even a little to spare now. I'm already laying aside the money for her fare home."

"I still think you could use a driver," Boyd tried again, but there was a resigned note in his words.

"I'll think about it," said Sarah, dipping her head to one side. "I'll do a little figuring and see what I can come up with."

"That new family. The Olivers. They have a grown son. He seems like a nice young fellow. Hear he's looking for work."

Sarah had seen him at church. Though she'd had no occasion to introduce herself to the young man, she had met his mother. A fine woman. Sarah found herself wishing she had time to develop a friendship with her.

"I'll think on it," Sarah promised Boyd again. It sure would be a relief not to have to take both freight runs each day.

Sarah lifted her simple skirt to step over a small puddle. She was so used to trousers now, she hardly remembered how to handle skirts in a ladylike fashion. She only wore a skirt on Sundays, and then she found herself choosing the plainest ones from her closet. She did not have time or energy to fuss with ribbons and frills. Besides, there seemed to be no good reason to do so.

Chapter Sixteen

Hired Hand

"I understand you're looking for a job."

Sarah spoke softly and matter-of-factly. She had learned to take a direct approach in all of her dealings with people. It saved her time and gave her a bit more confidence in living and working in a man's world.

"Yes, ma'am," the young man before her nodded.

Sarah found herself studying him. Tall and rather stocky, he certainly was big enough to not only drive the team but to load and unload his own deliveries as well. Sarah liked that. It would save her hiring a lad to help with the lifting and sorting. But after quickly noting his size and approving, Sarah's eyes returned to the young man's face. Something about it seemed to draw her.

He wasn't handsome—though he was appealing in his own way. He didn't seem cocky or overly daring or adventurous. Yet he did not look as if he would avoid a confrontation if presented with one. But there was something else about him. At first Sarah found herself puzzling over what it might be, and then she looked into his deep brown eyes and saw quiet strength looking back at her.

He's so—so—confident—for one so young, she mused to herself. It would have been easier to understand if it had been youthful brashness. What about him made him seem so serene—so at peace with a difficult world? Sarah hoped he would understand that the drayage business required a lot of hard work. That one had to be prompt and dependable—no matter the weather—no matter the circumstance—no matter how one was feeling.

"It's not an easy job I'm offering," she said almost abruptly. "One has to get the freight to the customer without fail."

He nodded. Sarah could see respect in his stance, but not subservience.

"There'll be days that you'd rather stay in out of the weather," Sarah warned.

He nodded again. His eyes were serious, but Sarah had the impression that they could sparkle with laughter were the occasion appropriate.

"I'll expect you to take both runs with me for a couple days, and then we'll decide which delivery run will be yours and which will be mine."

"Thank you, Miz Perry," said the young man; then he did smile, revealing even teeth and a slight dimple in one cheek. His eyes seemed to shine, and Sarah thought for one moment that he might explode into infectious whooping.

"You've just answered one of my prayers, ma'am," he said in explanation. "I told Ma this morning that God would see to it in His own time."

Sarah looked at him in surprise for one minute and then could not resist returning the full smile. She nodded silently, but inwardly she wondered if after several hard days on the rutted, difficult roads, loading freight until one's back ached and spirits sagged, if the young man would still thank God for the job she had just given him.

———

Rebecca stretched one dainty foot toward the luxurious mat beside her bed and stifled another yawn. It was much too early to be getting up after the party that wasn't over until almost two o'clock in the morning. But she still had classes to attend. Across the room, her three roommates still slept, covers pulled up close to their ears, soft breathing indicating that they had no intention of leaving warm beds to face the responsibilities of the morning.

Rebecca yawned again and crossed to where Annabelle lay sleeping. "Annabelle. Annabelle," she said, shaking the girl's blanketed shoulder slightly. "It's time to be up. We'll be late for breakfast if we don't hurry."

Annabelle groaned and would have turned over and gone back to sleep had not Rebecca shook her again.

"Now!" she said firmly. "We don't have much time."

Annabelle moaned again, but her eyes did open reluctantly. "You spoiler," she said sleepily. "I was having the most wonderful dream."

"Get up," scolded Rebecca, "or your dream might turn into a nightmare. You know we've been told we've used up all excuses for being late for breakfast."

Annabelle grumbled but threw back the bed clothes and stumbled from her bed while Rebecca moved on to waken the two remaining girls in the room.

"What was the party like?" Peony asked as the girls

hurried into robes and toward the shared bath facility in the dorm.

"Wonderful!" exclaimed Annabelle dreamily. "William Sheffler was my partner for almost every game. And we won two of them. He's so—so—"

"Romantic," squealed Peony.

Rebecca and Annabelle exchanged glances. To Peony everything was romantic.

"But it was Rebecca who was the belle of the ball," went on Annabelle knowingly.

Peony looked puzzled. "I didn't know you went to a ball. I thought it was just a home party. You said—"

Both girls groaned. "Oh, Peony," said Annabelle. "That was just an expression of speech. We did go to a home party."

Silence fell as the girls scurried to get on with their morning ablutions. They had to make it to breakfast on time or they would be in for more demerits—and more demerits would cost them. They would either need to pay a fine—money which they did not have and which neither wished to ask for from parents who might not understand the importance of parties—or else take a cut in grades. Annabelle could not afford that. She was just barely passing as it was. Rebecca would never have agreed to a grade cut. She was leading her class and intended to keep it that way. She wished the honor of being the class valedictorian at term end.

They managed breakfast. Even stayed awake during early morning classes. Even managed through the entire day without seeming to be too exhausted. It was not until they met back in their shared room that evening that the four were able to discuss at length the party of the night before.

"I don't know how you do it," said Peony. "It is all

I can do to keep up, with eight hours of sleep a night."
Annabelle nodded and yawned.

"This was a special party," she said. "We wouldn't
have been able to go either if Dr. Jeggers from the
Academy hadn't requested some young ladies to attend
the honor party for ten of the young men."

"Honor party?"

"They are all graduating—with top honors. The
Academy has this party each year. They always invite
discrete young ladies from the Dean's list at Tall Elms.
They feel it's most important that the young men know
how to properly conduct themselves in society—
though that 'proper conducting' is done under strict
supervision, of course."

"And you were selected?"

"Actually," said Annabelle honestly, "Rebecca was
selected. Then when one of the other girls got the
grippe at the last minute, Rebecca suggested me."

"And you had a good time?"

Rebecca and Annabelle exchanged glances. It was
Annabelle who answered, falling backward upon her
bed in unladylike fashion and throwing her arms wide.
"It was wonderful!" she exclaimed. "Simply wonderful."

"Oh-h," squealed Peony. "How—"

"Romantic," put in the other three girls in chorus.

"But it was," said Annabelle in sudden agreement,
sitting back up with her skirts still akimbo. "I mean—
just think—we were in the company of the ten most
promising young men in—in the country. Think of it!"

"Oh-h—" said Peony, "I would have just swooned."

Annabelle grew serious. "Well," she said, "Rebecca
didn't. I mean here she was with all of these—these—
possibilities, and she just—just acted like—like they

were boys from home or—or brothers—or something."

Three pairs of eyes turned on Rebecca. She felt herself coloring faintly. "Brothers," Annabelle had said. Rebecca knew that Annabelle had no idea what was in Rebecca's heart concerning Stanley. She had not admitted her feelings to anyone. Certainly not to Stanley. But things had been so different the last time they were together in the Foster home. Stanley had seemed so—attentive. Rebecca had often felt his eyes on her, and when she would turn toward him, he would flush and pretend to be looking elsewhere. Rebecca had enjoyed the attention, yet been uncomfortable too.

The Foster family encouraged correspondence among all of their scattered offspring. "It is so important to keep up communication among family members," Mrs. Foster said often. And as Rebecca was considered to be one of the family, she had been included in the weekly correspondence of family members. And Rebecca and Stanley continued to exchange letters.

In the past Rebecca had often chaffed under the unwritten family "law." Correspondence took up so much of her Sunday afternoons. She wished to read—or even sleep. It was so hard to write her mother, Mrs. Galvan, Uncle Boyd, the Fosters, Robert and Stanley. She was thankful that she didn't have to write the two younger girls. They could be included in the letter home to the Fosters.

But now, since her last trip home to the Fosters, Rebecca was no longer irritated by the task of writing to Stanley each week. She waited impatiently for his letter and then read it over and over, watching carefully for words that might indicate—well, that he looked forward to hers as well. Rebecca was never quite sure whether his letters were still "brotherly" or

if some of the phrases like "I miss you" or "I look forward to seeing you at Christmas break" held more
meaning than in the past. Stanley had always written
such things—but in brotherly fashion. Rebecca had
never paid attention to them before.

"—she's immune," said Peony.

Rebecca's attention jerked back to the conversation
in the room.

"Oh no, she's not," denied Annabelle. "I've known
Rebecca all my life, and she enjoys turning heads as
much as anyone."

The girls all giggled and Rebecca flushed. It was
true. She had always enjoyed the attention of fellows
her age. And there were always plenty around her.

"Then maybe she's—fallen head over heels," put in
Jo.

Again, giggles.

Annabelle sobered and looked directly at Rebecca.
"Are you keeping a secret from me?" she demanded in
mock anger.

"Don't talk nonsense," said Rebecca with a flick of
her skirts, but her cheeks did flush.

"Oh!" squealed Peony in her characteristic way.
"Rebecca has a beau. Oh-h—how romantic."

Giggles and hoots followed.

"I need some sleep," cut in Rebecca. "I have an
exam tomorrow."

"Afraid you'll only get a ninety-nine percent,"
taunted Jo.

"I'll not get fifty if I don't get some sleep," responded Rebecca dourly.

"Say," said Jo, "you are in a bad mood."

"Out of sorts?" asked the frank Peony, irking Rebecca further.

"No—I'm not out of sorts," she replied sharply,

slipping off her shoes and moving toward her cupboard to get her nightie. "I'm tired, that's all."

But it wasn't all. Stanley's letter should have arrived in yesterday's post. It always arrived on Wednesday. It hadn't. Nor was it in today's mail. What could have happened? Rebecca felt agitated. Concerned. What if—? But she pushed aside the troubling thoughts. She didn't even wish to consider the possibilities.

"How's young Seth doin'?" asked Boyd as he and Sarah walked back from church. Sarah took a moment to think about her answer. Seth's confidence had not been shaken by the difficulties of hauling freight. He looked as fresh at the end of the day as at the beginning. Oh, he might look tired, but he never looked down. He spoke with enthusiasm. He usually finished his shorter run before she herself did and was always on hand to help unload her return deliveries. He cared for his team with diligence. He even took care of her horses when she arrived home. He didn't fuss about the weather, and they had experienced some nasty storms since he had taken over the other run.

"He's—he's doing fine," she finally answered, her head nodding with her words. "He's a good worker."

But Seth was much more than a good worker. He was—was a—partner? An encourager? Sarah wasn't sure. She only knew that she looked forward to seeing him each day. He gave her spirits a much-needed lift. His boyish—yet settled—confidence did much to get her through her day. She often wished with all her heart that she knew the reason for his quiet, calm acceptance of life.

"He seems like a fine boy," went on Boyd. "his whole family—"

"Yes," responded Sarah. "Yes—he is."

———————

"What's your secret?" Sarah asked one day after she had worked with Seth for a number of months, watching daily his quiet demeanor.

"Secret?" He turned puzzled brown eyes to her, but even in his confusion she could see the laughter ready to spill out if something should amuse him.

"You always seem so—so at peace—even when things go wrong. If I'd had a broken wagon wheel and had to ride one of the horses back, toting the heavy wheel to the smithy, and then been late on the run and heard complaints about it, I'd have been ready to take to my bed."

He gave her a smile and looked down at his scuffed boots. When he looked up again the smile was gone, but that same peace was still in his eyes. "The secret . . ." he mused. "Guess it's no secret. I mean—it's not just mine—it's for everyone. Every child of God. I just remember John fifteen. Verse five. Especially the last part. I say it over and over to myself. It reminds me where my strength—my help—comes from. Ma was always strong on gettin' us to memorize from the Scriptures. She said we couldn't draw on them—if we didn't have 'em within to draw on."

He tapped his chest over his heart. "She said we need the Word not just in our head but in our heart," he finished.

Sarah nodded. She had the Word in her head. She knew her Bible quite well, though she would have admitted that she hadn't spent much time memorizing the verses. Perhaps she should have. Perhaps it would help her through some of the difficult days.

She looked at the young man before her and nodded her head. His eyes met hers with such serenity, such confidence, that she found herself swallowing in confusion. Then he smiled again and Sarah felt she had somehow just been blessed.

"I'll care for the horses," he offered.

She nodded again. "Good," she managed. "I've got a lot of bookkeeping to catch up on," and she turned and left him.

"But first," she promised herself as she walked away, "I'm going to look up John 15:5. I want to see for myself just what you're talking about."

————

I am the vine, ye are the branches: He that abideth in me, and I in him, the same bringeth forth much fruit: for without me ye can do nothing.

Without me ye can do nothing.

The words remained in Sarah's mind as she began her bookkeeping tasks. They stayed in her mind for the rest of the day. She reflected over her past years. She had done something. Not without God of course. She had always believed in God. But it was she, Sarah, who had done quite well working through her needs. She had provided for Rebecca. She had fought for and kept the freight run. She had acquired the second run and managed to keep them both operating smoothly, though she had nearly collapsed in the attempt. And now—now she was in a rather enviable position. Both runs were paying nicely. She had no debts. Rebecca was soon to graduate with a first-class education. Rebecca would soon be back home again and she, Sarah, would be able to lay some money aside for—for other things. Things had worked quite well. She had managed, through her own perseverance and hard work to make it—on her own. She may have felt just a bit of justifiable pride in her accomplishment.

Sarah stirred in her chair. She was pleased—even proud. But why—why didn't she have the same—same gentle peace this young man evidenced? The quiet assurance that he showed her every day—whether things went well or turned ugly? Why did she often fret and worry until well into the night?

"He's just a boy," she reminded herself. "He hasn't really been knocked about by the world yet. He'll learn. He'll learn that life can get pretty rough on one. We'll see how—"

Sarah abruptly left her chair and crossed to the window. She pulled agitatedly at the curtain and looked out across the yard to where the horses fed contentedly from the manger in the corral. They had been curried and rubbed until they shone. No harness sores to worry her. Seth saw to that.

Seth.

He was such an unusual young man. Sarah respected and appreciated him. In a motherly fashion she wished to protect him from the hard knocks in life. She would hate to see him crushed—destroyed. It would be so cruel. But life was cruel. She knew that. Didn't life rob her of Michael? Oh, she missed him. She still missed him after all the years. Now she had only Rebecca. Rebecca. Her little girl. The little girl who would soon be coming home.

Chapter Seventeen

Rights of Passage

So much happened in such a short time that Rebecca's head was swimming. Exams were over. She had earned the honor of giving the valedictory address at her graduation ceremony. Her mother was not there to hear her give it—nor was anyone from faraway Kenville, but the Fosters were there, including Robert and Stanley, who had come especially for the occasion. Rebecca had to remind herself that she was really not the reason they had come, because Annabelle also was graduating.

Mrs. Foster gave an elaborate party for the two girls, celebrating their graduation and the beginning of "a new life," as she referred to their future. Annabelle was nearly beside herself with gaiety during the occasion, but Rebecca, though outwardly enthusiastic, inwardly quaked. *What new life?* She had been quite satisfied with the old one. Now what lay in store? She could not even guess. She only knew that in her room, in the left corner of the top drawer in her small hankie box where she kept special treasures, smugly lay a one-way ticket for Kenville, as though dictating her future.

She was going home. *But home to what and to whom?* Rebecca tried hard to remember what her life had been like before she entered Tall Elms School for Girls. She tried to remember the people who were important to her before she had become such a part of the Foster family. But she could mentally picture only snatches of this or that, and the pieces didn't seem to complete any visual scene or concept. It made her uneasy to think ahead. At times over the past days, her stomach felt so queasy that she pushed the food around on her plate without eating.

"It is so-o romantic," Peony had bubbled as usual. "The West. You must be so-o excited! How I envy you."

But Rebecca had ignored the words. She wasn't convinced that she was to be envied.

In fact, more than her uneasiness about the future caused her to dread the thought of the quickly approaching day of her departure for her western home. She would be putting miles and miles between herself and Stanley.

"You will be back?" he questioned as the two stood on the veranda sipping glasses of icy lemonade. The other guests from the party had finally departed and the servants were scurrying about to clean away the remains of the celebration.

"I—I—don't really know," Rebecca answered in a voice softened by emotion.

She wished to hear him say that he wanted her to come back. That he would miss her when she was gone. But he didn't say any of those things. Instead, he said in his teasing fashion, "Don't let one of those rope-to-tin' cowboys lasso your heart."

Rebecca knew she was supposed to laugh, but for some reason she found it difficult to do so.

He sobered then and moved a bit closer, looking out

over the vast green lawns with her. He leaned his el-
bows on the railing and cupped his chin.

"Changes," he said. "I'm not sure they are all they
are claimed to be."

Rebecca stirred uneasily. She wasn't sure they
were either.

"What will you do when you get back home?" he
asked her seriously.

"I—I really don't know. I—I don't remember much
about my life back then—except that I stayed with
Aunt Min while Mother worked, and Uncle Boyd—Uncle Boyd used to—to—spoil me, I guess."

She managed a little laugh.

"Well, you won't need to stay with Aunt Min now,"
said Stanley, drawing up to his full height. He moved
near enough to brush against her shoulder. "You're
quite grown up, Rebecca."

Rebecca felt her face flushing and was glad for the
darkness that hid her discomfiture.

They stood in silence, deep in thought. Rebecca
knew that she should stir herself and say she must get
in. But her heart longed to hear some words of endearment—of commitment. Instead, Stanley shifted
uneasily and faced toward the green lawns again. She
heard a sigh escape his lips. It seemed to come from
his very soul.

"You are not the only one facing change," he said.

Rebecca turned to him.

"I need to make some decisions. Father wishes me
to turn to law. I don't want that. Yet I don't want a
career in the military either. Mother would like me to
be a doctor. I—I don't really know what I want." He
sighed again. "But I have to decide. I'm at the end of
my Academy courses. Now I—I have to choose and I'm

so—uncertain. Right now my whole future looks—bleak."

Rebecca was surprised at his little speech. She had thought his future was so settled. His education was so solid and gave him so many possibilities. And she was particularly surprised by his final word choice. Bleak? For Stanley? Why, he'd had every advantage, it seemed to her.

He wheeled to face her. "Why did you choose this time to go?" he demanded, his voice husky with agitation.

"I—I didn't choose," managed Rebecca.

"Then why—?"

"I must. Mother sent the—the ticket."

"Tear it up."

His words surprised her. What was he saying? Was he so distraught that he was becoming unreasonable?

She had no answer. She just stood looking at him, sensing his frustration—his anger. She wasn't liking what she was seeing, but she couldn't figure out what was prompting his dark mood.

She began at last, "I—I don't understand—"

"You don't?" His voice was almost a sneer. Then he turned and leaned back on the rail. "That's not surprising. No one ever does," he said.

"I—I think I—must go in," she said, her voice trembling. He did not answer, only nodded his head toward the door as though to give his consent. Rebecca wasted no time. She slipped past him and through the wide French doors of the patio.

She was shaking when she entered her own room. What had happened out there in the semidarkness? Why was Stanley so upset? She had been longing for expressions of endearment—or at least of interest—

and he had offered only words of frustration and gloom.

Rebecca slipped out of her full-skirted gown. It was her prettiest one yet. The cut showed off her slim waist, her rounded feminine curves. And the color enhanced her creamy skin and the deep brown of her eyes. Everyone had admired her throughout the evening. She had felt eyes on her wherever she went.

She began to peel off the layers of crinolines.

This was to have been the most exciting day of her life—the celebration of her graduation, her carefully prepared speech, the splendid "coming out" party. The pleasure of having Stanley home. But she didn't feel like celebrating. She felt like crying. Something wasn't right. Something wasn't fair. But she couldn't sort out just what had gone wrong.

———

Rebecca is coming home! Sarah reminded herself of the fact over and over. She could not believe that in just a few short weeks, the long, difficult years would finally end. It was over. She and Rebecca had made it. And the future looked so promising.

Sarah was actually making money now. She would no longer have to scrimp to make payments each month. She and Rebecca could do things, buy things. They would be cared for. Not live in luxury, but certainly not live in want. Things were going very well. Sarah felt a thankfulness welling up within her as she thought of her present circumstance. Already she had laid aside some funds. And she would add to it, month by month. Year by year. She and her little girl were going to get along just fine.

_____

Sarah had gone back to driving Gyp and Ginger and they once again pulled the heavier wagon. She was so glad for Boyd's advice to keep the team and wagon. She had turned the lighter team and wagon over to Seth for the longer run of the day, and she drove the sturdier team.

They were plodders. Up in years by now, they were slow but dependable. Sarah felt that she had slowed down a good deal herself. They were matched, she and the horses. Sarah appreciated the fact that she could just sit back, holding the reins for communication with her horses, not needing to fight them to keep them moving on course. She appreciated the more leisurely pace. She welcomed the chance to sit quietly and think while the miles slowly rolled by under wagon wheels.

She was so thankful for Seth. His desire to work and his quiet confidence were a daily encouragement. She had learned to depend on the young lad. Not just to haul the freight, but to link her once again to the world. She had locked away her thoughts, her feelings, for so many years that she feared she had become a mindless machine, meant only for hard work and counting money. Seth was freeing her again—to think—to feel—to search for God in new ways.

It was good for Sarah to have daily contact with Seth.

_____

"What happened?"

Sarah recognized Seth's voice. She attempted an answer but no answer came. She felt hands on her shoulders gently restraining her. She was lying down.

Where? Why wasn't she on her feet? What was the strange buzzing in her head? The dreadful pain? Why were the sounds and movements beside her so many miles away? She strained to sit up but the weight on her shoulders increased.

"Just relax, Miz Perry," the husky voice said near her ear.

"What—? Seth?" Sarah managed.

He was close beside her, leaning over her, one hand moved from her shoulder and gently rested on her arm. Even with the look of concern on his face, she still sensed a quiet peace.

"It's okay, Miz Perry," he said. "You had a bad bump. Just try to relax. It's okay."

He patted her hand rather awkwardly. "It's okay," he whispered again.

Sarah leaned back and let her body go limp. Seth was there. He said it was going to be okay. She wanted to believe him. She just wanted to sleep. To sleep and sleep. That's all she wanted.

Chapter Eighteen

The Lesson

Little by little they put together the pieces. From what they could determine by following the wagon tracks, Sarah must have either fallen asleep or else fainted. The sturdy team carried on, wandering back and forth across the rutted road to some extent, but generally following the well-trod trail.

They most certainly would have made it home on their own, but near the river crossing they had been spooked by a large grizzly. The usually gentle horses had thundered their way over the rough terrain in their frantic effort to get away from the bear. The wagon had overturned and Sarah was thrown out on the ground. The team had eventually been found by a passerby, miserably entangled in the harness and a length of wagon tongue, the only part of the wagon that still remained with them. The rest had been scattered piece by piece along the trail.

Both horses were badly shaken from the experience. Gyp had a gash torn along one flank where the bear must have assaulted him. Ginger had a lame leg, but no one knew where and when she had received the injury.

But Sarah, remarkably, was only shaken and bruised. The doctor informed her that she was a very lucky woman, much of it due to the fact that she had not been conscious before the accident and had flown from the wagon, limp and unresisting.

Sarah was thankful to be alive. But beyond that she didn't know how lucky she should feel. Her team was injured and her wagon was wrecked. Bits and pieces were gathered up. Three wheels were still in fair shape. But it was going to cost money to get a new wagon built. Sarah could have cried. She had just begun to lay money aside for Rebecca—and now she had lost it all.

"Rest for a week," the doctor had told her. "Let your body's bruises heal."

"But I have a freight run," she had tried to argue.

"Your boy will look after the freight," the doctor insisted. So Sarah had been required to go to Mrs. Galvan's. Folks didn't seem to trust her if she were left on her own.

She fidgeted and fretted. Mrs. Galvan tried to get her to relax. To rest. But Sarah had forgotten how.

"Here's some tea," Mrs. Galvan said, entering Sarah's bedroom one afternoon. "Boyd said if you're up to it, he'll play checkers with you when he gets home."

Checkers, Sarah wished to retort. *There's work to do—plans to make—and they expect me to sit around and play checkers.*

But Sarah did not voice her thoughts. They were trying to be kind. Instead she said, "Mrs. Galvan, can you get word to Seth? I need to see him."

Mrs. Galvan looked troubled by the request but

nodded her head. "I'll have Boyd give him the message," she said.

————————

Seth came by late that afternoon. His face showed his concern as he pulled a chair up to Sarah's bed.

"How are you?" he asked softly, searching her face with those calm eyes.

Sarah didn't answer. She was afraid that her voice might betray her. The only thing she really felt was anger.

"How are you making out with the runs?" she asked instead.

His quiet confidence showed through again. "Fine," he answered. "Just fine."

And then he leaned forward and took her limp hand and held it, gently massaging the back with one thumb as he spoke. "I do the runs the way you did before you hired me on. I leave early and do the first run. Get into town, unload, change teams, do the second run to High Springs. It works fine. But it does make a full day. Sure don't know how you managed all of those years."

He didn't give her a chance to comment.

"Then I care for the horses. Gyp is already healing nicely. I use a special ointment that my pa thinks is a miracle cure. Ginger still limps quite bad—but she's a strong horse. Doesn't seem to be anything wrong with the bone or muscle, so she'll heal."

Sarah felt relief.

"I talked with the smith," he continued. "He says he can have that new wagon done by end of next week. We saved all the parts we could. Boy—they sure were scattered. That must have been some ride."

He released her hand and patted her arm. "So—all

we need now is for you to get some rest," he said and smiled.

Sarah stirred uneasily. Everyone was telling her to rest. But it was so hard knowing that—that her business needed her. *But did it?* she wondered. Hadn't Seth just told her that everything was under control? What was she stewing about? Why didn't she just relax and get well so when Rebecca came home she would be back to normal?

She finally managed a wobbly smile of her own. Then she gave Seth a bit of a nod. "I will," she managed to say. "I will."

He patted her shoulder and stood to his feet. "Good," he responded with deep feeling. "Good."

Then he shifted his weight from one foot to the other and lifted his hat from the nightstand where he had placed it.

"Well—I'd best be goin'," he said. "Mornin' comes early when you have two runs." He grinned as though it were a private little joke just between the two of them.

He turned to go. "Now don't you go worryin'," he admonished her gently. "Whenever you are tempted to fret, just think on Philippians 4:13. And if that doesn't do it—then go on to verse 19."

He smiled again and was gone.

———————

Sarah could hardly wait to get home to her Bible and look up his verses. He always knew Scripture passages to fit the occasion. Sarah realized now that they were the source of his inner strength. They were what gave the young man such uncommon confidence and peace. Not just that he knew the verses but that he believed them with all his heart—and *lived* them out in his daily life.

Suddenly Sarah knew that she could not wait until she got home to look up the verses. She might be held here as a beloved prisoner for several more days.

"Mrs. Galvan," she said the next time the woman was in her room, "would you mind lending me your Bible. I don't have mine here with me."

"I'll get it," said the woman, then added, "I'll send Boyd over to fetch yours tonight. Something personal about a Bible. Like a dear, dear friend. You know right where to find things in your own. I'd be lost if I had to borrow someone else's."

While Mrs. Galvan went to get her Bible, Sarah had some thinking time. Was her Bible like a dear friend? Did she know right where to turn for what she needed? Or was her Bible simply something to carry with her on Sunday morning when she left for church? Sarah felt her face flushing. She had greatly neglected her Bible—her God—over the past years. She had been so busy—so busy—with her business, with earning money for Rebecca's needs, with the demands of her life.

Mrs. Galvan returned, a worn Bible in her hand. She patted Sarah's shoulder as she left her with it. Sarah hastily looked up Philippians. With a rustling of pages she located the fourth chapter. First she read verse thirteen:

I can do all things through Christ which strengtheneth me.

She read it again and again.

"I think I started out on the right track, but somehow—over the years I've switched my thinking," mused Sarah. "Somewhere along the way I began to stop after the first five words. I—I forgot to add the next two. 'Through Christ.' That's where my strength must come from."

Sarah let her eyes pass on to verse nineteen;
But my God shall supply all your need according to his riches in glory by Christ Jesus.

Had that verse—that promise always been there? Why hadn't she seen it before? Maybe she had seen it and just not believed it. She didn't know. Didn't she believe the Bible? Of course she did. But she certainly hadn't been living like she did.

To Sarah's mind came one of the other verses that Seth had shared. From John: *For without me ye can do nothing.*

She had to think. She had to pray. She had to get these things all properly sorted out. She needed time. She needed to—

Suddenly she stopped. Didn't she have time? Wasn't she lying in this bed? Had the accident not been an—an accident? Was there some purpose for her being here?

Suddenly Sarah's eyes filled with tears. "Yes, Lord," she whispered into the silence of the room. "I'm willing to listen. Speak to me, please."

Sarah lay back against her pillows and let her tears fall unchecked. She had so much to learn. She had neglected her spirit while trying so hard to care for the needs of her body. She had failed Rebecca as well. She had been so intent on caring for the physical needs of her little girl that she had forgotten about the spiritual needs. Oh, she had made sure that Rebecca was getting a good grounding in Bible knowledge, but was Rebecca, like Seth, able to appropriate the promises of the Scriptures to her life? Who had seen to that? Had Mrs. Foster? Had the teachers of the school? Had Miss Peabody? Sarah did not know. Had never asked.

"Oh, God," she prayed now in deep contrition, "I've not been caring for the needs of our souls while I've been scrambling to meet the needs of our bodies. Needs that you promised you would care for. I've been so—so totally—blind in assuming that I had the whole responsibility on my own shoulders. I should have learned to lean on you." Sarah stopped a moment as a sob shook her body.

"Thank you, Lord, for getting my attention, for showing me the truth before—before Rebecca comes home," she prayed. "I have so much to learn. So much. Help me to—to really be concerned about the right things. The important things. Help me to be the mother I need to be for Rebecca. Not just the—the provider of funds. Might we grow together, Lord—as you would have us grow."

And Sarah let the tears flow freely as she sought comfort and reassurance from her God.

———

Rebecca stirred uneasily. The morning sun traced around the heavy curtain with an etching of gold. Morning had come. It was a new day. The celebration of the preceding day was in the past. She was a graduate. She had made her debut into society. She should be feeling triumphant—but she was not. Why?

Stanley. Stanley had been awfully—morose. It troubled her. She had been so in hopes that Stanley would show some—some interest in her as a young lady. She cared for Stanley. She didn't know just how much she cared, but she was eager for his attentions so she might—might discover her own feelings.

She hadn't understood his mood. Hadn't liked it.

She hated to face him again. Yet she longed to see him. It didn't make any sense.

Suddenly Rebecca threw back the cover and sprang from the bed. Stanley was leaving today. Going back to finish his exams at the Academy. She might never see him again. What if she had already missed his departure?

Anxiously she looked toward the clock. It was ten past ten. Stanley was to leave at eleven-thirty. She must hurry. There would hardly be time for goodbyes. By the time Stanley returned home again, she would be gone—back to Kenville.

Hurriedly she dressed and prepared herself for joining the family. She must see Stanley before he left.

She was flushed when she entered the breakfast room. Robert was there, leisurely picking plump grapes from the cluster he held in his hand.

"You're up early—for a girl," he teased.

Rebecca paid no attention. "Has—have the others breakfasted already?" she inquired cautiously.

"If you mean Annabelle—no. I don't expect her until noon—or after."

Then he cocked his head and said pointedly, "If you mean Stanley—yes. I take it he's out at the stables saying goodbye to his horse."

He smiled rather cynically. "How do you like that? He's more intent on bidding his horse farewell than his family."

Rebecca said nothing, just brushed past Robert and his grapes and headed for the stables.

Chapter Nineteen

Homecoming

"Oh, good morning," Rebecca said as though caught by surprise. She hoped fervently that Stanley would think she had just wandered down to the stables to see the horses and accidentally found him there ahead of her.

"Well—look who's here," he replied.

She was relieved to see that his mood of the night before seemed to have left him. He even gave her one of his charming smiles.

"Did you sleep well?" he asked politely.

Rebecca hardly knew how to answer. In truth she'd had great difficulty in getting to sleep. But she had slept late—if that indicated a good sleep. She decided to let the question go unanswered.

"So you are telling Ramande goodbye," she said instead.

He nodded and rubbed the nose of the horse.

"It seems that life is full of goodbyes," he observed.

Rebecca nodded.

"Some of them are not easy," he continued.

Rebecca held her breath. Was he still speaking

about the horse? What might he say next?

As usual he was unpredictable. With a broad smile he spoke lightly, "Sorry about last night," he said easily. "I was just out of sorts. I hate this bouncing back and forth between home and the Academy."

He took a deep breath.

"But that will all be behind me soon. This is the last trip I'll need to make."

Rebecca nodded and reached out a hand to stroke the horse, who was begging for attention.

"Spoiled, isn't he?" observed Stanley. "Loves attention."

Rebecca said nothing.

"Maybe we're all like that. Like attention. Well—a person doesn't get much of it at the Academy—unless of course, you excel. Excel or fail. That's the only way to get any attention. If one is—somewhere in the middle—you are ignored."

He was sounding like doomsday again.

"Well—I don't excel," he admitted, "and so far I've managed to fight the urge to fail. So here I am." He shrugged his shoulders carelessly and laughed an empty laugh.

Rebecca did not know how to respond, so she said nothing.

"I was—rather hoping that you'd stay around, Rebecca," he said suddenly.

When she looked at him sharply, he laughed again and went on.

"I thought that maybe you could provide some of that attention I was longing for."

Rebecca's eyes must have shown her shock.

He laughed again, this time almost derisively. He noted the look in her eyes and his laugh became more genuine.

"I didn't mean to frighten you," he hurried on. "I

just meant that I thought—well—since you have grown up and—and become"—he stopped and let his eyes travel over her, causing her cheeks to flush—"quite attractive. I just thought that," he went on, "that we might—well—get to know each other better. Or—differently. I've always thought of you as a— a sister—or a sister's friend—or something—when I thought of you at all—and now that I see all of those other fellows hanging around with—with yearning eyes—"

He stopped and turned to watch her face. Truly she was uncomfortable with his statements.

"I really don't think—" began Rebecca, but he cut in.

"Do my words disturb you? Well—I suppose they do—you being reared such a proper girl and all." He laughed again.

"I don't understand what you are trying to say," said Rebecca. "I—"

He changed then. His eyes softened. He even reached out a hand to rest on her sleeve. "I'm sorry, Rebecca," he apologized. "I really am. I'm just so—so mixed up. So—so angry at—everything." He ran his hand over his face in agitation.

"It's just I'm here—I'm gone. You're here—you're gone. Nothing in life is—is settled. Is constant. You just start to feel for something and"—he waved a hand—"it's gone. What is life all about, anyway? Is this the best it can offer?"

Rebecca shook her head. "I—I don't know," she said in a whisper. "I—really don't know."

———

Sarah gradually gained back her strength. The rest helped not only to restore her body but to refresh her soul as well. In the days that she relaxed at the Galvan home, she spent many hours in prayer and in searching through the Scriptures. She was amazed at the change in her thinking, her attitudes. At times she shook her head in disbelief.

"I thought I believed in God," she often whispered to herself, "but I was living as if He didn't even exist—or else didn't care—or was totally powerless to do anything for me."

It was such a comfort to Sarah to learn that God, in a marvelous and powerful way, was interested in her well-being.

When at last she took up the reins of the team again after Seth had hitched them to the newly constructed wagon, she felt like a new person—almost.

She knew she still had a long way to go in her inner growth, in learning to really trust her life to God—but at least now she was on the right road.

———

Rebecca shook her skirts to free them of the penetrating road dust. It was everywhere. It seeped into the train and layered on her lap, her bonnet, her traveling bag. It would help if the passengers would close the windows, but even Rebecca knew better than to make such a request. The days were stifling. She could not have borne it were the windows to have been shut.

"And to think Peony called this romantic," she said to herself in irritation.

The Tall Elms School for Girls and the Foster household were now far behind her. She was on her way home. Home. Why did the word connected with Kenville hold so little meaning? She had scarcely any remembrance of the home she had left—the people who were supposed to mean something to her. She should be feeling—what? Happy? Excited? At least she might manage to feel—thankful?

Well—she felt nothing. Nothing but empty. Empty and a bit scared. And she felt lonely. Already she missed Annabelle. She missed the comforts of the Foster home with its servants to care for her needs and the predictability of how things would run. She even missed the girls' school. At least there she knew exactly what was expected of her. Now—now she knew nothing. Nothing about her hometown. Nothing about this—this woman who was her mother. The life that she would be expected to live in the future.

Again she withdrew the last letter she had received. She could have recited it by memory, but she let her eyes fall to the page.

> You will soon be home again. I can scarcely believe that it is finally happening. I have waited for so long for the day to arrive, and now that it is almost here I cannot believe it. I will not believe it until I actually hold my little girl in my arms again. We have so much catching up to do. So much time to make up for.

The letter was signed, "Lovingly, Your mother."

Rebecca let the hand holding the letter drop to her lap as she stared absentmindedly out of the window. Only dry prairie grass waved gently in the ever-present prairie wind. Occasionally a dust devil would pick up a handful of the soil and lift it in a whirling mass as though offering it to some unseen deity of the prairies.

Rebecca shuddered.

If only she could remember. If only she could put the pieces of memory together to form some kind of complete picture. If only she knew what lay ahead. What she was to expect.

"Think," she scolded herself. "Think. You must re-member something. You must."

And then to Rebecca's memory came a face. Bend-ing over her. Gentle hands wiping blood from a wounded knee. She had fallen. Had bloodied her knee on the boards of the sidewalk. The sidewalk that led to her house. Her house. She couldn't remember what the house looked like. But she did have a warm feeling when she thought of it. That meant she must have been happy there.

And the woman—the one who knelt before her, cleansing the wound, offering words of comfort and sympathy? That was her mother. Rebecca could almost see her face. Dark hair. Blue eyes. Love. Her mother. That was her mother. She remembered then. There had been a warm hug after the knee had been cared for. A warm hug and soon the tears had turned to laughter. Why? What was it her mother had said? Oh, yes, she said, "Careful you don't walk like ol' Billy."

Ol' Billy? Who was ol' Billy? And then Rebecca re-membered. Ol' Billy was a dog down the street. He had been hurt—once—a long time ago, and his owner in-sisted that Billy now limped out of habit or to get sym-pathy. The leg had long since completely healed. The dog should have walked without limping. Ol' Billy. And she had laughed as a child at her mother's little joke, and for several days after the little accident she had purposely limped, exaggerating the injury every time she saw her mother looking her way, and they would both laugh again.

Rebecca could not hide the smile at the thought. And then her thoughts carried her further. So that was her mother. This gentle, pretty woman with the soft voice and the warm arms, who dried Rebecca's tears and told her little jokes to make her laugh.

Rebecca found a measure of reassurance.

"I want to be here by the time the stage pulls in," Sarah told Seth.

"Why don't I just take both runs today?" he asked her again. "I'm sure you have lots of things to be doin'."

"Well—I—I really have everything already done. And it's too much to ask you to do them both. You know that Thursday's freight is always the heaviest."

That was true. But they both knew that Seth would have been able to handle it.

"Besides," said Sarah, "I don't think I could stand just sitting around waiting for the stagecoach. I'd go crazy."

Now Seth smiled. Now they were getting honest.

He nodded. He thought he could understand.

"I'll be home in time to meet the stage," went on Sarah. "Then—then I'll have my little girl home again. I—I just might not ever want to go to work again. We'll have so—so much lost time to make up for."

Again Seth nodded.

Sarah's eyes darkened. "Not that we'll be able to afford to do much else than talk—thanks to my falling asleep on the job—but—"

Sarah still had a pang of regret whenever she thought of the money she had put aside and then had to pay out for the new freight wagon.

"You needed the rest," Seth reminded her. "Remember?"

Sarah nodded. She had learned much during her recuperation time. Perhaps things were better now—without the money—than they would have been had she saved it.

She nodded solemnly. "I needed it," she admitted. "God used it for good."

"Romans 8:28," Seth said quietly.

Sarah did not have to wait to get home to look up
the verse. She knew Seth was reminding her that all
things do work together for good for the children of
God if they just allow Him to work as He sees best.

She smiled and nodded. "I need to get going," she
said.

"I'll take over your freight as soon as you get back.
You just enjoy getting reacquainted with your daughter."

———————

If there ever was a day that Sarah wished to have
things go well, it was this one when the stage pulled
into town bearing Rebecca.

But things did not go well. All day long little
things—irritating little things—seemed to happen.
The minutes ticked by and became hours and Sarah
found herself getting further and further behind in her
deliveries.

"The stage is going to be there before I get back,"
she fussed as she tried to hurry her plodding team. She
wished she had agreed to Seth's request to cover for
her. Or asked Mrs. Galvan to meet Rebecca. Sarah had
been rather selfish in expressing her desires.

"I want the first day all to myself," she had explained
to the Galvans. "I will share her with you later."

And they had understood.

And now she feared she wouldn't be there, and Rebecca would arrive home with no one to meet her. She
would feel totally—forsaken. Like no one really cared
if she came home or not.

Sarah chaffed and tried again to hurry the plodding
team. It seemed that they had two speeds—slow—and
barely moving.

"Gyp. Hi!" she called impatiently. "Ginger. Step it up."

But other than a flick of the ears, the horses paid no attention.

Sarah brought the rein down on the broad rump of Gyp, then Ginger. She had never before laid the rein to her horses in all of her years of driving, but her great agitation stirred her now.

Startled, the horses both responded, jerking forward on the harness only to be hampered by the weight of the wagon. At once Sarah felt remorse and allowed the two patient animals to settle back down to their usual plodding gait.

"I won't be there," Sarah wailed and was tempted to tie the team and run on ahead. But she knew that would be foolish.

"Maybe the stage will be late," she hoped. "It often is." But Sarah feared that this might be one of the days it would be on time.

She entered the main street of the town just as the stage was nearing the small depot. Hastily Sarah clambered down from the wagon, dropping her reins to ground-tie the horses. On foot she ran through the dust of the street, anxious to be there when Rebecca stepped down from the stagecoach.

———

Rebecca stretched a fashionable shoe toward the ground, her billows of skirts and crinolines lifted protectively in one white-gloved hand. Her thoughts were scattered and mixed. So this was Kenville. This was home. This was where her mother— Where was her mother? Rebecca let her eyes drift over the small crowd, trying to locate the face of the woman that hazily reflected in her memory. She could spot no one that looked at all familiar.

Just as Rebecca lowered her other foot, shook her skirts gently, and picked up her parasol, there was a shuffling through the small crowd. Rebecca raised her eyes.

Someone was rushing toward her. A man? No, the person was small. A boy?

Someone was calling her name, "Rebecca. Rebecca."

There was a catch in the voice—but it was unmistakenly a woman's voice.

Rebecca stood rooted to the spot while the figure rushed toward her. She was totally confused as this—this strange person with a woman's voice and man's clothing came rushing at her.

"Rebecca," the voice said again.

The person ground to a halt, suddenly as hesitant, as uncertain, as the bewildered girl.

"Are you—?" she began, her voice quivering.

"I'm—Rebecca," the girl managed to answer.

"But you've—you're—"

The girl let her eyes travel over the dusty, dishevelled figure before her. It was a woman. A woman with sun-darkened, weary-looking skin. A woman in dusty trousers and wrinkled shirt. A woman in hardened leather gloves that looked too big for her hands. But a woman with warm, blue eyes that somehow triggered a memory.

"Mother—?" queried Rebecca uncertainly.

"Oh, Rebecca," the woman sobbed, moving forward now without hesitation. "You're home. You're finally home," and she enfolded the young woman in her arms and let her tears flow.

Rebecca tried to respond. Tried hard to feel something. Something. Anything—other than horror and alarm.

Chapter Twenty

Beginning Again

Gradually Sarah's arms relaxed their embrace and she stepped back and looked at the young girl whose slender form she held.

"Rebecca," she said again, emotion making her voice tremble. "You've changed. I scarcely knew you."

Rebecca looked evenly at the woman before her. *Is this really my mother? But she is so—so—* Rebecca could not finish the thought. She did not wish to acknowledge what she was feeling.

But the woman kept looking at her. Studying her face. Perhaps searching for the little girl she had known.

"You've grown—you're a—a young woman." She laughed at herself. "Here I was still looking for my little girl," she said lamely. "I should have known—well, I did know—in my head, but—"

Rebecca stirred restlessly. The hands that still rested on her shoulders were creasing her gown—perhaps grinding dirt into the whiteness of the lacy collar.

Sarah released her hold and stepped back, her eyes

still full of tears of love and rejoicing. She blinked them away.

"You must be—dreadfully weary," she managed in a voice that was almost natural. "Come. Let's get you home. Seth will see to your luggage."

And Sarah took Rebecca's arm and led her across the dusty street.

Rebecca could hear the buzz of voices behind her. She was conscious of many pairs of staring eyes. She was also conscious of the drabness of the buildings, the dirt that seemed to lie everywhere that she wanted to place her foot, the dry, starkly bare hillsides that framed in the little town.

The West, she thought to herself. *This is romantic? Peony should see me now.*

But at once Rebecca changed her mind. She was so thankful that none of her friends could see her in her present circumstance. She would have died of embarrassment had they seen her mother come rushing toward her looking—looking—totally unwomanly. Totally—

Rebecca checked her thoughts. She did not want to even think in such a fashion. After all, this woman was her mother. She deserved her respect.

And Rebecca straightened her shoulders and marched on beside Sarah, trying to ignore the curious glances and the wagging tongues. She concentrated on lifting her skirts to avoid the swirling of the dust as she walked.

"I'm so glad we have nice weather for your arrival," Sarah was saying as she ushered her along, "It is so miserable when it has rained and the streets are full of mud. Somedays I just give up on even trying to keep myself clean."

Rebecca cast a sideways glance at the woman in the dirty trousers. Was she serious?

"I would have been here earlier," continued the woman in an excited voice, "but I had lots of trouble on the freight run today. Some days are like that. Oh, my! I left my team. Right in the middle of the road. I've never done that before. I hope— Well, I'll have to go check on them. Can you find your way on home? I'll just be a few minutes. Will you be able—"

"I . . . I don't remember," said Rebecca with a faltering voice.

"Well—you can just stop at the Galvans if you like. Mrs. Galvan—Aunt Min—is so anxious to see you. If you like you can just pop in there and wait for me."

Rebecca was even further confused.

"Right down the street. The white house with the green shutters," went on Sarah.

"I—I think I'd—just rather go on—home. If you don't mind," said Rebecca shakily. *I don't know the Galvans,* she was thinking. *I don't remember. Are they—are they like—?* But she didn't allow herself to finish that thought either.

"You must be tired," Sarah continued. "I'll just look after the team and then I'll be right home. We'll fix you a nice hot bath and then we'll have our supper. We'll have the whole evening to talk. The whole evening to catch up.

"You—you go on home," she said again. "It's the last house on the left of the street. You'll find it easily. The house with the barn and corrals."

Rebecca nodded mutely and turned to hasten down the street. She was glad that she was alone. Perhaps it would give her opportunity to recover her poise. She had been totally unprepared for what she had found. She just wished to get home—in the comforts of her own room, away from the staring eyes of strangers.

———

Sarah watched as her daughter walked on down the street. Then her eyes filled with tears again. It was touching. It really was. Rebecca had seemed to prefer the Galvans' home to her own before she had left for school. Now—now she was anxious to go home.

But she hadn't expected her to be quite so grown-up. Quite so attractive. Or so—so sophisticated. She hardly knew how to communicate with her. What to say.

She looked down at her mannish attire. "Look at me. Just look at me," she whispered. "Rebecca must have been shocked. I'd planned to clean up. To get home in time to put on my navy skirt and my striped shirtwaist—"

But even as Sarah described her plan, she knew instinctively that Rebecca still would have been shocked. The skirt and shirtwaist that she had chosen as appropriate were really quite out-of-date and unattractive. She still would have been woefully lacking in her fashion-conscious daughter's eyes.

———

It must be the right place. It was the last house on the street. And it did have a barn and corrals. But it was so small. It was so—so plain. Rebecca had seen servants' quarters that were more elaborate. But it had to be the right place. Rebecca moved forward and up the front walk.

But the door would not open to her knock. Apparently there were no servants about to bid her enter.

She tried the knob but it would not turn. With annoyance she left the front and preceded around to the back. There was another door there and Rebecca found that it opened willingly as she turned the handle and pushed.

"Well—at least I won't be left standing out on the porch," she said and entered a small kitchen—tidy but plain. Rebecca reasoned that perhaps servants in the West did not need as much working space. She passed on through to the rooms beyond.

But the next room was really of little consolation. The floors and walls were bare except for small scatter rugs and a few faded pictures with discolored frames. The furniture was plain and simple. Even the curtains at the windows were coarse and faded. Rebecca turned from the barrenness, seeking refuge elsewhere.

She found two bedrooms. Both were very small. By the look of the first she judged it to be her mother's room. She went on to the second. The room was small and crowded, but Rebecca concluded that it must be meant for her.

There was a small bed, made up with a handmade quilt. Lace curtains, that looked stiff with newness, fluttered at the window where a breeze teased them. The walls were a faded blue paint. The table by the bed was flounced with a blue and white check.

She had just removed her gloves and tossed them on the bed when she heard a knock at the door. Surely one of the servants would get it. She carefully removed her bonnet, patting disarranged curls back into place with a practiced hand when the knock came again.

Again, Rebecca ignored it, though she was beginning to feel uneasy.

Then she heard steps in the kitchen. Apparently

the person who was to have been on duty had finally returned and answered the door.

Reluctantly she went to take charge. She was used to dealing with hired help. It seemed they never knew quite how to go about things on their own.

Rebecca stepped through the kitchen door just as a tall, huskily built young man was setting two pieces of her luggage beside the table.

For one moment Rebecca was caught off guard. He wasn't quite what she had expected. But she quickly regained her composure and said with authority, "Just put them in my . . ." She hesitated, flustered. Did she really wish to claim it? "In the—the little bedroom—to the right," she finished.

He straightened. He was taller than she had thought. And he was younger as well. For one moment their eyes met. Rebecca wasn't sure which one of them might have showed the most surprise.

He lifted a hand to remove his dusty hat. "Ma'am," he said, and then smiled.

The smile unnerved Rebecca. She wasn't used to servants taking such liberties. She drew back and straightened to her full height. For the moment she envied Annabelle, who could demand so much more respect from her five-foot seven-inch frame. The servants all paid close attention to Miss Annabelle.

"In the bedroom," repeated Rebecca evenly.

"Yes, ma'am," he replied and reached down to lift the cases again, a twinkle in his eye. "They're none too light, I'm thinking," he quipped over his shoulder as he disappeared into the bedroom.

Rebecca was staring after him in bewilderment and dismay when the door was flung open. It was Sarah. Her face was flushed from her hurrying. She looked even more disheveled than when Rebecca had seen her last.

"Seth found the horses," she said, panting from her rush through the streets. "He's already cared for them. He's bringing your luggage."

So Seth was the name of the hired help. Rebecca would remember. It was one of the little unspoken rules in the Foster household. One called the servants by name. They always seemed to respond in better fashion when addressed personally. "Would you draw my bath, Lolly?" "Bring round the carriage, Manville." "I'll have tea in the drawing room, Wilbur." It was the way one spoke to servants.

But her mother should know that there had been no one on duty when she entered the house. Was Seth the negligent one? But he had been sent to pick up her luggage and care for the horses. Where was the kitchen help? Surely they should have been at their post.

The young man reentered the kitchen.

"Oh, Seth. Here you are," said Sarah. "I'm sorry about the horses. I got so excited when I saw the stage was in that I just left them and ran. Have you met Rebecca?"

The young man nodded in Rebecca's direction.

"Rebecca—this is Seth. I don't know how I'd ever manage without him. Seth—my little girl."

The young man moved forward easily and with no embarrassment or inhibition held out his hand.

Rebecca was further taken aback. She had never had a young man offer her his hand before. Manners dictated that the man wait for the woman to decide if she wished to extend a hand. And never, ever, under any circumstance, did a servant presume to be so familiar.

For one moment Rebecca stood, her cheeks staining red, her composure unsettled. Then she slowly extended her hand to have it firmly shaken by the young man before her.

"Pleased to meet you, miss," he said warmly. "Your mama has hardly been able to wait for you to get home. Now I think I can see why. Welcome home."

Rebecca thought that the spoken words were meant to be some kind of compliment, but she couldn't really sort them out. Here she was shaking hands with a servant, and her mother stood by beaming as though it was totally acceptable and even welcomed.

He gave her one more nod, then moved toward the door. His eyes turned to Sarah. "I know you have lots to talk about," he said with understanding. "I'll see you tomorrow."

Sarah nodded.

After the young man was gone, Sarah turned back to Rebecca. "Would you like your bath now—or your supper?" she asked. "I know you're both tired and hungry. Which comes first?"

"Well—I—I am hungry—and filthy. I will need to clean up before I can—even think of eating, so I suppose I— The bath must come first."

"I'll bring in the tub," said Sarah good-naturedly.

"Bring in the tub?" echoed Rebecca.

"There isn't room for it in here, so I hang it out on the back wall," said Sarah as though that was the most natural thing in the world.

"But—"

But Sarah had already left the room. When she returned Rebecca was again shocked. The tub was nothing more than a laundry tub. She was expected to bathe in that?

"I'll fill it with water from the reservoir. That's one nice thing about this stove. It has a nice big reservoir.

I've never run out of hot water yet."

And so saying Sarah went to place the tub in Rebecca's room and returned to take up a pail and a dipper to begin dipping water from the reserve tank at the end of the kitchen stove.

"While you're bathing I'll get our supper on. I already have the stew cooking."

Sarah failed to see Rebecca's look of horror. Stew? Did she mean the stuff that was cooked in one pot? The meat and vegetables all tumbled in together like—like common— Rebecca wrinkled her dainty nose.

"I left it at the back of the stove this morning. Mrs. Galvan promised to stoke the fire off and on through the day. It should be just right by now. I'll just get some biscuits in the oven and fix some of those fresh vegetables that Mrs. Galvan brought from her garden, and we'll be all set. Made some johnny cake for dessert. That was always your favorite. You would've eaten it every night if I'd let you."

Rebecca followed her mother toward the bedroom, her head whirling. This world was certainly different from the one she had known.

"Do you have to—to do everything?" she asked. "Don't the servants—"

Sarah stopped mid-stride. She whirled to look at her daughter, her eyes large, astounded. "Servants?" she echoed hollowly.

Rebecca nodded.

"We don't have servants," said Sarah with some force.

"We—we don't?"

"My land, no. No one here has servants."

Rebecca swallowed. How did one ever do without servants? Who did all the work?

"Then—?" Rebecca could not finish the question.

Sarah dropped her gaze and began to walk toward the bedroom with the pail of water in her hand. "Anything you want done here—you have to learn how to do yourself," she said quietly.

"Then—then who is—Seth?"

"Seth," Sarah said evenly, "is a neighbor. He is from our church. He works for me—that's true. But not as a servant. As a—a hired hand. Paid and respected. And he does far more than he would need to do to earn his wage. Far more.

"And another thing—he is the closest to God of any person I know. That's Seth."

Rebecca swallowed, nodded her head, and moved toward her bedroom and the tub that waited on the rag rug. If she was to rid herself of the trail dust, she had to disrobe and climb into that ugly metal tub. She hated the thought. She hated everything that had greeted her in this miserable town. Oh, if only she could have stayed where she was. If only she was back where she belonged. Rebecca longed to cry, but under the circumstances it did not seem like the proper thing to do.

———

Sarah stared at the closed bedroom door. Rebecca really was young. And she was so beautiful. She was also naive. She had lived in splendor and opulence. She would have to learn to live all over again. Could she? It was a totally different world. Sarah had not realized how different until that very moment.

Love filled her mother-heart as she thought of her bewildered offspring in her dusty, fashionable clothes. She looked as if she belonged in a rich man's parlor. Not on the dirty, windswept streets of Kenville.

Chapter Twenty-one

Hard Days

Rebecca longed to linger in the tub—but the size and shape made it most uncomfortable. She could not stretch out her legs for a proper soak. So she found herself hurrying through her bath.

Besides, she was hungry. The aromas from the kitchen that drifted toward her room made her stomach rumble.

"But it's stew," she complained under her breath. "I won't even be able to eat it."

When Rebecca had finished her bath and changed into fresh, though wrinkled, garments, she found herself drawn toward the inviting smell.

The small kitchen table was set with simple dishes. There were no linens. No candles. Nothing that Rebecca was used to. Still, in spite of herself, she felt ready to eat.

She eyed the biscuits. They did look good. She would just fill up on biscuits until her mother supplied something more suitable to her taste. But even before she took the chair at the table, she had changed her mind. She would try a small bit of the steaming stew just to see how it tasted.

Sarah was still scurrying about the room. Rebecca had not looked her mother's way until she spoke.

"Well—we're ready. You sit right there."

It was then that Rebecca noticed that Sarah too had changed for the meal. She wore a simple black skirt and a white shirtwaist, very much like the apparel that Hettie, from the kitchen, wore—except that Hettie always wore a white frilled apron over the skirt. It made the outfit decidedly more attractive, Rebecca thought.

When Sarah bowed her head, Rebecca did too. Silence followed and then Rebecca realized her mother was fighting for control so she could voice her thoughts in prayer.

"Dear Lord," Sarah began. "You are so good—and I thank you. Thank you for bringing Rebecca safely home. Thank you for the fine young lady she has become. Our years of separation were such—hard years, but now they are behind us and we look forward to—to many days of being together. Bless our days and make us a blessing to each other and to those we meet. And bless this food that you have so bountifully provided for our use. In the name of Christ our Lord and Savior. Amen."

Sarah was still blinking away thankful tears when she lifted her head. Rebecca felt both amazed and slightly ashamed.

———

"Here," said Sarah, tossing Rebecca a kitchen towel. "I'll wash and you can dry—just like we used to do."

Rebecca was not used to drying dishes—though

she would not have admitted it under the circumstances.

"You—you even do the dishes—yourself?" she queried, hoping that her voice didn't give her away.

Sarah turned to look at her daughter. "Of course," she said, and even managed a bit of a laugh. "Didn't Mrs. Foster do dishes?"

"Never," said Rebecca with emphasis.

"Then who did?"

"The kitchen help," replied Rebecca, her voice indicating that this was only right and proper.

"Well—we are the kitchen help," Sarah said stoutly. "Anything that gets done here will get done by our own hands." Rebecca could not avoid an expression of shock, and Sarah, seeing it, went on lightly, "You'll get used to it."

They finished the dishes in silence.

"I have dreamed of this day," Sarah said as she hung the emptied dish pan back on its peg behind the kitchen stove. "Just think—we have the whole evening to talk."

Rebecca nodded.

"Now—let's get cozy," encouraged Sarah. "Where do you prefer? Here in the kitchen—with the fire crackling and the kettle singing—or in the other room where you can curl up in one of the chairs?"

Rebecca swallowed away the retort on the tip of her tongue. She found nothing cozy about either place. The kitchen was hot after the evening meal, and the chairs in the other room where she was to get cozy were solid and uncomfortable.

"You choose," said Rebecca.

Sarah chose the small room she referred to as the "other" room. Rebecca selected a chair and tried to get comfortable.

"Now—tell me all about your years at school," invited Sarah.

"Well—I—I rather—told you all of that in my letters," replied Rebecca.

Sarah nodded.

"I was really proud of you—being valedictorian and all that. I wish I could have heard you . . ." Her voice drifted to a halt. Then she said, "I was—I am proud of you."

Rebecca nodded. Her school days already felt so distant now.

"And your piano. I was so pleased about all the nice things they said about you in those—reports on your recitals. I'm proud."

Rebecca reached down and smoothed out her skirt. If they'd had servants she would have had her dress pressed to remove the packing wrinkles.

"I—I wish we had a piano," went on Sarah. "Then I could hear you play. I'd—really like that."

There was silence.

"The pastor's wife—do you remember her? The church organist. She said you could play at church. She said she'd be glad to have you do the playing. Folks are all anxious to hear you. I showed some of them the newspaper write-ups about you. Everyone here was proud."

Rebecca nodded. She wondered if her fingers would still remember the keys. She wished her mother had a piano. Then she could at least lose herself in her music.

"Tomorrow night we are to have supper with the Galvans. They can hardly wait to see you again, but I—I wanted this night together to—for just us—to just talk—to—"

But the talking did not go well. There seemed so little to say to each other. At last Sarah stood to her feet. "You must be dreadfully tired," she said, and Rebecca patted away a yawn in response. She was weary. Maybe that was what was the matter with her. With the world. Maybe things would not seem quite so abrasive—so crude—once she had rested.

"Our talk can wait," said Sarah. "We have years and years to catch up." She smiled. When she smiled she was almost pretty, Rebecca noticed with surprise.

"I think I would like to retire," Rebecca admitted and stood up.

She was almost to her door when Sarah spoke. Rebecca was afraid she would see tears in her mother's eyes again.

"You know I had this—this funny idea—that when you came home—it would be—well sort of like it used to be when I—I used to tuck you in and tell you a story and hear your prayers. I—I guess—I'll have to—to—adjust. I mean—look at you. You're not my little girl anymore. You've—you've grown up while you were gone. It might—take a while for me to get used to—to who you are now. I—I hope that you can be—patient with me while I—kind of sort it all out."

Rebecca felt confused. How should she be responding to this woman? How should she feel? It was all so strange. The used-to-be was so different than the now. She looked at the woman before her, and for a moment something foreign tugged at her heart. She crossed back to where Sarah still sat in her chair and reached out to gently kiss her on the forehead.

"Good-night, Mother," she said, her voice a mere whisper. That was the way she had said her good-night to Mrs. Foster in all the years she had lived in her home—but Sarah did not know that. She blinked at tears again.

"Good-night, Rebecca," she answered in a choking

voice. "Sleep well. I'm—I'm glad you're home. So glad."

———

Rebecca's eyes fluttered open and she stared at the ceiling. *Where am I?* she thought, coming gradually to her senses. The bit of light coming in the window indicated it was barely dawn.

Then it all came back to her. Her horrid trip west on the miserable train. Her arrival in Kenville in that dusty old stagecoach where she was met by the stranger who was her mother. And then this. The house she was supposed to think of as home.

She looked around at the small, crowded room. So plain. So simple. Unthinking, she reached to her right to ring the bell for a servant—and remembered again that there were none.

With a groan she lay back against her pillow and pulled the covers tightly up to her chin. Did she really have to face this day? Couldn't she just stay right where she was? Why had she awakened at such an early hour?

A noise from outside reached her. That was it. There were unfamiliar sounds. They had awakened her from her sleep.

"Well—as long as I'm awake I may as well get up," she muttered and threw back the covers and stretched her foot out to the rag rug by her bed.

The house seemed awfully quiet. Rebecca took a robe from the hook on the wall, found her slippers among the pile of garments that had not fit in either the little chest of drawers or on the hooks at the end of her bed, and ventured forth.

There was no one around. Rebecca wondered if her

mother was still sleeping. Then a note on the table
caught her eye.

I have gone on the freight run, it said simply. *I will
be back around three. Make yourself at home. Mother.*

"Make myself at home," repeated Rebecca dourly.
Home? This didn't feel like home. Being in the West
was like living in a foreign country. She truly hated it.

––––––––––––

"Did Rebecca arrive?" asked Alex Murray when
Sarah swung her team in behind his store and climbed
nimbly down over the wagon wheel.

"She did," beamed Sarah. "And—" She shook her
head. The shine left her eyes and she looked troubled.

"Oh—Alex," she said quietly, "I was totally unprepared."

He looked puzzled.

"But I thought—" he began. "I thought you surely
must be ready by now. You were in quite often lately
to get supplies—"

"Oh—I was ready. Just—just unprepared."

At Alex's puzzled frown Sarah hurried on. "She's
not a child. I mean there is no resemblance to the little
girl I sent away. She's a young woman. I mean she's—
she's beautiful. Just beautiful. And so—so refined
and—and dainty."

Alex's smile seemed relieved. Sarah's motherly
pride again shone from her brighter than the noonday
sun.

"Isn't that why you sent her away?" he reminded
Sarah as he hoisted up a crate and moved toward his
open back door.

"Of course it is," agreed Sarah as she followed him.

"And it was worth every penny. I can—can hardly wait for you to see her for yourself."

"I'm looking forward to it," said Alex. "She was always a sweet one."

"She is," enthused Sarah. Then she sighed and her voice dropped. "But I'm afraid we will need to get to know each other all over again. I mean—so much has changed. Rebecca has changed. I had thought that our letters would—that I would still know her. But I—I don't think I do. I mean—" Sarah dropped her voice further in embarrassment at what she was telling her friend of many years. "She was expecting servants," she finished.

"Servants?"

Sarah nodded.

"Where did she get that idea?"

Sarah shook her head. "She is just used to them. The Fosters had several. Can you imagine? Rebecca was shocked that I have to wash my own dishes. And get my own meals."

"We used to have servants," mused Alex. "When I was growing up. I'd quite forgotten. Hoffman—he was the—butler I guess you'd call him. We used to call him Hoffie when my mother wasn't around. Then there was Berdette in the kitchen and Mrs. Crane came in to clean. Funny—I'd quite forgotten all that. It was a long time ago."

Sarah was surprised. "When was that?" she asked candidly.

"In England. Before we sailed. It wasn't Mother's idea to leave the comforts of England to sail to a 'heathen' country—even if it was supposed to be a land of promise. Resettling was dreadfully hard on my mother. She only lived for three years after we landed. Papa had to take over raising five scared kids—until he re-married."

Sarah had never heard the story. She suddenly realized that she knew very little about this friend she had known for so long.

"She'll adjust," Alex assured Sarah. "She's young. She'll adjust."

But his words had unintentionally put fear in Sarah's heart. Would she adjust? Her Rebecca? Had she been wrong to send the girl out to school? Or was Sarah wrong to expect her to return? She was confused and filled with doubts and fear.

"Oh, God," she prayed, "I'm going to need your help in the days ahead. We are both going to need your help."

———

Rebecca managed to find some biscuits in the cupboard, left over from last night's supper, so she had a breakfast of biscuits and honey. Then she puttered away the morning trying to find room for all her clothes as she removed them from the cases.

She ate the last of the biscuits for her lunch and tried to decide what she should do with the rest of the day. She attempted to read and ended up napping. When she awoke from her nap she was hot and irritable.

Feeling trapped and bored, she wandered about the house, longing for something icy cold to drink to cool her. She found nothing. The pail that sat on the stand by the back door contained water, but Rebecca discovered it was as warm as the day itself.

She glanced at the clock. It was already past three and her mother had said she would be home by three.

"Well—I need to get out of this stuffy house," she murmured in annoyance and left by the back door. The front door, to Rebecca's displeasure, was held firmly in place by a large inside bolt. No wonder she had been unable to open it from the outside. Back doors were for servants and delivery men. The front door was for the family and for guests. So, since there were no servants here, shouldn't it be the back door that was bolted and the front door that was used? To Rebecca, that would have made some sense.

She wandered out into the yard and took a deep breath. Though hot, it was better than the stuffy house, and the faint breeze felt so good on her hot cheeks. She lifted her hand to brush the tendrils of drifting curls back from her face when her eye caught sight of the corrals. Rebecca liked horses. At least here was something of interest. She moved toward the animals standing in the simmering heat of the afternoon.

There were three horses in the corral. A bay and two blacks, one with a stripe down his face. Rebecca hoisted her skirt and climbed the first rail of the fence, leaning over to reach a hand toward the horses.

"Here, boys," she coaxed. "Here. Come let me get a good look at you."

The black with the stripe tossed his head and snorted. The bay ignored her completely. But the other black came toward her, nose outstretched, head high.

Rebecca was pleased to have his company. She stroked his neck and rubbed his nose and plucked handfuls of grass for him from outside the corral.

"You should really have a bonnet." The voice behind her made Rebecca jump with the suddenness of it.

Rebecca whirled. It was that fellow Seth. Rebecca had not heard his team pull into the yard. They stood behind her, still hitched to the wagon.

"I'm sorry," he apologized. "I didn't mean to startle you."

Rebecca stepped down from the fence rail, her face flushed with embarrassment.

"It's pretty hot to be out without a bonnet," he said again and began to unhitch his team.

"I haven't been out for long," Rebecca argued. "I just came to see the horses."

His face brightened. "Fine horses," he said with a nod. "Boyd picked them out for your ma. I see you were favoring Ebony. He's my favorite too."

Rebecca looked back at the horse that still stood at the rails stretching his head toward her.

"He's nice," she acknowledged. "Is he broken?"

"For harness. Don't know if anyone has ever tried to ride him or not."

Rebecca had never had her own horse. It had been one of her secret dreams since she had mastered the art of riding. At the Fosters, she had always had to ride one of the horses that nobody else wanted. She looked longingly at Ebony. She'd love to go for a ride.

"You want him broken to saddle?" asked Seth.

"I'd—I'd really like that," replied Rebecca.

"I'll talk to your ma. If she doesn't mind, I'll break him for you."

Rebecca swung back to face him, her eyes glowing. If she had a horse, then she wouldn't be stuck in the house—day after day.

"Oh—would you?"

"Sure."

He moved away with the team. Rebecca watched as he pulled off the harnesses one by one and carried them into the barn to hang on the pegs. Then he began to brush and curry one of the horses.

He seemed so absorbed in his work that it irked Rebecca. She had never been around a young man who paid so little attention to her before. Well, she sure wouldn't beg for it.

She moved back toward the house. There really didn't seem to be anything else to do.

Chapter Twenty-two

Making Do

When they went out for supper that night, Rebecca was surprised that she actually remembered Aunt Min and "Uncle Boy" better than she had remembered her own mother. Was it because they had changed less over the years or was it because she had spent so much time with them before she had been sent away to school? She wasn't sure. She only knew that the house had a familiar presence—as though she connected with it somehow. In spite of its sparseness, she felt a drawing because of the memories stirring inside her.

"Rebecca—look at you," said the woman who greeted her with open arms. Rebecca allowed herself to be warmly embraced while Sarah stood to the side beaming her pleasure.

Then Rebecca was passed on to another pair of arms.

"Uncle Boyd," she said with a smile.

"I—I hardly know how to greet you," he admitted. "With a hug—or a deep bow."

They both laughed and he did give her a welcoming hug.

Rebecca even remembered Mr. Galvan. He greeted her somewhat stiffly—but then he had always been a bit stiff. Rebecca was not put off by it. In fact, she found his proper manner more in keeping with what she was used to.

"Your ma said you'd gone and growed up," went on Mrs. Galvan, letting her hand rest on Rebecca's shoulder. "But I was scarce ready for such a young lady. My—you've changed. But I still see the little girl shinin' out of those brown eyes."

"No hair bows to pull now though," teased Boyd.

"Well—we're all set to sit down," Mrs. Galvan said briskly. "You two just set yerselves there at the back an' I'll dish up."

Sarah moved to sit down as bidden and Rebecca followed. She was not used to taking her seat before the hostess was seated. She let her eyes take in her surroundings, finding herself searching for more memories. The house was larger than the small one she and her mother shared. The kitchen was actually a fair-sized room with ample cupboards and a good-sized pantry whose door stood wide open, allowing her a view inside. It seemed to Rebecca that one could actually prepare a real meal in these surroundings, and the meal that was set before them bore that out.

Rebecca was hungry after the scant meals on her own, and the fried chicken and fresh garden vegetables lived up to her expectations.

"You always liked fried chicken. You used to say, 'Let's fry chicken, Aunt Min,' jest as though you had something to do with it."

Three adults at the table laughed. Even Mr. Galvan smiled.

"Well—I used to let you do some dippin'. That kept you happy."

Yes. I remember, thought Rebecca. "And we used to cut gingerbread men," she added. "You'd let me make the raisin eyes."

Mrs. Galvan beamed. "I think more raisins got et than ever made it to the oven," she teased.

"Just like the doughnuts," cut in Boyd. "You'd gather all the newly fried holes after you'd sugared them and make a nest of them. You said you were gonna hatch baby chicks. But the eggs kept disappearing, and I never did see those chicks."

It was a jolly meal. Everyone at the table seemed so pleased to have her back that Rebecca began to feel some kinship with those around the table. The light chatter brought back many childhood memories. Little things that she had long since forgotten. She had been happy in this house. She remembered it now.

A strange thought crossed her mind. If she had to be out West, she wished she could be here. Back with Aunt Min and Uncle Boyd—just like she used to be while her mother was off doing whatever she did during her day.

Rebecca stirred uneasily at the thought and dismissed it. She was a big girl now—she did not need a nanny.

After the meal was enjoyed and the dishes were washed and placed back on the pantry shelves, Boyd entered the kitchen.

"I have something for you," he said to Rebecca, words that had a familiar ring to Rebecca. She remembered hearing them many times in the past.

He came toward her with something in his arms. Rebecca's eyes widened. It was a cat.

"Remember her?" he asked softly.

Rebecca reached out and let her fingers trail through the soft fur. She loved cats. Mrs. Foster had never allowed pets. She said she was allergic to them, but Rebecca always secretly wondered if she didn't just hate them.

The cat looked up at Rebecca and she did remember. "Uncle Boyd," she said—and then laughed. "I—I did call it that, didn't I?"

"You did until she had her first batch of kittens—then you changed her name to Cat," laughed Sarah, joining Rebecca and running a hand over the cat's back.

Rebecca laughed again.

"You asked me to keep her—remember? You thought she would get lonesome with your ma gone all day."

"She—she must be pretty old now!" exclaimed Rebecca.

"She is. But she still seems healthy. Hasn't had kittens for a number of years now. But she still has a life or two left."

He held the cat out to Rebecca and she accepted her carefully. It felt good to have the cat snuggled up in her arms. It was warm and purring and contented to snuggle against her.

"Can I take her home?" asked Rebecca.

"She's yours. You can do whatever you like."

Rebecca nodded. This was something that was really hers, still hers, from those long-ago years.

———

"It's a lovely evening. Would you care to go for a walk?" Sarah asked Rebecca after they had finished the supper dishes. Rebecca looked out the window. It *was* lovely. She ached to get out and stretch her legs. She felt as if she had been caged up for nearly the whole week. Then her eyes took in the form of her mother, and her head dropped in confusion.

"I—I don't think so," she answered. "I—I—it is so dusty that one gets one's skirts all covered with—"

Sarah nodded. "Well, maybe we should just sit out on the front porch."

That seemed harmless enough. They were at the end of the street. No one ever came down their way. "Fine," said Rebecca and followed her mother out the back door and around to the front.

"I think we're going to have another hot day to-morrow," said Sarah, "so we'd best enjoy this nice cool breeze tonight."

Rebecca nodded her agreement. Her cheeks were hot. She felt deep shame for the thoughts she was thinking, but nevertheless they were there. She was ashamed of her mother. Ashamed of the way she dressed. The way she carelessly wrapped her hair and pinned it in a tight bun at the nape of her neck. Didn't she ever look in a mirror? Didn't she realize how un-attractive she looked? How unfeminine? Surely she could see that she should do something about her ap-pearance. Her hands were—were brown and calloused and often dirty with jagged, unkept nails and—they were disgusting. And Rebecca flushed a deeper red. She was ashamed of being ashamed.

———

They sat quietly for some time, enjoying the stir-ring of the evening breeze. Sarah even appreciated the squeak of the complaining old rocker that seemed to sing a little off-key melody in time to the movement.

"It's nice here in the evening," Sarah remarked. "No matter how hot it gets during the day, it always cools off so one can sleep at night."

Rebecca nodded. She had been glad for the light blanket on her bed. At the Fosters' home she had needed only a sheet in the summer months. And she had still tossed and turned in the muggy heat.

"But I always feel lazy without something in my hands," went on Sarah. "Well—guess I'll go get my knitting."

She had no sooner left the porch than Boyd came up the boardwalk.

"Enjoyin' the evenin', Becky?" he asked. He still called her by her childhood nickname and for reasons she could not explain, Rebecca did not mind.

"It's nice out here, isn't it?" she answered, motioning to the chair beside her on the porch.

"I was wonderin' if you might like to go for a walk?" he asked her.

"I'd love to," she replied, and fairly skipped down the steps to join him.

He left her for a moment and went around to the open kitchen window. "Sarah," he called, "I've invited Becky for a walk. We'll not be gone long."

Rebecca didn't see Sarah in the kitchen where she was gathering up her knitting. Sarah lifted her head, tipped it slightly, then nodded. Rebecca had not wished to go for a walk. She had told her so. Was Boyd's offer so much more inviting? She shrugged and headed back to the porch to spend her evening alone.

———

"I'm afraid Rebecca is terribly bored," Sarah said to Boyd a few days later.

"I don't suppose life is quite the same for her," he admitted.

"She seems to just—just wander around aimlessly while I'm gone."

"Well—she'll need some time to find herself. She likely hasn't got over the long trip out yet."

Sarah nodded. She could only imagine, never having had the chance to make the difficult trip herself.

"What does she do with her day?" Boyd asked.

Sarah thought for a moment. "I don't really know. She—she visits the horses some, I guess. Seth asked if he could break the black to saddle. Rebecca has taken a fancy to him. She does ride, you know. Was taught at the school back there."

"Even that will be different," put in Boyd. "They likely taught her English saddle."

"English? How's that? A saddle is a saddle."

"No—our western saddles are different—but she'll likely adjust fast enough." He thought for a moment longer. "What did you say—to Seth."

"I told him to go ahead if he had the time. He took Ebony home with him. Wants to gentle him into riding."

"He'll do a good job. He's patient—and good with horses."

Sarah pushed back her bonnet. It was hot again. She looked down at her dusty trousers and dirt-streaked shirt. She longed to get home to a tub of warm water.

"Rebecca help with the chores around the house?" Boyd asked off-handedly.

Sarah's brow furrowed. "No—not yet."

"I'm sure she will—once she learns where things are—feels more familiar. It would be good if you could have some help shoulderin' the load."

Sarah nodded. But in her heart she wasn't sure if Rebecca would ever help. She wasn't sure that Rebecca knew how to do any of those things that a woman was supposed to know. She hadn't even understood how to use an iron. It was Sarah who'd had to stay up late pressing wrinkles from creased dresses and crinolines.

"I don't think they taught them much of that at that school where I sent her," she admitted slowly.

"Well—she'll catch on soon enough," Boyd assured her and moved to check off another crate against his list.

Sarah longed to agree. She felt a bit of shame at how little Rebecca seemed to know about simple things around the house. "I guess so," she answered, unable to say more.

———————

Rebecca *was* bored. There was nothing to do. Even Ebony was gone now, and the other horses left in the corral could not be coaxed to the rails for pampering.

No longer the young kitten that had been given to Rebecca years ago, Cat seemed to wish to just lie and sleep. She wasn't even the energetic mother cat that had been all bounce and business in caring for her offspring.

Rebecca wandered restlessly about the house. She wished there was something to do. Something new to read. The few books she did find were old and worn and meant for a child. Rebecca flipped through the pages of one in irritation. She remembered the stories. She had enjoyed them then—when she had been four or five.

She tossed the book carelessly into one of the chairs and went to see if she could find something to eat in the sparsely stocked kitchen.

———

Each new day was as boring as the last. Even Cat brought little company. Rebecca longed for the day when Ebony would be returned and she could go for long rides to escape the monotony. Seth had told her the horse was coming along nicely and that it wouldn't be long until he could be trusted for her to ride. Rebecca could hardly wait.

Seth. He was a puzzle to Rebecca. She was used to young men noticing her, admiring her. And though Seth was mannerly and friendly, he seemed to quite ignore her beauty. Rebecca was embarrassed to find herself fixing her curls, choosing a dress, just to get some response from the young man. But except for a good-natured greeting and friendly conversation, he paid little attention to her preening.

It puzzled her. It annoyed her. Was she losing her charm? Was the West robbing her of even that? No. She got plenty of stares from other young men on the few occasions she went out and about the town.

Then why didn't Seth notice her? He seemed to pay far more attention to the horses he worked over so diligently.

Even more annoying was the way her mother spoke of Seth. As if he could do no wrong. As if he was the final authority. She was always saying, "Seth would say to remember Proverbs 3:5-6," or "Seth says that one must guard against the appearance of evil," or "Seth would ask what the Bible has to say on the matter."

Rebecca got terribly tired of listening to Seth's little sermons secondhand.

Yet there was something about the young man that fascinated Rebecca. Perhaps it was just his rugged good looks. Peony would have swooned over him and declared him to be "So-o romantic." Rebecca wished to see some evidence of that. He seemed totally taken up with his work for her mother and his attendance at the local church.

Rebecca just couldn't quite figure Seth out.

———

"I have to rush. It's washday," said Sarah, sounding weary.

"How are things going?" Boyd asked.

Sarah shook her head. "She's—she's still adjusting, I guess," she answered, understanding his question.

"Takes a while," he admitted.

Sarah thought about the statement. She shrugged and picked at the hole in her glove. She would soon need new ones and she didn't have the money. She had been spending far more on groceries, trying to please Rebecca's more sophisticated taste.

"I—I don't think she's happy here," she said slowly.

He looked up. "Maybe she's just missing her friends," he put in, his tone comforting.

"Could be. Could be. I'll have to think on that. See what I can do. Maybe the Fosters would let their girl come out for a visit. I'll have to look into it."

———

"Something bothering you, honey?" Sarah asked Rebecca later. "You seem so—so withdrawn."

Rebecca looked up and shrugged her shoulders. "Just bored," she replied. "There's nothing to do in this town."

Sarah lifted her head slowly. The whole house was filled with work she had to try to crowd in after coming home from her daily deliveries, and Rebecca claimed there was nothing to do.

"Seems I always find more than enough to do," she answered, trying hard to keep her voice even.

Rebecca shrugged her shoulders and looked away.

"I know—I know," cut in Sarah, sensing the girl's irritation. "It is a quiet little town. We don't have many young folks. Especially not in the church. Are you lonesome?"

Rebecca did not answer the question, but looked as if she might cry.

"I've been thinking," Sarah hurried on. "How would you like to have Annabelle come for a visit?"

Rebecca sat upright, the cat in her lap deposited unceremoniously on the floor. For one moment excitement flashed across her face, but it was quickly replaced with a look her mother could not interpret.

"Here?" she said, casting a quick glance around her.

Sarah smiled. "Sure. Here. She could have my room, and I'd sleep on the cot."

Rebecca leaned back. "I don't suppose her folks would let her travel so far alone," she said, her tone casual.

"You did," reminded Sarah.

"Yes, but I—I was born in the West," said Rebecca quickly.

"I suppose," replied Sarah thoughtfully, pleased to hear that Rebecca was in some way identifying with the West.

"Well—would you like me to write and ask Mrs. Foster?" Sarah went on.

"I—I don't think it would be wise. Not just now.

Things are—are rather unsettled, and it—it just wouldn't be the right time. Believe me—it's not a good time for such a—an invitation."

"Very well," said Sarah. "We'll let it go for now."

———

As Sarah left the room Rebecca watched, then let out her breath. That would be a dreadful mistake. Annabelle would jump at the chance, and Mrs. Foster had already promised the girl that should the occasion arise, she would purchase the ticket. Rebecca felt she had just avoided the most dreadful catastrophe. She did not wish to hurt her mother, but she would be absolutely mortified to have one of her friends, especially Annabelle, see her here.

———

"Is Ebony ready yet?" Rebecca asked sweetly as she approached Seth, who was running the curry comb over the sides of the skittish Rhubarb. She had put on one of her most fashionable gowns, tied her bonnet casually on her shoulders rather than placing it on her head so she could show off her dark curls to the best advantage.

"Don't come too close, miss," he advised, then flashed her a bright smile. "Ol' Rhubarb is one sour horse. You never know what he might decide to do."

"Why do you use him then?" asked Rebecca, feeling a bit put out. He would not even be able to smell her cologne from that distance.

"He pulls good," he answered simply. "As long as I keep my eye on him—he behaves himself. I just don't trust him. You never know what might spook him."

"Spook him. Like what?"

"Um-m-m, anything. Flying birds. Barking dogs. Fancy-smellin' perfume."

So he had noticed. Rebecca felt her spirits lift.

"You're good with horses," she said. She had always found that young men loved compliments.

"I like 'em. Generally quite predictable—once you get to know them. Not like some things."

"Like?" queried Rebecca, tilting her head so the sun could splash off her crown of hair.

"Oh—grizzly bears. New mamas. Pretty girls."

"Pretty girls!" she exclaimed, her voice feigning annoyance.

He lifted his head from his work to look up at her. His deep brown eyes glinted with subdued laughter.

He was teasing, she could see that. But she liked it. She tilted her head and pretended to be perturbed. "I'll bet you tease all the girls," she accused him.

"Girls? I don't even talk to 'em if I can help it," he said matter-of-factly. "I've much better luck talking to horses."

Rebecca tipped her head and observed him. He really was quite nice looking. She paused for a moment, then responded, "Maybe that's because you have never given a girl proper attention. Perhaps if you tried as hard with—with her—as you do with a horse—you might be pleasantly surprised." Rebecca swung on her heel and walked toward the house. She had taken only a few steps when he called out to her. "You asked about Ebony. He should be ready sometime next week."

Rebecca turned and looked back at him. He was still currying the horse, but she saw him lift his eyes for just a moment and give her a bit of a nod.

Chapter Twenty-three

The Clash

"I think you're still working too hard," said Boyd.

"I *am* tired," said Sarah and eased herself into a chair. "I think it's just this hot weather."

"Are you still taking the daily route and doing everything at home, too?" Boyd asked her frankly as he crossed over to her and offered her a cold drink.

Sarah nodded.

Doing it all—and then some, she admitted to herself silently. The work at home had been even heavier since Rebecca had arrived with all of her starched crinolines and frilly dresses and expectations.

"Maybe she's just hesitant to go ahead on her own. Work with her for a while."

"I've tried. She just looks at me absentmindedly, shrugs, and walks off."

"Well—she certainly has come to a different lifestyle than she was used to."

Sarah admitted that. She had been trying to be patient with Rebecca. She knew that the girl was struggling. Was feeling alone and bored and out-of-touch.

"She plays the organ real nice," went on Boyd.

"She says she hates it." Sarah's comment brought a surprised look to Boyd's face. "I guess it is a rather beat-up old instrument compared to what she was used to," Sarah continued. "It bothers her no end when a key sticks and puts out a sour chord. After last Sunday she says she'll never play it again."

They looked at each other and could not suppress a laugh.

"You have to admit—it *was* rather funny," said Boyd.

"Not to Rebecca. She was embarrassed to death."

Boyd nodded in sympathy. "Hear the youth are thinking of an outing," he said.

Sarah lifted the glass from her lips. "Really? That would be wonderful." Perhaps this was the answer she had been praying for.

"Pastor was talking to me about it. Wondering where would be a good place to hold it. I offered our backyard. Guess it's one of the biggest in town. I told him I'd put together a few tables so they could picnic there. It was Seth's idea. He's concerned about the youth of the town that never go to church. Thinks they could be invited to something like this."

"It sounds wonderful," said Sarah.

"I'm sure Rebecca will look forward to something to do with other young people," Boyd went on.

Sarah hesitated. "I don't think I will tell her," she said at last. "It—it might mean more if the invitation comes from one of the young people—from Seth."

For a moment Boyd looked surprised and then he smiled. "Might at that," he agreed.

Sarah stood and handed the glass back. Already she was feeling better. The cold lemonade helped, but it was the news about the coming youth party that had given her the lift.

———

A letter finally came from Stanley. Rebecca had been waiting for it. Longing for it. She tore it open with trembling fingers.

The first paragraphs were news about family and plans for coming events. He had finished at the Academy and managed to pass in all his subjects.

Then he wrote that he still hadn't decided what he would do next. His mother had been enlisted to help appease his father. Between the two of them they had argued his case. They were apparently successful, for his father had agreed to let him put off choosing a vocation for the next year or so. "Maybe I should be a lawyer after all," Stanley quipped. "I think I must have presented my case remarkably well, for one does not influence Father easily." So now he was off to Europe—for a year. Or more if needed. "Father says I may as well get it out of my system now. Maybe then I will be settled enough to study." Stanley sounded very pleased with the arrangement. Rebecca was heartbroken. He hadn't even said that he would miss her dreadfully or that he wished he could see her before he left.

Rebecca crumpled the letter in a trembling hand and gave way to tears.

———

Seth finally brought Ebony home. "He's gentled fine," he said. "I'm quite sure we can trust him now, but just to be sure I think we should ride together the first time or two."

Rebecca had no objection. "Very well," she nodded, trying hard not to let her real enthusiasm show.

"I'll get him saddled while you get changed," he offered.

Rebecca walked demurely toward the house, though she wished to run. She took down her most attractive riding habit and proceeded to dress, trying to be careful but also hurry. She didn't want the young man to change his mind.

When she returned to the corrals Seth was waiting patiently against the corral fence, one hand stroking the dark neck of Ebony. Rebecca stopped in confusion. The horse Seth was to ride stood nearby without a saddle.

"I thought you intended to come with me," said Rebecca.

"I do," he answered.

"Then why is your horse not saddled?"

"I'll ride bareback."

"Bareback?" Rebecca had never heard of such a thing.

"Without a saddle. I do it lots of times," Seth answered easily.

Rebecca's eyes then went to Ebony. Ebony had a strange-looking piece of gear on his back.

"But—but—what—where'd you get that?" Rebecca floundered, pointing with her crop.

"It's mine," he answered. "Your mother doesn't have a saddle."

"But I—I've never ridden with—with anything like that before," went on Rebecca.

Seth turned to look at her and then it was his turn to look surprised. "I thought you were going to change for riding," he said.

"I did," replied Rebecca, now in a bit of a huff.

"But you can't ride in that," said Seth, indicating her riding habit.

"I can't ride in that," rejoined Rebecca, pointing at the saddle.

"What do you mean? I can adjust the stirrups to wherever you need them."

"Stirrups? It's not only the stirrups."

Seth looked calmly back at Ebony, who stood patiently waiting for his rider.

"I get it," he said, seemingly unruffled. "You're used to an English saddle."

"I don't care what nationality it is," said Rebecca in mock annoyance. "I just want to be able to ride."

Seth chuckled. The laugh soothed Rebecca's irritation.

"Well, miss," Seth said slowly, "you are now in the West. I guess if you want to ride, you'll just have to learn to use a western saddle."

Rebecca was still flushed.

"Now—you run on in and change into something sensible and we'll—"

"Sensible," echoed Rebecca. "What do you mean sensible? I'll have you know that this—this is quite proper—in fashion."

Seth turned to her and lifted his hat to scratch his head. When he spoke again his voice was calm and gentle. "It looks lovely, miss. Real lovely. But all that ribbon and lace a flutterin' . . ." He paused, then went on. "Ebony's gentled but he's not used to that. It could spook him so's he'd never stop runnin'. Honest! I would never dare put you on a horse wearin' that."

Rebecca tried to calm herself. She wanted the freedom of riding. She hated to be cooped in the house day after day. She would pay almost any price to be able to escape.

"What do you wish me to wear?" she asked, trying hard to control her voice.

"Just—just something that—that won't rattle in the wind," he replied.

"Like?"

"Like a pair of your ma's trousers."

Rebecca's eyes filled with horror. She would *never* wear those. Never. Not if she grew old sitting in the small kitchen. She gave him one long glaring look and spun away.

"I am not made for trousers," she hissed. "I am a lady."

He stood for one moment looking at her evenly and then he nodded and stepped past her.

"Yes, ma'am," he said. His voice was still gentle. "A lady to be sure."

And he casually began to remove the saddle from the back of Ebony.

———

Rebecca was both surprised and pleased when Seth invited her to the youth outing. After the saddle incident, she had thought that the two of them might never speak again.

But apparently Seth did not carry a grudge. He appeared, hat in hand after finishing with the horses one evening, and explained about the picnic to a flushed Rebecca.

"I was hoping you'd consent to go with me," he ended his little speech.

Rebecca nodded. She did not wish to appear too eager.

"I'll give it thought."

"Yes, miss. But there isn't much time for thought. The party is tomorrow evening."

At first Rebecca felt annoyance. Why hadn't he

asked her earlier? And then she forced herself to swallow her pride. It wasn't like she had other plans for the evening.

"I'd—be pleased to go," she managed to say.

He smiled. There was something dreadfully disarming about his smile. Rebecca flushed, regardless of her poise obtained at Tall Elms School for Girls.

"I'll pick you up at eight, miss," he said, smiled, tipped his hat, and turned to go.

Rebecca hesitated for a moment and then called after him, "Just a minute."

He turned back toward her.

She felt embarrassed. She wished she had just let him go. But now she was committed to continuing. She took a deep breath and began before she lost her nerve. "I—I was just thinking," she said. "If—if we are going to the picnic—together—then maybe—maybe we should—well—call each other by name."

He nodded.

"I'll see you tomorrow night then—Rebecca," he said.

She stood in the soft glow of the twilight and listened to his whistle until the sound faded into the night.

It was a strange event. Rebecca had never been to one quite like it. Oh, they had fun—and the young people that she met were much like the ones she had known back East. She supposed that young people all around the world were probably much alike even though they might dress differently or speak a little differently. Rebecca was rather surprised to discover that she was quite enjoying herself as the evening moved on.

Seth, though not gushy or romantic like the other boys she knew, was really quite attentive and actually a lot of fun to be with. Rebecca sensed that there were other girls there that night that would have more than welcomed his special attention.

It wasn't the fun or the food that surprised Rebecca. It was the ending of the evening. Rebecca had already gathered from the conversation that many of the young people who were in attendance at the picnic were from the town—yet not from the church. So she was more than a little surprised when at the close of the evening, Seth stepped forward and said he wished to leave a little devotional thought with the group.

There was a bit of uncomfortable stirring at first, but once Seth had begun his little talk, they listened— all of them. Rebecca found herself listening carefully too, her eyes on the young man before her.

He's like—like a preacher, she thought to herself, though she didn't remember the preachers that she was familiar with being quite as earnest as Seth appeared to be.

He spoke of God's plan for the human race. Of the sin that entered the world through Adam. Of God's great love that made a way to redeem mankind from the fallen state.

"He loves us. He loved us so much that He was willing to send His only Son to die—but He wants our love in return. How can we show our love? By obedience. But we can't follow His commands if we don't know what they are. We find them by studying His Word. He tells us there how He wants us to live. The most important thing that we—any of us—can do in life is to discover what Jesus wants us to be—and let Him help us to become that."

They were strange words to Rebecca. Oh, she knew all of the facts from the Bible. They had to study the Bible at school. She had learned dozens of Bible passages. But she had never heard anyone talk like this before.

"We need to put aside our own selfish desires and find what God wants for our lives," he went on. "He always has the best plan. We can trust Him. We can trust Him completely with every part of our life. Our past—that He will forgive and forget our wrongdoing if we ask Him. With our present—because He knows our thoughts and feelings and what we are struggling with. Our future—because He has a plan for our life. He loves us."

Rebecca had never heard such strange words. She began to put the words together with all the things she had heard her mother say about this young man. She had much to think about.

Rebecca was reminded of the fact that it was Sunday again the moment she rolled over and opened her eyes. The delicious aroma of breakfast came drifting into her room. Her mother was never there to cook breakfast on other mornings. It would be nice to have something hot—something palatable—again. Rebecca stretched and groaned. She had the vague notion that she would be expected to be up soon.

But Rebecca hated getting up to face another day, even Sunday. She tugged the blanket up closer to her chin, dislodging Cat, who slept at her side. The cat complained, then leaped easily to the rag rug and began to groom her fur. After a few good licks she curled up into a ball on the rug and closed her eyes again.

"You lazy thing," said Rebecca. "All you ever want to do is sleep."

Rebecca's words were self-condemning. With a flushed face she threw back the covers and crawled from her bed.

"It's not that I'm lazy," she excused herself. "There's just no good reason to be up and about. There's nowhere to go. Nothing to do. I hate it. It's nearly intolerable."

"Rebecca," came Sarah's call. "Breakfast. We need to be ready for church soon."

Church. Rebecca had never been overly fond of the Sunday morning ritual. But at least there were no longer the daily chapels as there had been when she was a student.

She drew on her robe and proceeded to the kitchen. Hot cinnamon buns greeted her, sending their pungent aroma throughout the room.

"Good morning," greeted Sarah. "Did you sleep well?"

For an answer Rebecca yawned again.

"Church starts in an hour. We'll need to hurry," said Sarah.

Rebecca seated herself in her place at the table.

"We've been invited to the Galvans' home for dinner," went on Sarah. "She has asked Mr. Murray as well."

"Who's Mr. Murray?" queried Rebecca without real interest.

"He owns the store."

"Oh—him." Rebecca easily dismissed the man.

"He says business is so good that he might hire a clerk. Are you interested?"

Rebecca frowned. "In being a clerk? Really, Mother."

Sarah turned to her daughter and spoke rather sharply. "When I was in need of work, clerking for Mr. Murray would have seemed like a godsend. In fact, he offered me the job and I was tempted to accept."

"So why didn't you?" asked Rebecca carelessly.

"Because I knew he didn't need a clerk at the time. He was just offering me the job out of the goodness of his heart."

Rebecca smiled disdainfully. "Some goodness," she said and reached for a cinnamon roll.

"Now just a minute, young lady," began Sarah, and Rebecca looked at her in surprise. "I might be willing to let you take advantage of me. But I won't allow you to speak of my friends in such a fashion. Alex Murray has helped me to get through the tough years. He even gave credit at his store when I couldn't pay. Fact is— when he asked about you working for him—I put him off. I wasn't sure that you'd—that you'd be worth your pay." Her flushed face looked as shocked at her frank words as Rebecca was.

Rebecca stared at her with wide-open, horrified eyes. Then she sprang to her feet and faced her mother, her own cheeks flushed with anger. "I had no idea when I came back West that I would be expected to be hired help," she hissed.

"Hired help? No. No—not hired help. A member of the family—that's what. Just a living—working—acceptable member of the family."

"So I'm not acceptable. Then why did you bring me back?"

"I brought you back because you are mine. Because I thought we belonged together," said Sarah, her voice ragged with emotion. "I thought that you would be as—as anxious to be back with family as I would be to have you."

"Well, you were wrong," stormed Rebecca through tears. "You were wrong." Her voice rose. "I don't belong here. You know I don't belong here. I hate it here. *I hate it!*"

And she ran from the room, loud sobs seeming to fill the space around Sarah, choking her.

———

Sarah sat in a kitchen chair with her face in her hands. The tears came freely. "Oh, what have I done?" she cried. "What have I done? I'm supposed to be the mature one. The mother. I wanted so much to have her home. To make her belong. To have her love me, and now I've gone and spoiled everything. Everything. We'll never share a closeness now. Never. Oh, God— I've really messed this up. I—I need your help. Patience. Help me with Rebecca, Lord. Help me to understand why—why she feels so—" Her prayer ended in sobs. But Sarah could not go on. She felt like having a good long cry. Instead, she roused herself, cleared the table and washed up the dishes, and prepared herself for the morning service. She knew Rebecca would not be going. She could still hear her crying in her bedroom. Sarah longed to talk with her. To offer an apology—but she wasn't sure just yet what her words should be. What approach she should take. How could they communicate when they had not been together? She didn't understand her daughter. She didn't know her little girl. And her little girl did not know her mother. Their two worlds were so far apart. She never should have sent Rebecca away to school for so many years. Now the girl was a stranger in her own home. She no longer fit.

Sarah bowed under the weight of her burden. She couldn't have Rebecca hating every minute of her life here in the West. She couldn't force the young girl to love those who loved her. Nor could she demand that she cooperate when she obviously was so miserable. She wasn't sure what she should do. Would Rebecca learn to love, or at least accept, her home in time? It seemed unlikely.

"Oh—God—help me. Help me to know what's the right thing to do. I don't want to lose her, Lord. I don't want to lose her. But—I just don't know. I don't know what to do."

Chapter Twenty-four

A Difficult Decision

"Rebecca—may I come in?"

Rebecca wished with all her heart she could say no, but she knew that she could not. She didn't wish to see her mother. Not now. Maybe not ever. She wasn't sure. She was hurt. She was angry. She wanted to be alone.

The door pushed open and Sarah appeared. In her hands was a tray of food.

"Mrs. Galvan sent you some dinner," she said as she set the tray on the nightstand. "She was—sorry to hear that you were—not feeling up to joining us for dinner at her house."

Rebecca wondered what her mother had said about her absence. Had she admitted to the neighbors that they'd had an awful spat?

"I'm—sorry about this morning," Sarah began. "I had no—no right to talk to you like I did. I'm ashamed—and I'm sorry. I've—I've done a lot of thinking—and praying. I— Can you forgive me?"

Rebecca had not expected her mother to come to her in apology. She didn't know quite how to respond. She had been prepared to defend herself. To speak her mind about the way they lived. The condition of the house—Sarah—everything. Now what was she to say?

"I'm—I'm terribly sorry," went on Sarah. "I know that—that I have no right to expect—well, just to expect you to feel about me as I feel about you—just because I'm your mother. You see—I—I welcomed you as a baby—me and your father—you—you brought us so much joy—both of us. We longed to give you everything.

"Then—when we lost your father—I still wanted you to have—the best. I—I doubted that the—the West could give you that. I was wrong. You would have been fine here. I—I look at our other young people— upright, intelligent, hard-working individuals, and I think—I—"

But Rebecca cut in, tears forming in her eyes again, anger showing in her voice, "And you think that I'm not upright and intelligent?"

"I—I didn't say that—didn't mean that," quickly put in Sarah.

"Then what did you mean? You as good as said. You—"

"I meant that you could have been that anyway. The West—or the East—has no—no monopoly on goodness. It's the person—they are—we are each responsible—ourselves—for how we turn out—what we do with our life—not our circumstances."

"So it's my fault that I didn't turn out to your liking?"

Sarah stopped and looked at her daughter. Rebecca was pushing too far. She didn't even try to understand. But Sarah refused to speak further harsh words. She stood slowly to her feet and turned to look out the window, her back to Rebecca.

But Rebecca was not finished.

"Look at you," she hurled at her mother's back.

"Just look at you. You—you dress like a—like a man and you don't even—don't even—fix your hair or— or— You're not—not to my liking either."

The angry words stung Sarah more than she would have thought possible. She felt the tears gathering in her eyes. She felt the slump of her shoulders—the rending of her broken heart.

She stood silently. She could not speak. Did not trust herself with words. In spite of the pain that she was suffering, her glance went down to her plain skirt and simple white shirtwaist.

It's true, she admitted silently. *It's true. She has a right to be embarrassed. I must—I must look—horrible to her.*

But Sarah made no comment about the slashing remarks. Silently she prayed while Rebecca sobbed behind her.

Oh, God, she prayed silently, *this has all gone wrong. It is not what I wanted. Not what I longed for. I wanted so much for us to be—to be mother and daughter. I wanted so much for her to love me. But it's all wrong. We don't seem to be—be able to connect with each other. We are not even able to understand each other. To be mother and daughter.*

In tears, Sarah finally gave her little girl entirely to her Lord. He would have to work in Rebecca's heart. She, as mother, could not dictate and demand. She had to simply trust her child to God, asking that His will be done for each of them. For Sarah's part, there seemed only one thing to do. She could not force Rebecca to accept her way of life. She had to be willing to let Rebecca go. To choose her own way in life. Perhaps that freedom would lead her back to the life that she knew and understood—away from her mother and the West. Sarah's heart ached at the thought.

When the worst of Rebecca's storm of tears seemed to have passed, Sarah spoke, quietly, evenly, her voice hardly cracking in her efforts to keep it calm and controlled.

"I—I don't have the funds—right now—unless I borrow. I—I hate to do that. But I will if I have to."

She took a deep breath and let it out in a soft sigh.

"If—if you feel you cannot be happy here—I'll allow you—let you go back. It—may be a while before I can make the arrangements. But I'll—see to your ticket. I'm—I'm sorry. I hate to see you go. I had such—such hopes and dreams—of us being together again—but I can—I think—understand that you—you've—got to be free to live—where you—you desire to live."

Sarah turned suddenly and looked at her daughter. Rebecca's slim shoulders still shook with sobs, and tears lay on her cheeks.

"Is that what you wish?" Sarah asked softly.

Rebecca did not trust herself to speak. It was a bitter triumph. She hated to see the woman who was her mother hurt. She hadn't wanted that. And Stanley was somewhere in Europe. She would not be going back to Stanley. And Seth— Rebecca still hadn't sorted out her thinking concerning Seth.

Still—it was what she wanted. What she longed for. She hated the way her mother lived.

Slowly she nodded her head, avoiding eye contact with the woman near her bed.

There was silence.

"And what I wish—what I long for—more than—even more than for you to—to accept me—is for you to—to learn to know—God—His will for your life—whatever that might be."

Rebecca heard the soft swish of Sarah's Sunday

skirts and then her door closed softly. She was alone in her room.

————

"You've been keeping pretty much to yourself. Care to go for a walk?"

Rebecca smiled. She always enjoyed the company of Boyd. If there was a bright spot in having to spend some time in Kenville while her mother made arrangements for her return back to civilization, it was her self-adopted Uncle Boyd.

"Will I need my shawl?" she asked.

"I don't think so. It's a pleasant evening and we won't be gone long."

Rebecca stepped lightly down the stairs and joined him on the boardwalk.

For a time they walked along in silence; then Boyd spoke. "Must be rather—different for you livin' here—after bein' used to the Fosters. Thet big house—with servants. All the parties and outin's and nice places to wear your fancy dresses. You miss it?"

Rebecca nodded. There was no use denying it.

"The school? With all the girls yer own age—and the—the fancy doin's. Ya miss thet too?"

Rebecca hesitated on that. She wasn't too sure she'd like to go back to school with all its demands.

"Remember much about when you were a little tyke?" he continued.

Rebecca turned to him. "Not much," she said. "Little pieces here and there. I remember you—how you went with me on the stage and then the train."

He nodded.

"Remember anything about your pa?" he asked her.

Rebecca shook her head.

Boyd was slow in continuing. "He was tall—I s'pose women would've called him a good-looker. Clean cut, sort of mannish young fella. Little bit of a crook in his nose. Hardly noticeable, but we fellas his age teased him."

He paused.

"They made a real strikin' couple—yer ma and yer pa."

Rebecca's face showed a bit of surprise. Boyd did not even look her way.

"Several fellas in the area had their eyes on yer ma when her folks first moved in here. Yer pa—he was the lucky fella she chose." He shook his head and walked in silence as if remembering, as if seeing mind-pictures that captured his full attention.

"She had this beautiful hair—dark but with rich shades of—of—I don't even know what color you'd call it—and she always wore it up in this—this pretty fashion with just little bits of—of soft curls, sort of—flutterin' down around her perky little face—an' her skin was so soft—so creamy—I don't know how a woman would describe it, but I—I used to wonder what it'd be like to just run my finger down her cheek. An' her eyes. Yer ma has always had the prettiest—most—most alive eyes of anyone I've ever seen. They used to dance and—and sparkle. And she was so tiny and dainty— with frills and bows and lacy hankies and pert little bonnets and frilly parasols. She looked like a—a— walkin' doll."

Rebecca was so startled at his words that she was tempted to stop and stare at the man. He certainly could not be describing her mother.

She was about to question him when he picked up again. "An' then—then she lost yer pa—and her whole world changed."

Rebecca heard his voice tighten. She chose the moment to interrupt the brief silence. "How—what happened—to—to—my father?"

Boyd looked at her, surprise showing in his face. "You don't know?"

Rebecca shook her head. "No one has ever told me."

"I thought your mama—"

"No—she never talked about it." Rebecca hesitated. "I don't think she wants to talk about it. Oh, she—she talks about my father—some—but she doesn't—" Rebecca stopped, then went on softly, "Maybe it's—too hard."

Boyd nodded. "Maybe," he said, but he did not lift his eyes to hers. Then he seemed to take a deep breath as though needing extra strength. "He was killed by lightning—in a freak storm. He was opening a gate for the team. They figured the bolt traveled the wire."

Rebecca's eyes widened in horror. "How—awful," she whispered through stiff lips. "How awful."

Boyd stopped talking. He seemed to be sorting through painful memories—perhaps wondering if more needed to be said. Rebecca wondered if he would go on. At length he did.

"She could have remarried—of course. It could have—have been so much easier for her—but she didn't. Chose not to. She was so—so set on caring fer her little girl. She wanted her little girl to have the—the best education—and she wouldn't saddle a man with those responsibilities, so she just concentrated on—on doing it all herself.

"Now you might argue that she chose the wrong way. I—I don't try to sort thet out anymore—but she chose her way. She has a right to thet. But in the—the doin'—and strugglin' and—and hard, backbreakin' work—she had to put aside her frills and—and womanly things—an'—an' live—differently. It cost her—it really cost her. Oh—not in the person she is. She's still the same—underneath, but outwardly—she changed with the years. Her—house changed. Every time she ran short of money—she found something more she could do without. Little by little she—she sold most of her 'homey' things. Her house was so—so pretty and refined at one time. It's—quite plain now."

Rebecca was trying hard to follow his words. She didn't really understand what he was saying. It all sounded so—so foreign and incomprehensible.

"But the house is—is still sound. She's seen to that. The foundation is strong—it's never been allowed to deteriorate. Always painted and kept in repair.

"An' yer ma. She's strong. I've never met a stronger woman. Nor one with so much—so much character. All of the—the important things—her faith in God—it's grown—I've seen it grow—her appreciation of neighbors—that's always there—her love—for her little girl—that's never wavered. Never. She's always wanted—the best for you, Rebecca."

He turned and looked at her for the first time.

"She loves you, Becky. She truly loves you."

Suddenly Rebecca thought she knew what he was trying to say. Her face flushed with resentment and anger. Uncle Boyd was on her mother's side.

"Did she tell you to talk to me?" she asked sharply.

He looked surprised.

"No. Why?"

"I suppose you're going to say that you don't know about our spat."

"I don't know what spat you are referring to. I do know that your ma is—troubled. I know her well enough to see when something is botherin' her—when she is—is feelin' down. She—she's counted on yer comin' home for—for years—but she doesn't look happy now that you're here. An'—it's easy to see thet—thet you're not happy. You've been—been frettin' and poutin' ever since you got home. I—I thought it might help you to understand if I—you knew how things used to be and—why they are as they are now."

Rebecca was caught by his description of her. "Fretting and pouting." Was that the way he saw her? Was that how everyone in the town saw her? Tears stung her eyes. That wasn't fair. No one understood. No one. She couldn't wait to leave this town. She couldn't wait.

"—she could hardly wait. She worked so hard—and she wants you to be a part of her life," Boyd was saying.

Rebecca's head jerked up, tears in her eyes. "Well—I can't," she said, trying to keep her voice controlled as she had been trained to do when angry at school. "I can't—be a part of—of this. You speak of a young—beautiful woman—a walking—doll. I see an—an unkempt—disgustingly clad—woman with—with snarled hair and—and dirty hands."

Boyd whirled to look at her. "Doesn't it mean anything to you that she dirtied those hands for *you*?"

Rebecca stopped walking and looked at him. The tears were coursing down her cheeks. "Should it? Should it? Couldn't she have—have worked hard—someway other than—than becoming a—a freight hauler? And—and even if she went to hauling freight—did she have to forsake being a woman—dress in—in disgusting, dirty trousers?"

"Don't you understand—?"

"No! No, I don't understand! I've tried to understand but—but I am only—only embarrassed. Humiliated by the way we live—by—by the woman who is—is supposed to be my mother."

She was sobbing uncontrollably as she finished her
torrent of words; then she spun away from him and ran
down the boardwalk. She had to get away. She had to.
She would insist that her mother borrow the money so
she could leave now. She couldn't wait until her mother
had saved enough from the hauling of freight.

"I want to leave," said Rebecca coolly to her mother
that evening. "I want to leave soon."

She saw the hurt in her mother's eyes, and then a
weariness seemed to take its place.

"I was hoping—"

"Hoping I'd decide to stay. No—no—it won't
work."

Sarah nodded.

"I'll see what I can do about a loan—and I'll write
to Mrs. Foster—right away," she said, her shoulders
sagging. It seemed it was settled.

After Rebecca had retired for the night, she kept
replaying over and over the words of Boyd. Was it
true? Had her mother really changed so much because
of her love and devotion to her only daughter? Had she
sacrificed—her looks—her home—her very self?

It was all so hard to sort out. Rebecca had never
loved anyone like that. She couldn't understand such
love. Didn't a love like that ask for—deserve—some
kind of response?

It was all so troubling. Rebecca tossed and turned
even after she had finally managed to fall into a restless sleep.

Chapter Twenty-five

Stubborn Will

Seth was in the yard harnessing the team. Rebecca ached to go out to talk with him. Her thoughts were so troubled—and Seth seemed so—so at peace. She wondered if he had ever battled with disturbing emotions and then dismissed the idea. She was quite sure that nothing had ever bothered Seth.

Rebecca paced back and forth in the kitchen. Now and then she cast a glance out the window. She knew that he would soon be leaving. She knew she would hate to see him go. But what excuse could she use to interrupt his work?

A knock sounded at the door. Rebecca reached a hand down to smooth her skirts, then quickly up to pat her hair. Could it possibly be—?

It was. Seth stood there, his hat in his hand, a calm, disarming smile on his face.

"We are havin' another youth gatherin' tonight," he said after greeting her. "Could you come along?"

Rebecca flushed. There was nothing she would enjoy more. She nodded her head and answered with a soft, "That would be nice."

"At the same time then," he said, gave her another smile, replaced his hat, and went whistling off to the team.

————

The meeting did much to lift Rebecca's spirits. She even enjoyed Seth's devotional—though she had to admit that his words troubled her. She had gone to church and to chapel services all her life and felt that she knew the Bible as well as anyone. But she had never thought that she was in any way responsible for what had happened so long ago on Golgotha. But Seth did. "He died because of my sins—because of your sin," Seth had said, and for the first time in her life Rebecca felt a pricking of her heart.

"We don't have to murder—or steal—or all of those big sins. Each of us has done something— enough to deserve to be condemned. Pride. Selfishness. Deceit. Arrogance. All of these—and more— make us sinful. We need a Savior just as much as the murderer. Christ's death was for us, too."

Rebecca had cast her eyes around the small circle, hoping to pick out one or two to whom this message might apply. But within, her own conscience told her that she was the one who needed the words. She pushed the thoughts aside.

She was able to forget about it while the young people shared the lunch and chatted merrily with one another. She could even put it out of her mind on the way home—with just Seth—as they talked of lighter topics. At one point he took her elbow to help her over a patch of uneven ground, and Rebecca's heart beat faster in the moonlight, very aware of his nearness.

"Thank you, Rebecca," he said sincerely as he bid

her good-night at her door. "I—I've enjoyed the evening. I—I'm glad you came home—back to Kenville. I—I'll see you—maybe tomorrow."

Rebecca closed the door softly, feeling that he had really wished to say more but didn't know how to. She leaned back against the door and breathed deeply. There was something very special about Seth. She hadn't quite figured it out yet, but it was there. And then she thought of his words during his short devotional, and her thoughts became troubled again. She headed for her room, hoping that she could quickly go to sleep to shut out all the confusing thoughts.

————

"Hi!" He grinned at her as she walked slowly toward him. "I was hoping you might come out."

She flushed. Was it so obvious that she was being forward? She had tried to think of a good excuse for coming out to see him as he worked with the horses and had finally decided that she would ask him about his devotional the night before.

"Well—I—I just wanted to—I enjoyed your little talk last night to the—the group. I wondered—" She was flustered. "I wondered if anyone asked to—to talk to you later—like you said. You told them you'd be glad to talk to anyone."

He shook his head slowly, his eyes showing concern. But they soon brightened. "Sometimes it takes a good deal of bridge-building before one sees acceptance of the gospel truth," he said. "We just need to keep praying and sharing the Word—and leave the rest to the Holy Spirit."

Rebecca nodded—though she really didn't understand his words.

He continued to rub down the sweated black, just released from harness.

"If you wouldn't have come out—I'd have knocked," he admitted.

Rebecca looked surprised.

"I know that—that I really have no right to—to such—such—dreams, but—I've been wondering if—if you'd mind if I—I come calling," he said, giving her his full attention.

Rebecca could not believe her ears. Her face flushed and she dipped her head demurely.

"'Course I will ask your ma first," he continued quickly.

Fear filled Rebecca's heart. What if her mother said no? What if her mother told him about some of their recent discussions?

"I'm sure Mother will not mind," replied Rebecca quickly. "She—she thinks highly of you and—and besides—I am of age—I am allowed to answer for myself."

Rebecca was not sure that her statement was totally true. She had never tested such matters. Since their disagreement, her mother had been polite and gentle, but a strange tension had settled over the house.

The young man looked relieved.

"Tonight, then?" he asked politely.

Rebecca nodded. "Perhaps we can go for a walk," she said softly, not wishing to have Seth and her mother in the same room for an evening. Then she added quickly, "The evenings are so—refreshing this time of the year."

Seth nodded again. The arrangements were made.

———

It was a pleasant evening. Rebecca enjoyed the stroll

to the nearby stream. She enjoyed Seth's company. He talked easily yet seriously about many things. Rebecca found herself admiring the young man more and more.

When they reached the spot where the stream narrowed and scurried hurriedly over outcropping rock, he removed his hat and casually dusted off a large rock for her to be seated. She laughed gaily as she accepted, and he took a place on the ground beside her.

"I love it here," he began simply. "I used to come here to think and pray when—when our family was going through all its turmoil."

"Turmoil?" asked Rebecca, turning to look at him in surprise.

"I've never told anyone about this before—but we moved here because—because of my older brother. He—he never did like to—to take orders—from anyone. Not from Pa—not from his teachers—and especially not from the Lord. He rebelled—against all authority—defied everyone."

He stopped and toyed with a small twig he picked up from the ground beside him.

"I loved him. Even—sort of—worshiped him," he went on, "but even I knew that he—he thought only of himself. Had to always have his own way. I used to beg him to—to think about Ma. She had a weak heart—we both knew it. But he wouldn't listen. I prayed and prayed that—that he'd change before—"

He stopped for a moment as though he wasn't sure how much he should reveal. "Well—eventually he got in a lot of trouble. Drinking. Fighting. Stealing. Both Pa and Ma were really worried but we just kept praying. And then it got even worse. He killed a man. Some said it was self-defense—others said no. The judge decided that it was murder. He was in jail waiting to be sentenced."

He hesitated again. Rebecca knew by his face and his voice that the memories were very hard for him.

"We're not sure how it happened. Or who did it. But there was a jail break—or an attempted jail break. They didn't make it. At least he didn't make it. He was shot and killed trying to escape."

He stopped again. "I'll never forget Ma," he went on at last. "She clung to him and sobbed and sobbed; then she wiped her tears and straightened her back and said, 'Thank you, Lord, that you took him before he could hurt anyone else.' Just like that. But it near killed her. Pa and I tried to be brave for the sake of Ma and the younger ones—but I know I cried every night when I went to bed. I often wondered if my pa did, too.

"It's a terrible thing to know that your brother is—lost. Beyond hope. Once you're gone—" He shrugged helplessly. Rebecca could feel the weight of the burden he carried.

There was silence for a long time. Each seemed to be thinking thoughts too personal to speak. At last Rebecca spoke.

"So—how—how can you seem so—so cheerful all the time?" she asked in a shaky voice.

He turned and looked at her then and the sadness left his face. "We moved here—that was supposed to help—but it took a while," he answered. "Took me quite a while to get beyond the hurt and the anger. At first I didn't seem to be getting anywhere. I prayed but I still felt—angry and—and betrayed, I guess. Finally—one day—here—I just asked God to take it all from my heart and give me joy in its place. You know—He did. I don't know how, but He did."

Then he continued. "I can't bring my brother back. I know that. But I can try to help others see the light before it's too late. I made up my mind that as long as

I'm here in this world—surrounded by people who
need to hear the gospel, I'd keep telling them and telling them every chance I got—in every way I know
how—that God loves them and wants them to accept
His love—not destroy themselves by seeking their own
selfish ways. God will forgive all those who ask for His
forgiveness and turn from their sin."

He seemed to shift his heavy thoughts. He stirred
from his spot on the grass and held out his hand to her.
She stood up slowly. He was standing close to her, looking at her in the soft light of evening.

"I'm sorry," he said. "I didn't mean to spill that all
out. It's just—just you are the first one I've met who
is—is—who I thought might understand. We moved
here because Pa thought a fresh, new start would be
good for Ma and the younger ones. I'm glad we moved.
It's easier here for them. And besides—" He still held
her hand, "I'd never have met you if we hadn't."

Rebecca felt her heart skip a beat.

"You're very special, Rebecca," he went on. "I
guess you've sorta guessed how I feel."

Rebecca could not speak. She could not even meet
his eyes. She stirred restlessly. He took her elbow and
moved her gently toward the path that led to the town.

They walked home together through the gathering
twilight. The talk returned to more casual things. They
were almost at home before he spoke more seriously
again.

"I hope—I hope my talking tonight about my family wasn't—wasn't taking advantage of our friendship."

"Oh no," replied Rebecca quickly. "I—I feel—hon-
ored that you spoke your heart."

He took her small hand in his strong, calloused one.
Rebecca had never walked hand in hand with a young

man before. She was surprised at the feelings it
brought. As though they belonged together—shared
something deeply personal and precious. She felt her
heart racing.

"I wish I could help your mother more," he said
softly. "She is—is a very special person. Folks here—
all have a deep respect for her. She—she was trying so
hard to save up money so that she could—get extra
things—have things nicer for when you got back home.
She could hardly wait for that, you know. Now I understand why."

The pressure on her hand increased and she saw
him turn and smile at her in the soft darkness that en-
circled them.

"And now—just when she was getting back on her
feet after paying for the new wagon—she needs this
here next loan."

He seemed to bite his tongue.

"I'm sorry," he said quickly. "That's breaking confidence. I don't know if you know about that or if it's
supposed to be . . . It just slipped out. It's—I don't even
know why she needs the money or—"

Rebecca laughed softly. "It's okay," she said, feeling
close to him and able to confide. "It's for my ticket."

"Ticket?"

Rebecca sobered. Now she had carelessly said
something that she regretted.

She nodded slowly into the darkness, half hoping
that the movement would be concealed.

"Ticket where?" he asked her.

"Back—back East," she managed to say, her heart
beating even faster.

"Back East? Do you have to go?"

Rebecca swallowed. She wished she could withdraw
her hand—distance herself before she had to answer.

"I—I wish to go," she answered, trying to keep her voice even.

"For how long? When will you be back?" He sounded deeply concerned.

"I—I'm not—not planning to come back," she managed to answer.

He was the one who released her hand. He put his hands to her shoulders and turned her slightly to face him so that he could see her face in the semidarkness.

"What are you saying?" he asked, his voice husky.

Rebecca tipped her head and tried to appear self-assured.

"I'm going back East," she said. "To stay. Mother is making the arrangements with the Fosters. As soon as their reply arrives I will be taking the stage back to the eastbound train. I expect to leave—"

"You can't," he said quietly into the stillness of the evening. "She's lived for the day when you'd be home."

"I can't help that," said Rebecca, tilting her head. "I don't fit in here. I don't like it. I'm going back."

He seemed to stare at her long and hard. Rebecca could see the muscles in his jaw working. She could feel the intensity in the dark eyes. She tried not to flinch under his scrutiny—then he stepped back. "If you do that—to her," he said slowly, "you are as selfish and uncaring as my brother."

Then he turned on his heel and left her to go alone to her house, the darkness gathering about like a shroud.

For one moment Rebecca wanted to run after him. To assure him that she had changed her mind. To plead with him not to be angry. And then her own anger took hold of her. They were all against her. All of them. She had to get away.

Without further thought she rushed toward the corrals. Ebony was there. He lifted his head and looked at her curiously. Rebecca slowed her step so she wouldn't cause him to bolt as she approached him.

Seth had said that he rode bareback. Well—she could ride bareback. She would flee this place where everyone condemned her and no one understood her.

Hurriedly she bridled the black, who seemed surprised but patient in being drawn from his feed trough as night was descending.

She climbed on the rail of the fence and flung herself onto the silky smooth back that Seth had curried a few short hours earlier, then turned the horse through the gate she had opened and not bothered to close behind her.

Out of town she rode, her skirts swirling in the wind, her hair loosening from its pins. Down the dusty road that led her toward the foothills she raced. She put her heels to Ebony's side and slapped him with a rein. She couldn't go far enough—fast enough. Tears whipped from her eyes. Was it the wind—or was she weeping?

On and on she galloped, the distance slipping slowly beneath the pounding hooves of the horse. Rebecca no longer knew if she was pushing the horse or if the black was running out of control. She did not care.

She could hear Ebony's breathing deepen and knew she was running him too hard. He was laboring from the fast pace. But she did not draw back on the reins. The night pressed in around them, but she urged Ebony on even though she could no longer see ahead into the blackness.

Suddenly she felt a terrifying jerk. Ebony was going down and she was being thrown over his head through the darkness. She screamed into the black silence that rushed to meet her. Then darkness totally engulfed her as she lay in a crumpled heap where she had fallen.

Chapter Twenty-six

The Awakening

When Rebecca awoke later the moon was high in the sky. She came back to her senses slowly, puzzled at where she was and how she had come to be there. Gradually it all came back to her. She had raced away on Ebony to escape from them. Anger filled Rebecca's heart. "Now look what they've done. Look what they've made me do!" she cried in the eerie stillness of the night, fear and anger making her voice tremble. "Now look."

A strange thought followed. They hadn't done anything. She had fled of her own free will. Because she was angry—because she was selfish.

It was true. All that Seth had said. It was true. She had lived her whole life thinking only of herself. Her mother had tried to tell her. Uncle Boyd had tried to tell her. And then Seth had tried to tell her, and she had still determined to run away from the truth.

She was selfish. She had never considered others. She had been mean and spiteful to her mother. She had only wanted her own way—had not cared how cruelly she hurt the one who had loved her so deeply.

What had Seth said in his devotional? Pride—self-ishness—deceit—arrogance. Rebecca knew about them all. Enough reason to be condemned. Enough? More than enough. God knew her heart and that she had never—ever—surrendered herself to seek His will. She had never allowed Him to be her Savior and had certainly never considered Him as her Lord. She had seen Him only as the God of the Bible—never as her God.

It was the first time Rebecca had fully faced the fact that she was less than perfect. It was the first time she had realized she had a heart full of sinful and wicked desires. It was the first time she knew she needed the forgiveness of God for who and what she was.

Rebecca dropped her head in her arms and wept into the darkness. After a time she slowly, haltingly began to pray, opening her heart and her most intimate feelings to the God she could not see but could sense was with her in the dark night.

At last a peace stole over Rebecca. She couldn't have explained it, but she knew that her prayer had been heard. She knew that she had been forgiven.

"If—if Mother—and the others—will just—just give me another chance. If only they can—can forgive me—for what I've done—and been," her heart cried.

———————

With the first light of morning, Rebecca tried to stir. The night had been cold and she was lightly clad. Her dress with its many skirts really had not been of much warmth. She felt cold and stiff and miles from nowhere. She did not even know in which direction the town lay. She was not only far from home but she was lost as well.

Had Ebony been hurt in the fall? She hoped fervently that he had not. She peered into the morning light for the horse but saw no sign of him.

She managed to pull herself to her feet, though weight on one ankle sent pain shooting through her. With the help of a tree limb to steady herself, she looked around for some landmark. She saw nothing familiar. How would she ever get home again? Her mother would be worried. What would she say? Rebecca knew that she deserved a scathing reprimand. This time—this time she would accept what was justly hers. She had done wrong—again.

Had her mother summoned Boyd? Rebecca had done much thinking during the night about her Uncle Boyd. She had replayed his words over and over in her mind and gradually sorted them through and felt that she understood him. She was sure that he was one of the young men who had loved her mother. One that her mother could have chosen to marry and live in reasonable comfort instead of working so hard. Rebecca understood now that she couldn't cause her mother pain without also hurting Boyd. "Uncle Boyd will be so angry," she whispered to herself.

And Seth. What of Seth? He had—had almost told her that he—that he cared for her in a special way and then— Then she had become defiant and headstrong and had raced off into the night on one of the horses he tended carefully. She was selfish. Had been selfish. After her long prayer throughout the night, she hoped she would never be so selfish again. She felt—changed. She *was* changed. She hoped to have opportunity to prove it. But first. First she had to get back home. First she had to ask forgiveness from those she loved the most. Had to try to explain to them that she'd had a change of heart. No. No, that wasn't quite right. God had changed her heart. What was the Bible verse she had learned so long ago?

Create in me a clean heart, O God. That was it. King David had prayed the prayer. He had been selfish, too. Rebecca remembered the story. And God had answered King David's prayer—just as He had answered hers.

————

It was Boyd who found her. Rebecca expected reprimand, but he was off his horse before the animal had even stopped. He gathered her into his arms.

"Rebecca. Are you hurt?" he asked, his face ashen. "We've been searching all night."

"I'm fine," managed Rebecca, clinging to him—and then her tears started again. She was so ashamed. So embarrassed. She clung to him and he held her close and let her weep, brushing back her tangled hair with a clumsy hand.

As soon as she was calmer he released her and eased her to a large rock, taking off his coat and wrapping it around her shaking shoulders.

"I must let your mother know," he said and crossed to his horse to withdraw a rifle from where it hung on the saddle. He fired his gun into the air, startling his horse even more than he startled Rebecca. The animal leaped forward and ran a short distance, tossing its head and snorting in fright, then stood trembling as the sound echoed and reechoed in the distance.

As soon as the sound of the shot had evaporated in the morning stillness, Boyd whistled for the horse who obediently retraced its steps, still looking skitterish and uneasy. The man put the gun back into its case and lifted down a small bag that Rebecca would discover contained first-aid supplies and a flask of water.

"Where are you hurt?" he asked with concern.

"I—I bumped my head—and—and hurt my ankle," she answered.

He was still kneeling before her, gently wrapping the injured ankle, when Sarah rode up.

"Oh, Rebecca. Thank God!" she cried before she even dismounted.

"She's fine," Boyd quickly assured her.

"Thank God!" Sarah cried again as she ran toward the girl and threw her arms around her. "Oh, thank God."

They cried together, clinging to each other. Sarah kept whispering little words of love and praying prayers of thanks all jumbled together.

Later, with the ankle protected as best he could, Boyd placed Rebecca in the saddle, mounted up behind her, and cradling her close against his chest, they rode toward home.

"We'll soak that ankle and get you to bed," said Sarah from her mount, her eyes still misty. "I'm so glad—you'll never know how frightened I was when Ebony came limping home."

"Is he—?"

"He'll be all right. It's not a break."

Rebecca felt so thankful.

———————

She was fussed over and put to bed. The warmth and softness felt wonderful to her aching, chilled body.

"We need to try to find Seth. Let him know she's found," Rebecca heard Sarah say quietly to Boyd as the two left the room.

Seth? Seth was still searching. Seth was searching

for her after she had made him so angry?

Rebecca wasn't sure that she wished to see Seth. What would he say? What could she say?

She had tried to apologize to her mother. She had shared with her the experience she'd had the night before in the darkness—with only God to talk to—and her prayer of repentance and remorse. She had tearfully asked for her mother's forgiveness for her terrible attitude and the spiteful words she had said.

Sarah had wept and held her close against her breast. She had kissed her forehead and assured her that she was loved. That she was forgiven. That they'd make a new start. And Rebecca, through her own tears, had said that she would like that. Would try hard to be the daughter that Sarah had wished to welcome home.

Then Rebecca had reached for the man's hand. "Uncle Boyd," she had said sincerely, "I understand now. I'm—I'm sorry. I—I know I've been selfish and ungrateful. Please—forgive me."

It had been almost like having a father. He had held her close, unable to say much, but Rebecca knew that she was loved—and forgiven.

But Seth? Seth knew the wickedness of her heart. He understood just how selfish and proud she was. He knew. Could Seth ever, ever wish to even speak to her again after her childish behavior?

Rebecca closed her eyes and willed herself to go to sleep. Her mind was spinning. She just wanted to rest. To sink into blissful oblivion.

But at least, at last, she was at peace within her own heart. At peace, even though she still felt uneasy about facing Seth with her confession.

A light rap on the door caused her eyes to flutter open. Her mother peered in. "Are you still awake?' she whispered.

Rebecca managed a nod. The door opened wider and Seth moved his broad shoulders through the narrow crack. Rebecca caught her breath. She didn't know what to say. She didn't know what he would say.

Silently he knelt by her bed and took one of her hands in his. Wordlessly he caressed the slender fingers with one thumb. When he raised his eyes they were filled with tears. "I hear you're home," he whispered, his voice hoarse.

Rebecca nodded.

"To stay?"

"To stay," whispered Rebecca, her whole heart in the words.

He smiled softly and lifted her hand to press it to his lips.

Like the prodigal son, Rebecca knew the wonder of complete, though undeserved, forgiveness.

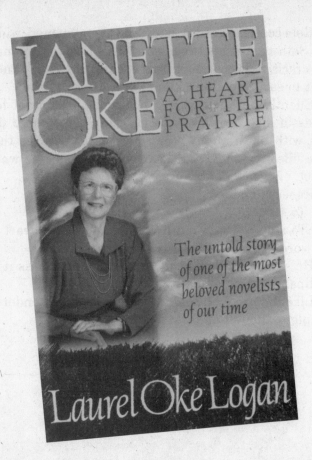

For those readers who enjoy Janette Oke's prairie fiction,
here is the untold story of one of the most beloved novelists
of our time. Written by her daughter, Janette's biography
gives intimate glimpses into her life and heritage, and her
fiction fans will find hints of characters and events that she
has incorporated into her captivating stories.